FREN

'You have lovely legs, Leonie,' said Charles. 'You ought to enter one of those contests in Paris.'

'I don't agree,' she replied and pulled the dress up slowly, 'I've always though they were a little heavy.'

Her thighs were full indeed but the fullness was perfect and made him mad with lust.

'Turn around.'

He heard her chuckle as she slowly turned her back to him. She lifted her dress to give him a complete view of everything from her buttocks down to her ankles, all of it covered by the beige tights, the darker part of the nylon sheer enough to reveal the deep split between the cheeks of her buttocks and the full shape of the delicious globes themselves.

'Do I get the job, Monsieur Boudin?' she asked.

Also available from Headline

The Lusts of the Borgias
Amorous Liaisons
Lustful Liaisons
Learning Curves
My Duty, My Desire
Love in the Saddle
Bare Necessities
The Story of Honey O
Night Moves
Eroticon Dreams
Eroticon Desires
Intimate Positions
Play Time
Carnal Days
Carnal Nights
Hot Type
The Sensual Mirror
French Frolics
Claudine
Wild Abandon
Fondle in Flagrante
Fondle on Top
After Hours
French Thrills
Kiss of Death
The Blue Lantern
Bianca
In the Mood
Sex and Mrs Saxon
Reluctant Lust

French Secrets

(and Demon Heat)

Anonymous

HEADLINE

Published in association with
Masquerade Books Inc

First published in Great Britain in 1993
by HEADLINE BOOK PUBLISHING PLC

10 9 8 7 6 5 4 3 2 1

ISBN 0 7472 4037 X

Printed and bound in Great Britain by
HarperCollins Manufacturing, Glasgow

HEADLINE BOOK PUBLISHING PLC
Headline House
79 Great Titchfield Street
London W1P 7FN

French Secrets

Contents

I.

THE WIDOW'S PASSION

Germaine Borel liked to think of herself as a woman of accomplishment. After her husband died, she used the money he'd left her to open a restaurant in an old barn outside the town of Dampierre. Everyone said she'd go broke, but it didn't happen. Instead she coaxed the restaurant along. She hired an expert chef from one of the schools in Paris, and eventually she turned the place into a gourmet attraction with a rating of three stars. She made a great deal of money from the business, and she now had one of the larger houses on the road between Dampierre and Versailles. In the town of Dampierre to have a house on that road meant that you'd arrived, and to have one of the larger houses meant that everyone in town knew you were someone important. She had three grown children in Paris and a pile of money in the bank. She was forty-five years old, still attractive enough to draw the eyes of men, and undoubtedly one of the more eligible widows in the region. She was also lonely enough to marry again, but she thought all the men she knew were either too dull or too obviously after her money. She consoled herself with the understanding that she was one of a million women in France with the same problem. But at least she had her comforts, didn't she? She went off to the Côte d'Azur whenever she was in the mood for it. She kept her body firm, her skin tone good to look at. She had an occasional intrigue with this or that man in her circle, went to one party or another in Dampierre or the towns around it or sometimes in Paris, but these days she'd almost given up any idea of a serious liaison. She minded it not at all, but what she did miss was the active sexual life she'd had with her husband. Poor Albert, if only he were alive to keep her content! None of the men she knew could live up to his memory. When she did let something happen with a man, he was usually too clumsy or too selfish to satisfy her completely. Since the death of her husband, her affairs had been with older men, men in their fifties and sixties, and she'd come to realize they were not suitable for her. What she liked was a man adept enough to know how to get her clothes off without a fuss, and then gallant enough to make certain she had sufficient pleasure out of their connection. What she'd learned was that very few men in her circle were adept, and those who were adept usually had more interest in younger women or were more directorial than she could tolerate. She would not be subservient to a man, not completely anyway. She'd made a success in a highly competitive business and she understood the value of her personal independence. All of which made it extremely difficult for her to find a man who might be a suitable replacement for her dead husband. She was a different woman anyway from what she'd been when Albert was alive. She was something else now, more mature, more poised, more in control of her life. She understood all of it. The entire profile ran through her mind each time she studied herself in a mirror, each time she wondered what she ought to do to make her life a happier one. So far the answer continued to escape her. What do you want, Germaine? A new hairdo? She wore her red hair short now, long bangs in front and the hair cut close to the shape of her head. She thought it looked interesting with large hoop earrings and a loose colorful blouse. Anyone could tell what was under the blouse. She was well provided in that department, ample enough to get the stares from the men, the envious looks from the women with small developments. Her dead husband Albert had adored her large breasts, and now that she was a bit older they were even larger and more sensitive. What she wanted was a man to enjoy her body, kiss it, fondle it, but it had to be someone who would complement her life and not destroy it, a lover easily controlled, a skillful lover who would bring her the ecstasies she needed so much. Did such a creature exist?

One hot afternoon in June, Germaine's amorous desires took a turn she afterward realized was quite remarkable. She was alone in the big house, the cook and one maid on holiday, thinking about whether to give the other maid the afternoon off, when she noticed a young man riding the grass cutting machine on the broad lawn. For a moment Germaine had no idea who he was. Then she realized it was one of the busboys from the restaurant, a local boy she'd asked to comc out and trim the grounds around the house. She'd had to fire the gardener last month because he drank too much and often ruined her flowers. What a babbling old fool that one was! And now the grounds needed tending. She never liked the way the professional services did it and she also thought they were much too expensive. Did they need to charge her as though the house were a grand chateau? The boy had said he'd be more than happy to earn extra money trimming the grass, and now there he was doing the job. She guessed he'd arrived at the back of the house, told the maid who he was and obtained the keys to the tool shed.

What a fine-looking boy! Germaine thought. She looked at him now. He was nineteen or twenty, not more than that, dark hair and a lean strong body, sweating in the hot sun and the sweat showing as a large stain on the back of his cotton shirt. She tried to remember his name, but it escaped her. Which busboy was he? She ran through the names in her head and she decided he had to be Tony Sadou. Yes, that was the one; it was young Tony Sadou she'd asked to work at the house. She stood there at her bedroom window looking at him, and the more she looked the more intrigued she became about certain feelings he provoked. Why him? Maybe it was the way he was sweating, that wiry body on the machine reminding her so much of her dead husband Albert when he was in his prime. A long time had passed since she'd been with a boy like this one, so many years. He was younger than her son, much younger, and it seemed awful to be thinking of him in a sexual way. But the knot in her belly won out and she decided it wasn't any different than a man her age thinking about a twenty-year-old girl. Was it any different? Such a long time had passed since she'd had a man in her arms. How many months was it?

She went downstairs and sent the maid away for the rest of the day. "I'll see you tomorrow," Germaine said.

Rosalie nodded. "Yes, madame."

After that Germaine went up to her room and she had a shower and some rum to fortify her convictions. She'd started drinking rum one time during a holiday in Mexico and after that she'd adopted it.

She drank one rum and then another, and then after that she went down to the lawn to see what she could do about Tony Sadou. She talked to him about the grounds awhile, and then about his job at the restaurant, and then about his family in Dampierre. She discovered two things about him: first, that his family was from Marseilles; and second, that young as he was he had much experience with women. She could tell all about his experience with women by the way he looked at her, by the way he dropped his eyes to her breasts and smiled, by the way he flirted with her without any awkwardness. She quivered as she imagined him sucking at her tetons, those attractive masculine lips tugging at her fat nipples. He seemed to understand her needs, this boy, and it wasn't long before she had him in the kitchen opening a bottle of wine and then pouring some of it into two glasses.

"I'm sure you'd rather be here than riding that machine in the heat," she said, her eyes moving over his chest and shoulders so clearly revealed by his tight cotton shirt. What a lovely specimen he was, so young and healthy!

He smiled at her. "It's a pleasure, madame."

"Is it really?"

"I think I'm under your spell."

"Maybe I'm a witch," she teased, keeping her shoulders pulled back to give him the full effect of what she had under the blouse she wore.

He said if she was a witch, she was the loveliest witch he'd ever seen. Germaine liked that; it amused her. It occurred to her he was as much seducing her as she was seducing him, and that amused her even more. After all the mature and moneyed men she'd known, here she was maybe about to bed a busboy who worked in her restaurant. She looked him over, the finely boned face with a hint of a hard edge at the corners, the mouth twisting now from a boyish grin into something approaching a leer as he looked at the swell of her breasts again. She could see his young body hard and muscular under his jeans and cotton shirt, his trousers clinging to his sturdy-looking legs and strong thighs. And there, just below his belt, a sloping bulge stood out unmistakably. He certainly looked capable enough. From the look of the mound in his jeans, it seemed he had all the equipment a woman might want. A large and aggressive sex had always been of prime importance to Germaine, and suddenly with this boy it became a compelling attraction. She remembered her dead husband's magnificent penis and she wondered if Tony Sadou could compete with Albert. The boy was large down there, wasn't he? What a lovely big bulge it made! As they looked silently at each other, she couldn't help wondering what his obviously large penis would look like unsheathed, erect, emerging from the loins of such a youthful hard body. She imagined a long thick shaft rising over a pair of bulging testicles. She chastised herself, tried to get the picture out of her mind, but she only succeeded in sharpening the image, and in a moment she found herself trembling, her belly in a knot again. "Why don't we sit in the living room?" she said.

The boy nodded, his hands in his pockets, the fabric of his jeans pulled even tighter. There was no doubt about what he was showing her. It was evident now that he had an erection and that he was boldly exhibiting it. She could not miss the clear outline of the erect penis, the brazen display, the offer. She'd thought seducing him would be a difficult trial, but now it seemed so ridiculously easy.

As he followed her into the living room, she sensed his eyes boring holes in her as she walked.

She allowed her hips to sway, and with every step she imagined she could feel the wetness soaking through the gusset of her panties and dampening her inner thighs. By the time they were in the living room she was trembling again, this time in a complete surrender to the excitement of the moment. How strange it was to be doing this with a boy half her age!

"This is more comfortable," she said, facing him again with a smile, and then feeling a sudden jolt in her chest as she saw what he had done while her back was turned.

His organ was out of his open fly, the knob a fiery red and dripping at the tip.

"Dear God, what are you doing?" she said.

He locked his eyes with hers. "You disapprove?"

Her face flushed, Germaine stared at the enormous swollen penis. "Aren't you rushing things?"

He made as if to tuck his member inside his pants again. "All right, we'll return to the pretense again."

"No, please..."

"I thought you wanted it."

"Yes, I do."

She was vanquished. She hadn't expected him to be sophisticated enough to be so bold, to understand everything so completely.

He smiled at her with satisfaction, slowly stroked his penis with his fingers and then slipped his hand inside the opening of his jeans and struggled to get his testicles out. Germaine felt hypnotized as she watched him. By the time he had everything completely out of his trousers, she saw that her estimate of his masculine development had been correct. She could see all of the penis now, an enormous organ that made her heart pound with excitement as she realized how much it reminded her of her dead husband's. Both the penis and the testicles were absolutely perfect. The member pulsed with thick blue veins, the base fringed by a forest of dark pubic hair protruding from the opening in the jeans. His balls were pink spheroids of enormous size and promised an exciting deluge of sperm. At the sight of these lovely masculine attributes, Germaine's sex, already oozing steadily, virtually exploded. Feminine syrup swamped the gusset of her panties and moistened the insides of her thighs. All sense of decorum vanishing, she had a sudden urge to abandon herself, an urge to show him she could be as uninhibited as he was.

"Would you like to look at me?" she whispered.

The boy gave her a knowing smile. "Is it hot?"

Germaine shuddered with excitement at the brazen question. Losing no time, she lifted her skirt and tucked the hem inside her belt. She stepped out of her sopping panties and moved her legs apart to give him a full view of her generous red-haired sex. Did he find it exciting to look at? She wished she were lying down so he could see more of it. She adored exhibiting herself, showing the full-lipped mouth to eyes with lust in them. What an amazing thing it was to be so free! She had never in her life felt so lewd and ready to abandon herself to pleasure. She moved close to the boy, close enough to bring her pubic bush in contact with the tip of his penis. He tried to kiss her, but she avoided it. Instead she looked down, maneuvered her pelvis, squirmed her hips, her wet sex searching for the enormous knob of his penis. When she felt the glans rub insistently against her labia, a wave of excitement coursed through her. There was no turning back as she lowered herself onto the upright organ. Within moments she had the member halfway inside her, filling her sex with its girth, the stalk hot and pulsing in her channel. The boy was strong, strong enough to lift her body and make their connection more certain. Germaine was amazed that he could do it, amazed they were actually managing such an acrobatic position. My God, how lovely! Her legs straddled his body, her thighs and knees clutching him so he could remain upright and begin moving inside her. By now his penis was in her vagina almost to the hilt, pumping solidly in and out of her dripping sex. Although partially suspended in mid-air, she could not stop wriggling her buttocks, and the shaking movement of her loins caused his penis to twist even deeper inside her body. Finally he was inside her completely, his hot testicles pressed against the bottom of her sex, the enormous member like a huge club inside the barrel of her vagina. She could feel the cheeks of her buttocks spreading wide as her sex was forced to accommodate the full engorgement of the huge penis. Her anus pulsed with excitement, throbbing in spasms as she felt the immensity of the penis filling her channel.

He finally carried her to the sofa and pressed her down against the cushions. He pulled himself out of her and unbuckled his belt. He quickly dropped his jeans, his penis swaying from side to side like a heavy baton. In a moment he was on her again, plunging inside her with a lusty grunt of satisfaction. Germaine groaned as she felt the huge organ again stretching her insides. They embraced, their bodies locked, holding each other to avoid falling onto the rug while they were connected. Now their mouths found each other, Germaine's tongue darting against his. As they kissed, one of his hands closed over the front of her blouse to maul her breasts. He tore the front of her blouse open and brought one breast out of the brassiere cup. As his hand clawed at the large breast, she slammed her pelvis upward, thrusting at him so hard she nearly wrenching his penis out of her vagina. The huge organ swiveled inside her like a twisting corkscrew, bringing her depths of pleasure she had never known before. She felt the slap of his testicles below her sex, the two enormous eggs striking her each time he thrust forward. What a lovely feeling that was! What a glorious accompaniment to the piston-like movements of the organ hammering back and forth inside her vagina! He moved with great skill, strokes that were sometimes long and graceful, then suddenly short and violent. The more animal-like he was, the more she adored it. My bull! she thought. She pulled her mouth away from his and hissed in his ear. "Come inside me like a bull! Fill me with your sperm!"

"How's this?" he said through clenched teeth.

His thrusting more fierce than ever, he began spending inside her. She was certain she could feel him erupting in her vagina, the scalding sperm shooting out of the head of his penis against the rear wall of her sex. Immediately she felt full of it, brimming with his steaming man-milk. "Come, darling, come," she repeated, but now the urgency was gone, the male product already inside her female receptacle. She helped him finish, holding his buttocks until the end, thrilled by the wetness she could feel flowing out of her stuffed sex.

Finally she made him dismount. She kept her eyes on her belly as he pulled himself out of her, and the sight of the swollen wet penis leaving her sex thrilled her immensely. "Lie down," she said, urging him to recline at the other end of the long sofa. In a moment she was off the sofa and kneeling on the rug beside him, her hands gently stroking the slime-covered masculine apparatus, her lips finally closing over the wet glans to nurse at it, to suck the last of the sperm from the swollen member. As she gently squeezed his testicles, a final spurt of milk squirted out of the tip of the organ to bubble on her tongue.

At last she pulled her mouth away from his member. "Come to the bedroom now," she said. "You're not finished, are you?"

The boy smiled. "Do I look finished?"

"No, you look stronger than ever."

They hurried together out of the living room and up the stairs to her bedroom. There they quickly undressed and threw themselves on the bed together, Germaine laughing as he began kissing her breasts and sucking at her nipples. She held the large breasts in her hands, offering each nipple in turn to his mouth. What an animal he was! What a perfectly divine lover! She finally pushed his face away from her breasts and she moved down on the bed to again close her lips over his penis. She sucked at it furiously, taking advantage of the fact that in its present deflated state it was small enough to fit entirely inside her mouth. She fondled his testicles to excite him further, adoring the taste and smell of his genitals, the hot male smell of his testicles. He finally managed to twist his body around to get his hand between her open thighs. His fingers found her sperm-soaked sex and her swollen clitoris. A shudder of delight passed through Germaine as the boy rolled the engorged bud of her clitoris between his fingertips. She continued sucking his penis, working her lips over it, and before long she had the result she wanted. The organ was hard again, thick, filling her mouth to capacity as he rocked his hips back and forth. When she realized he was moving closer and closer to another orgasm, she thrilled at the idea of taking his sperm in her mouth. She sucked the knob with more vigor, and when she felt the sudden torrent of hot milk on her tongue she moaned with happiness around the spurting penis.

When the boy finally stopped coming in her mouth, Germaine lapped his penis dry, scraped her lips over it as she pulled away from him. "Was it good, darling?"

He groaned. "Fantastic."

"Why don't you rest awhile?"

"We can do more."

"Later, my sweet."

She left him there on the bed and she locked herself in the bathroom to make herself fresh for him again. How marvelous it was that he was young enough to go on and on! None of the older men she knew would have such stamina. Did he want to take her again? Or maybe it would be better to give him another emission and send him home to anticipate the next occasion. Naked in the bathroom, she brushed her hair and repaired her makeup and perfumed herself. She toyed with her nipples a moment, exciting herself as she remembered the boy's hot kisses.

When she came out of the bathroom wearing a silk robe, she found him lying on his back with his erect penis in his hand.

She smiled at him. "Do you want to go off again?"

"What do you think?"

"I'll use my hand, then."

He seemed astonished. "But why? Let me make love to you."

"No, not now. I'll do it with my hand and then you'll be very gallant and leave."

"You're unkind," he said, pouting at her.

"I'll be very kind to you with my hand."

"It's absurd."

"Don't you want to be with me again?"

"Yes."
"Then do as I say."
"At least let me see your breasts while you do it."
Germaine laughed gaily, slipped the robe off her shoulders and lifted her breasts in her hands. "Next time you'll pay more attention to these."
"Yes."
She felt a great happiness as she realized how easy it was to control him. She pushed his hand away from his penis and she took the enormous member in her fist. The firm pulsing man-flesh excited her tremendously, and for a moment she relented and she thought how lovely it would be to have him inside her again. Then she decided it would be just as thrilling to see the explosion of sperm erupting from the swollen knob. The boy groaned as she began stroking him. Was this better than when he did it himself? She slid the foreskin back and forth over the fat glans, then pulled the skin firmly down on the shaft and held it there as the knob swelled even further. He began moving his hips, encouraging the rhythm of her hand as it stroked the long penis. Her fingers squeezed the organ, fondling it and stroking it firmly at the same time. She could feel the flush in her face, the heat of her passion as she kept her eyes fixed on the tip of the bloated glans. When his testicles visibly tightened at the base of his penis, she knew it wouldn't be long. To prolong the agony of his excitement, she leaned down and ran the tip of her tongue into the vertical slit at the end of his member. As her tongue gouged the tiny opening of the ultra-sensitive glans, she could feel him flinch and his groin tighten. His member lurched forward in her hand as his orgasm approached, and she pulled her face back just in time to have a full view of the sperm erupting from the swollen knob. The first salvo shot a good

twenty centimeters into the air, the semen flying, each following dollop seeming larger than its predecessor, the milky spurts finally falling on his belly and chest. At the end, as his penis dribbled the last of the sperm, her hand was covered with his sticky substance.

"Happy, darling?"

He had strength only to mutter a vague response, and Germaine smiled as she bent to kiss the very tip of the already softened organ. He belonged to her now, didn't he? This wonderful boy-lover belonged to her. The boy and the lovely penis both belonged to her completely.

II.

A NEW SECRETARY

The large shoe factory at the southern edge of Dampierre was in the hands of the Boudin family, and these days it was forty-five-year-old Charles Boudin who was both head of the factory and head of the family following the recent death of his older brother from cirrhosis of the liver. The old dowager Marie-Louise Boudin was still alive, but now a recluse in her ancient house, and all the financial power in the Boudin family rested in the hands of Charles. They owned large pieces of Dampierre, and considerable real estate in Paris and Bordeaux. They were a family devoted to the acquisition of capital, and it was only Charles Boudin and his wife Annette who seemed to care about spending the money they had. All the other Boudins were content to count the money; Charles and his wife were determined to enjoy it.

It was now Saturday morning, and from his desk in his office in the shoe factory Charles could watch the cars as they arrived and departed from the factory parking lot two stories below. He had no need to stand, merely turn to the left and peer down at them as the factory workers hurried to their cars and yet another crowd of them waited patiently outside to be let into the lot to begin their Saturday shift.

But he was not interested in the reduced weekend shift, or the workers that spilled in and out on their way to their boring menial jobs or back to the dullness of their boring menial lives. That was all they meant to Charles, just pegs to fit in the holes, his robots. He had a great indifference for those who toiled under him—except for a special few.

Like that one now talking to the guard at the gate. Charles immediately rose from his oversized walnut desk to have a better look at her. He squinted into the morning sun to be certain. Yes, it was her. He could see the red hair and the full breasts under the modest little dress. He saw the guard go into the hut for the telephone, and in a moment, when it buzzed, Charles reached for the phone on his desk.

"Yes?"

"Someone here to see you, Monsieur Boudin. She says she has an appointment. Mademoiselle Vogelin. Shall I let her through?"

Boudin paused a moment, muttering as if he had to recall the appointment. Finally he said, "Yes, I remember. It's a job interview. Give her a pass to my office."

Charles could see the girl take the blue slip from the guard and walk across the parking lot to the building entrance. There she handed the pass to another guard and Boudin went back to his desk to wait for her. He picked up a newspaper and glanced at it, but he was too much on edge to read anything. These little interviews were always unsettling because they were so unpredictable. Mademoiselle Vogelin was the sister-in-law of Juliette Wedekind, a young woman in the factory with whom he'd been occasionally intimate before her marriage. Juliette still worked at the factory, but now that she was married she refused all invitations to Charles's office. She had telephoned Charles to tell him that her sister-in-law wanted a secretarial job at the factory and would he be kind enough to interview her? When Charles seemed reluctant, Juliette casually mentioned that her sister-in-law had a lovely figure that would certainly be an asset in the executive offices. "She's a friendly girl too," Juliette said, and with that Charles realized that Juliette's sister-in-law might be as "friendly" as Juliette herself had been before her marriage. Juliette had been very friendly indeed, visiting Charles in his office any time he wanted her, ready for any fancy he had, even certain things she had previously thought shocking but later learned to enjoy immensely. Hoping that Juliette's sister-in-law might be a replacement for Juliette, Charles had agreed to interview the girl. One tried, didn't one? It might turn out to be an empty morning, but one had to try. He would rather have a girl available to him here in the office than travel to Paris for it or have them send a girl out here when he wanted one. He somehow always found it more exciting with the factory girls, the Dampierre girls only recently innocent, these lovely healthy girls with none of the cynicism of the Parisian whores. This girl wanted a job, and if she pleased Charles she would get the job, and then in a few years she would marry some local boy and none of it would matter to her. For Charles what mattered was that at the moment he needed someone to replace Juliette. If the girl was capable enough, he might even hire her as his personal secretary.

In a few moments a knock came at the door and Charles went to open it. The girl stood there, her hands clasped across the gentle slope of her belly. She was a tall girl in a pale blue dress.

"Monsieur Boudin?"

Charles nodded. "Yes, please come in, Mademoiselle Vogelin. You're Léonie, aren't you? May I call you that?"

"Yes, thank you."

Charles noticed her legs and shoes as she walked past him into his office, perfect legs above white high-heeled sandals. She had dainty feet for such a big girl, and they immediately excited him. She had a curvaceous upthrust bottom with a delicious apparent firmness, and barely hidden by the tight bodice of her dress were a pair of melon-sized beauties.

"You're very pretty," he said as he sat behind his desk and gestured to Léonie to take the chair beside the desk where his secretary usually perched.

The girl blushed, a manifestation of innocence that made her all the more enticing to Charles.

"Thank you, Monsieur Boudin. My sister-in-law Juliette..."

"Yes?"

"She said that you might have a job for me in the secretarial pool."

Charles nodded. "Either in the pool or as my personal secretary." He explained that the position as his personal secretary was also available, and of course the girl immediately showed an interest in it. For a few moments they talked about her experience, credentials, schooling, and so on. Léonie smiled sweetly, her crisp white teeth gleaming with youthful exuberance. She looked so sweet and innocent, Charles began to wonder if Juliette had made a mistake about her. Was it possible? The girl was beautiful, all right, but so far there wasn't a hint that he might reach an understanding with her.

They continued discussing her secretarial qualifications. Léonie had put her small purse down beside her chair, and now she reached for it to get something out of it. Charles took advantage of the opportunity to mentally undress her. He allowed his eyes to wander over the firm mounds of her breasts and the long sweep of her thighs. Her short dress rode up as she leaned over the side of the chair and he could see a good deal of her nylon-covered thighs.

What she brought out of her purse was a certificate from a secretarial school attesting to her skill as a typist and stenographer. Charles made a pretense of looking at it when she handed it to him, but in a moment he said, "Would you like some cognac, Léonie?"

The girl appeared surprised, but obviously pleased. "Why yes, Monsieur Boudin, if you..."

"It's the weekend after all, isn't it?"

"Yes, it's Saturday."

Of course it was too early in the day for cognac, but he knew the girl wouldn't refuse him. He swiveled his chair around to find the decanter on the buffet behind him, and after he poured two short glasses of cognac he handed one to Léonie and smiled at her. "A bit of cognac is always good for the soul, isn't it?" He moved his swivel chair close enough so their knees almost touched. "I hope it isn't too much for you."

She looked into the brownish liquid and shook her head. "No, I think it's fine."

They sipped the cognac and he watched her shiver as the alcohol ran down her throat. He imagined her young full breasts shivering under the dress. He wondered what type of brassiere she wore, how much support those beauties had. He gazed at the full swell of her breasts and then down at the long tapering legs and the pretty high-heeled shoes.

"Do you like it?" he said.

She nodded as she licked her lips. "I like the taste of cognac."

"Some people say it's a wicked drink."

"Wicked?"

"They say it causes people to relax too much. May I ask you something, Léonie?"

"Yes, of course."

"How badly do you want the job?"

Now he allowed his knees to touch hers and he was happy when she did not pull her legs away. Her eyelids fluttered and a soft flush came to her cheeks. Was it the cognac or a growing understanding of what he wanted from her?

"I want it," she said quietly. "I would like very much to work for you as your personal secretary."

"Ah yes. It pays more, of course."

"I also think it would be more interesting."

Charles felt his pulse quicken as he saw the knowing look in her eyes. All the innocence in her face seemed to have vanished now, and he was thankful for it. His penis was already swollen with eagerness. Dear Juliette had not disappointed him. He had a sudden memory of Juliette bending over this desk with her broad rump naked and waiting for him. She was very hairy, Juliette was, and from the back her sex looked wild and tropical. She liked to be taken from the rear, but she liked it best when he finished in her mouth. She had a firm conviction the vital juices of the male could keep a woman's breasts from drooping. Charles felt his penis twitch as he remembered Juliette's thick red lips pulling the sap out of his testicles.

"Monsieur Boudin?"

His attention suddenly returned to Léonie. "Yes?"

"Do I get the job?"

"Perhaps." He touched her knee with his hand. Instead of moving her leg, she remained motionless, unmoving, silent as his fingers pushed the edge of her dress a bit further back on her thigh. "You have lovely legs," he said. "You ought to enter one of those contests in Paris."

She seemed pleased by the compliment. "Do you really think my legs are that pretty?"

His hand moved beyond her knee and onto the soft warmth of her thigh. He let it rest there, his palm pressed against the nylon-covered flesh, his fingertips moving only slightly as he stroked her.

Unexpectedly, she rose. For a moment Charles thought he'd gone too far with her, but when he looked at her face he realized it was otherwise.

"I don't agree," she said. "I don't think my legs are that pretty. I've always thought they were a little heavy...especially at the tops." She bunched her dress in her hands as they moved up her thighs, and she pulled the dress up slowly until her legs were exposed all the way to the dark part of her nylon tights.

Her thighs were full indeed; not heavy but full. Maybe in a few years they'd be heavy; maybe after she had a few children the weight of maturity would appear. Now the fullness was perfect and it made him mad with lust. He touched one of her legs again, first her knee and then her thigh, and then further until he reached the place where the edge of the dress still hid the nylon-covered mound of her sex. After a moment's hesitation, he lifted the edge of the dress enough to have a look at what was hidden there. She did not refuse it; she helped it by holding the dress higher with her hands.

A deep sigh of pleasure escaped his lips as he saw the nylon over the mound was sheer enough to reveal the full bush of reddish hair.

"Perfect," he said.

"My legs, Monsieur Boudin."

"Everything. Now turn around and show me the back."

He heard her make a sound of amusement as she slowly turned her back to him. Now she lifted the dress in back to give him a full view of everything from her buttocks down to her ankles, all of it covered by the beige tights, the darker part of the nylon again sheer enough to show the deep split between the cheeks of her buttocks and the full muscular shape of the globes themselves.

After holding the pose another long moment, she suddenly began sliding the dress upward again to remove it.

"Can you help me with the zipper, Monsieur Boudin?"

She still had her back to him. Charles managed to pull his eyes away from her buttocks, and he rose to find the zipper tab and pull it down along her back. As soon as that was done, she hoisted the dress over her head with a single smooth motion, freed it from her arms and tossed it over the back of the chair she'd been sitting on earlier.

Then she turned around to face him again. "There, that's better, isn't it?"

Charles sat in the swivel chair again, making a half-hearted attempt to conceal the throbbing bulge in his trousers. He sat only a foot or so from the narrow curve of her waist and the flaring invitation of the girl's hips and belly. He could see her pubic bush through the nylon more clearly now, an untrimmed reddish-brown triangle flattened a bit by the tights. As he raised his gaze over her belly, his eyes feasted on the brassiere and the bulging swell of her large, firm breasts. They looked firm enough to stand as well without support.

"You're quite a girl," he said.

"Thank you," she said. She smiled, a sweet girlish smile, moved her arms across her breasts as if to hide them and then uncovered them again and looked uncertain. She wet her full lips with her tongue and said: "I suppose if you've seen this much, you might as well see all of it." She reached down for the elastic waistband of her tights, but then changed her mind and stretched backward for the clasp of her white brassiere instead. She took a deep breath, unhooked the brassiere and let it slip down her outstretched arms.

Her breasts spilled forward like two pink melons, full and round, the small nipples apparently erect. Charles had been correct about her breasts needing no support: they stood out full from her rib-cage, like sweet fruit waiting for the hands and kisses of a lover. She mumbled something about her breast exercises, but Charles paid no attention to what she said. He extended a hand to touch one of her breasts. A long sigh escaped Léonie's lips as she felt his fingers fondle and squeeze her flesh.

After that the pact between them was as good as signed. Confident of her success, Léonie smiled down at him. After he withdrew his hand, she lifted both her breasts with her own hands, bounced them gently, held them up as if to gauge their weight, playfully aiming the pink nipples at his face. Then she dropped her breasts and she reached for the elastic waistband of her tights, pulled at it, tugging it down, rolling the sheer nylon down over her belly until the top of her red pubic bush was revealed. She held the top of her tights there and gently wiggled her hips from side to side. Charles wondered where she'd seen that, on what stage or in what film. The young people these days were so marvelously sophisticated. As if to confirm his appraisal of her artfulness, she did a slow turn on the white high-heeled sandals, and when she had her back to him her fingers slowly tugged the rolled tights down further to reveal completely the globes of her buttocks.

"Do you approve?" she said, her voice more confidant, her pink buttocks weaving back and forth so close to his face that it made him dizzy. Without waiting for his answer, she continued pushing the tights down her thighs. "I'll have to get my shoes off to get out of this."

Charles found his voice. "Yes, by all means." He had an urge to kiss her bottom, but he refrained. Later, he thought; let the refinements come later.

Her tights halfway down her thighs, Léonie turned to face him again before shuffling backward to sit in the chair. "Will you help me, Monsieur Boudin?" She extended one of her legs, wriggling her foot to remind him that her shoes needed to be removed.

Charles was convinced now that whatever innocence she had displayed earlier had been affected. This girl knew her onions! He told himself he had to remember to send Juliette a gift of some kind, something carefully chosen that would not produce difficulties with her new husband. Meanwhile he had Léonie, her knees open enough so that now for the first time he could see nearly all of her sex, the tangled fringes of red hair along the lips, the tendrils growing wild down the two grooves to where her buttocks began.

He took the offered foot in his hands and he unbuckled the high-heeled sandal. "Pretty shoes," he said, slipping the shoe off her foot and then fondling her heel and instep as she made a sound of pleasure and wriggled her toes. Oh, there would be games to play with this one!

He removed the other shoe, then after that he

took hold of the nylon tights and pulled them completely off her legs and feet. As he tossed the tights onto his desk, she opened her knees without modesty.

"Do I get the job, Monsieur Boudin?"

Charles gazed at the now unfurled lips of her sex, at the glint of the pink groove between the hairy labia. "As of this moment you're my personal secretary."

The girl sighed and looked around. "Are we going to finish this? Where should we do it?"

"Over there on the sofa. Get on your hands and knees and wait for me."

She blushed when her eyes met his. "On my hands and knees?"

"It's better that way when it's on a sofa. You don't mind, do you? Maybe you can just kneel on the cushion if you like that better."

She shook her head and gave him a look as if to say it didn't matter to her one way or the other. "All right, Monsieur Boudin."

"Call me Charles, won't you?"

"Only when we're doing this."

"Agreed."

He watched her as she rose from the chair and walked gracefully to the sofa along the far wall. What a confection she was, with those long legs and robust buttocks now faintly marked by the upholstery she'd been sitting on. She assumed a position on the sofa, kneeling lengthwise, her weight resting on her knees and elbows. "This way, Charles?"

"Perfect," he said.

She casually watched him as he undressed, as he stepped out of his pants and carefully draped them across the back of a leather chair. If she expected an inelegant middle-aged body, he surprised her. Except for a slight roll around his middle, he was as muscled and trim as a twenty-year-old. Was she pleased by that? But after he removed his shorts, it was obviously the muscle between his legs that pleased her even more. Charles could see in her face that she was pleased by the vigor of his erection.

"Do you take the pill?" he said.

"Yes, of course."

Full of confidence now that her interest in his appendage was apparent, he walked toward her with his hand on his stiffly extended penis. When he was close to her, he stopped and teased her by stroking his foreskin back and forth over his swollen glans. "And you, Léonie?"

"And me, Charles?"

"Do you approve?"

She stared at his penis and blushed. "It's a nice one."

Charles was amused, wondering if her sex twitched at the sight of the male organ. His wife had told him that sometimes happened with her. He continued teasing Léonie with his penis. He ran his fingers lightly along the long hard shaft of his member, peeling the foreskin back to uncover the glans and then pushing it forward again. As the purplish head slipped out of the sheath, it glistened with the first oozing of his lust.

Finally, he climbed onto the sofa behind her and he positioned himself between her long legs. She immediately moved her knees further apart and lowered her breasts to the cushion. He had no doubt she'd been taken in this position before. As her buttocks wriggled lewdly in front of him, he could see the tiny pink eye of her anus. Was she a virgin there? He doubted it. These working class girls were usually quite experienced in that domain. Maybe at another time...

Now he took her buttocks in his palms and he spread them open to reveal her secrets more completely. Her thighs were warm against his own as he maneuvered the bulbous head of his erection up between the hairy lips of her sex.

She made a sound of pleasure, shuddering as the swollen knob pressed into the pink groove. He pushed forward, and in a moment the head of his penis slipped into the clasping mouth of her vagina. Instantly, he could feel the liquid heat of her passage. He ground forward, sinking his member deeply into the hot opening. She groaned again, squirmed her bottom, grinding her hips backward onto the impaling thickness of his erection until it slapped home with his heavy testicles touching her thighs.

"Ooof!" she said.

"Do you like it, Léonie?"

"Yes, it's good. Come on, do it to me."

He reached around her hips, leaning over her, his fingers sliding over the firm young belly and into her sex until they found the bud of her clitoris. As he stroked the tiny organ, she moaned her approval. She worked back against his pelvis with rhythmic movements that forced his member even more deeply inside her vagina. She continued moaning as his fingertips worked over the oily marble of her clitoris. She began grinding back harder, each fervent movement of her hips and thighs stronger and more insistent than the one before. Charles hunched over her, working feverishly, the sweat beading on his neck and shoulders and dripping onto the girl's skin, dribbling down her bare sides and onto the full jiggling mounds of her breasts. Her clitoris seemed to grow beneath his practiced touch, pulsing and throbbing, swelling with her arousal. He continued rubbing it, rolled it between his fingers like a wet pebble as she responded with a wanton dance of her hips. She groaned and squirmed, her buttocks moving in tight concentric circles around the intrusion of his hard penis.

Finally he came, groaning loudly as he spurted deep in her belly. He continued pumping his hips until his balls were empty, his frothy sperm now oozing out of her vagina and around the sliding shaft of his penis. When he let her go at last, his member already drooping, she moaned as she eased her body down on the sofa.

"You can start on Monday," he said. "Make sure you're always neatly dressed. I like high heels on a girl, and fresh lipstick during the day. When you answer the telephone, never tell anyone I'm in until I accept the call."

After that he left her and he went to the washroom.

III.

THE TWO FRIENDS

Marianne Lamarche had been a beauty as an adolescent, but now at the age of thirty-two her beauty had refined itself and become even more significant. She was tall, slender, dark-haired, and always fashionably dressed. She was married to Robert Lamarche, a successful architect, and although they lived in Dampierre they considered themselves Parisians. Both had more friends in Paris than anywhere else, and travelling back and forth between Dampierre and Paris was a commonplace in their lives. Robert had his Citroen and Marianne had her little Peugot, and hardly a week passed that Marianne did not drive to Paris for one reason or another. She worked several hours each day at a small art gallery in Dampierre, mainly to "keep busy" as she told her friends, but shopping in Paris, visiting in Paris, enjoying Paris was in truth her primary occupation. The Lamarches had no children, and in the absence of this usual domestic preoccupation, Marianne told herself she had to dissipate her nervous energy somehow, and why not in Paris?

Today, however, Marianne entered Paris in her Peugot for reasons more elaborate than shopping. She had a rendezvous with an old friend, Sylvie Roux, a very dear old friend who lived and worked in

Lyon but who occasionally visited Paris and always let Marianne know beforehand so they could arrange a meeting somewhere. The two women would shop together, talk together, and eventually move on to the more important aspect of their friendship. They had been occasional lovers for nearly ten years, since they'd known each other at the lycée they had attended, and each time Sylvie managed a trip to Paris she and Marianne would renew their more intimate connection. Sylvie was a confirmed lesbian, although she occasionally went to bed with a man when it suited her fancy and her business interests. Marianne, on the other hand, did not consider her relationship with Sylvie a "real affair" but only an unimportant diversion from the growing boredom of her marriage. She certainly enjoyed the time she spent with Sylvie, the warm intimacy and feverish caresses, but she could not imagine herself as a lesbian and the once or twice a year that she diverted herself with Sylvie seemed sufficient for her.

This afternoon Marianne would meet Sylvie at the Deux Magots on the Left Bank. Sylvie had already telephoned in the morning to confirm the rendezvous, and she had hinted to Marianne that she had something "special" she wanted to discuss with Marianne when they saw each other. Marianne wondered now what it was that was so special. Sylvie was such a busy woman, a successful advertising executive in Lyon, no doubt with numerous female lovers in that city. Were they numerous? Since Sylvie never talked about her sexual life in Lyon, Marianne had no idea if the lovers were numerous. As she drove her car into a garage in St. Germaine, it occurred to Marianne that Sylvie knew more about her intimate life than she knew about Sylvie's. Marianne always talked to Sylvie about her life with her husband, first because Sylvie seemed so interested and second because she felt that Sylvie was her true confidante, certainly more so than any woman she knew in Dampierre.

From the garage, Marianne walked to the Deux Magots. It was an overcast day, threatening rain at any moment, and when she reached the cafe she saw that most of the people were inside, only few of the tables on the terrace occupied. She did not see Sylvie on the terrace, so she entered the bustling interior of the cafe to look for her. She stood on tiptoe to see better, and finally she located Sylvie sitting alone at a table, sipping a drink and reading a magazine.

Sylvie hadn't changed much since their days at the lycée. Her face showed a few signs of maturity, but not many. Her blond hair was cut short in a boyish style, but she looked feminine enough and extremely chic.

When Marianne approached the table, she said: "Am I late? You look marvelous." She then slid into the seat across from Sylvie.

Sylvie put her magazine away and smiled. "No, you aren't late. And thank you."

Marianne took Sylvie's hand and squeezed it affectionately. A warm smile passed between the two women, expressing the friendship they had shared for so many years. As girls in the lycée they had been best friends. They had shared all the dark secrets that young teenage girls had to share. They shared clothes, boyfriends, homework assignments and eventually their bodies. Before either of them had breasts, they had their first orgasms together, and then many more after that. When they graduated the lycée, they had a tearful parting in Sylvie's bedroom. She left for Lyon to live with her mother and Marianne remained in Paris to find a job and a husband.

Sylvie adored Marianne. Of all the women Sylvie had known, Marianne excited her the most. The influence of those first sexual times together had always stayed with her. The remembrance of Marianne's soft hands caressing her body, Marianne's innocent squeals of joy as she orgasmed for the first time while Sylvie stroked her clitoris with her fingers, the lovely scent of Marianne's body—these had caused Sylvie to prefer women to men. Sylvie had tried often during those early years of sexual experimentation to find happiness with men, but they never satisfied her emotional needs or sexual desires. She liked men enough, and she found that working with men, even competing with them, was never a problem for her. She had men who were close and intimate friends, but none who were steady lovers. By the time Sylvie turned twenty-two, she had accepted herself as a lesbian. The knowledge of what she was did not upset her; there was no guilt, no fear, only regret that she had spent so many years attempting to be something else. She had lost all those early innocent years of lovemaking.

When the waiter approached the table, Marianne ordered coffee and a toasted ham sandwich. After he left them, the two women talked in earnest again, reviewing their lives, discussing the details of the shopping trip they'd planned for the afternoon. Marianne intended to buy some shoes and Sylvie said she wanted a new dress. But by the time they finished in the cafe a fierce rain had started and the shopping trip suddenly lost its appeal. They huddled under the awning of the cafe, each waiting for the other to make the obvious suggestion.

Finally, Sylvie said: "Let's not be ridiculous, darling. What we ought to do is go directly to my hotel. We'll have some wine and talk and so on."

"And so on," Marianne said with amusement.
"Would you rather get soaked by the rain first?"
"Certainly not."
They climbed into a taxi, and when Marianne heard Sylvie order the driver to the Ritz she made a sound of astonishment.
"There?"
Sylvie smiled. "A gift from my firm."
"But that's lovely!"
A sense of excitement came over Marianne as the driver headed the taxi for the Place Vendôme. What a glorious thing it would be to have an afternoon with Sylvie in such an elegant hotel! She envied Sylvie her ability to travel in such luxury.
As soon as they arrived at Sylvie's room in the hotel, Marianne made a careful inspection of the appointments.
"My God, it's divine," she said.
Sylvie was amused. "Look at the bathroom, darling."
"The bathroom?"
"Look at it, won't you?"
Marianne looked, and what she found was an enormous room with a sunken onyx bath the size of a small pool. "I'm overwhelmed," Marianne said.
"It's exquisite, isn't it?"
"Oh, Sylvie, I want to take a bath in there. Do you have any bath oil?"
An erotic shiver passed up Sylvie's spine as she imagined Marianne splashing around in the onyx tub. "Now?" Sylvie said.
"Immediately," Marianne said.
"All right, I'll draw your bath while you tell more about this problem with Robert."
The problem with Robert that Marianne had already mentioned to Sylvie was Marianne's sense of

a growing boredom in her marriage. Now she sat on the bench in the bathroom and kicked off her shoes as she talked again to Sylvie about it.

Sylvie, meanwhile, knelt beside the large tub to draw Marianne's bath. At intervals, her round bottom jutting out behind her, the blonde looked over her shoulder at Marianne as Marianne talked about Robert. Sylvie's short skirt soon rode up her thighs far enough to reveal the more intimate nylon-covered portions of her anatomy.

Marianne could not help looking at Sylvie as she talked, and as she gazed at Sylvie's bottom the memory of their last time together brought a flash of sexual heat to her belly. She squirmed on the bench, shifting position, then lifted the hem of her skirt to find the waistband of her tights and pull them down her thighs.

"Don't make the bath too hot," she said to Sylvie.

Sylvie looked back at her again, her face flushed. "Just hurry and get your clothes off."

With a teasing smile, Marianne rose to peel her dress off. In a few moments she removed her brassiere, her breasts jiggling as she turned her body to toss the brassiere on top of the dress on the bench. "I suppose it's a little crazy to rush into a bath like this," Marianne said.

Sylvie did not think it was crazy at all. The sight of Marianne's half-naked body made Sylvie dizzy. Marianne's nylon-covered sex was just inches away from Sylvie's face and it was more than Sylvie could bear. "Let me help you," Sylvie said.

She helped Marianne finish undressing. As Marianne watched Sylvie kneel in front of her, Marianne shivered with excitement. Sylvie took hold of Marianne's tights and pulled them completely down. The blonde's fingertips trailed along Marianne's flesh and Marianne responded by spreading her legs. Now with her tights at her ankles, Marianne's dark-haired sex was exposed through the sheer nylon of her panties. Sylvie stared at the furry mound, and then she finished removing the tights from Marianne's feet and she tossed them aside.

"It's too much," Sylvie said.

"What is?"

"You know very well what I mean."

And the next moment Sylvie buried her head between Marianne's thighs. Her tongue darted out to lick at Marianne's sopping panties. Marianne gasped, her hips rotating as she held Sylvie's head with both hands. Sylvie pushed her face deeper into the recess between Marianne's legs, licking at the panties, running her hands up and down Marianne's thighs and across her buttocks. Now the blonde made no attempt to take the panties off Marianne, who continued grinding her sex against Sylvie's face as much as she could without losing her balance. Sylvie crouched down even further and put her head completely under Marianne's crotch. She licked the panties underneath and trailed her tongue where the elastic bands tightened around the tops of Marianne's thighs.

Marianne groaned. "I'll come if you keep doing that."

"Go on," Sylvie said.

"But my bath is getting cold."

Sylvie sighed as she pulled her face away from Marianne's crotch. "I ought to make you do it in your pants."

Marianne giggled. "Take a bath with me. It'll be fun, won't it?"

"All right, I'll get in the tub with you. But I want to do you. I want to bathe you. Come on then, pull off those wet panties and get in."

Marianne pulled her panties down, kicked them off, and went into the tub slowly. "It's hot."

"Get in."

"It's hot, no matter what you say." She felt her feet burning in the water.

"Marianne, sit in the tub. Your clitoris will appreciate it, even if the rest of you doesn't."

Marianne giggled again and sat down, and in a few moments she did begin to feel comfortable. The hot oily water covered her body almost up to her neck and white bubbles floated all around her. She stretched her entire body out in the huge tub and arched her back. Her face barely cleared the water, the rest of her hidden by the bubbles.

"All right, bathe me. I think I like this now."

Sylvie removed her skirt and tossed it to the corner of the room. She lifted the sweater she wore over her head, and immediately her breasts swung loose, unfettered by a brassiere, the large rose-colored nipples like two berries on the white orbs. The nipples were long and fat, quivering as the cool air assaulted them. She dropped the sweater and then pulled down her panties and kicked them off quickly. Then she stepped into the tub to join Marianne. She knelt down next to the brunette, studied her for a moment, and then kissed her gently, tenderly.

The kiss lingered. Marianne floated in the warm water, her eyes closed and her thoughts drifting. As she felt Sylvie's lips press against her own, she settled her body and sat up in the tub. The two women put their arms around each other and embraced with a gentle affection. But as the kiss became more passionate, as their tongues entwined, they soon submitted to the urging of their sexuality. They looked into each other's eyes and each saw the reflection of their feminine needs and each understood what to do. Sylvie pulled Marianne into a kneeling position and the two continued kissing and clutching each other, their breasts rubbing together, their pelvises gyrating against one another, Sylvie's blond pubic hair rubbing against the coarser dark hair of Marianne's sex.

"Sit down," Sylvie said. "Sit down and let me wash you."

Marianne raised one hand to Sylvie's face and stroked her cheek. She traced her fingertips around Sylvie's mouth. "Yes," she whispered.

Sylvie searched under the water for the bar of scented soap she had left in the tub, and finding it, she lathered Marianne's back and neck. Her hands moved over Marianne's flesh as she massaged the brunette's back with the soap.

"Lift your arms."

Marianne lifted her arms and Sylvie ran her soapy hands up Marianne's sides, over her rib cage and around her armpits. She washed Marianne's entire torso, coating Marianne's body with white lather. Her fingers moved in slow small circles, massaging, tickling, while the palms of her hands pressed lightly against Marianne's muscles. As Marianne's body awakened to new desires, small groans escaped her lips. Sylvie looked at the writhing woman in front of her and understood it was time for the next stage of their lovemaking.

"Sit down again and raise one leg," Sylvie said.

Marianne sat down, and leaning back on her elbows she raised her right leg out of the water. She remained silent, her eyes closed, a placid look softening her face.

Kneeling between Marianne's legs, Sylvie washed Marianne's foot and calf. She kissed Marianne's toes and trailed her tongue up the side of Marianne's leg, all the way up to where Marianne's thigh vanished into the water again. Marianne shuddered.

"The other leg." Sylvie said. She repeated the same movements, the same foreplay, and Marianne shuddered again. "Now stand up," Sylvie said.

Like an obedient child, Marianne rose from the water, staring dazedly as Sylvie slid the bar of soap between her legs. Parting her legs to accommodate Sylvie, Marianne watched as Sylvie crawled closer to her. The brunette felt her clitoris hardening, her sex dilating, the muscles within her vagina contracting with her excitement. The cool air titillated the rigid clitoris as the pleasure made her knees tremble.

Sylvie looked up at Marianne, wetness running down her own thighs, and as she drew in her breath her breasts rose and heaved. Marianne looked at them, then reached down with both hands to knead the soft flesh. She squeezed and pinched the fat nipples, stroking the full breasts with her hands.

"Well, you're not a boy," Marianne said. "Not with these."

Sylvie chuckled. "Would you rather I be?"

"No, I like you the way you are," Marianne said as she straightened up again.

Sylvie dropped the bar of soap and put both hands behind Marianne to take a firm hold of the brunette's buttocks. Her fingers dug into Marianne's bottom as Marianne thrust her pelvis forward in response, offering her mound, her sex waiting. Sylvie immediately extended her tongue and licked a wide circle around Marianne's clitoris. Marianne gasped and spread her legs further apart. Sylvie's tongue darted again, touching the insides of Marianne's thighs, licking just under the clitoris and around the labia. Moaning softly, Marianne kept her hips moving as she attempted to increase the pressure against her clitoris. She could feel her clitoris protruding, rigid, waiting for Sylvie's tongue to bring her to orgasm.

But Sylvie teased her, denied her the pleasure she wanted. "Let me rinse you," Sylvie said. "Sit down and let me get the soap off you."

"What?" Marianne was in a daze. She wanted to come. She cared nothing about the soap, or the bath. She wanted nothing except to come. "No, make me come first."

Sylvie laughed and shook her head. "I want you in a bed. I want to suck you until you scream, but I want you in a bed."

Marianne visibly trembled. "Sometimes you're a vicious tease."

"I'll have you dripping in my mouth like a faucet."

"My God, what you do to me!"

They left the tub and dried themselves, then hurried to the bedroom. Sylvie showed Marianne the body oil on the night table, and in a moment Marianne untwisted the cap and poured some of the amber liquid into the palm of her hand. "I remember this," Marianne said.

Sylvie smiled. "Yes, I suppose you do."

As Marianne coated her neck with the oil, it made her skin feel warm and she continued to apply it to her flesh. She rubbed the scented oil all over her body, giving her breasts a more generous layer, making them glisten, getting the nipples erect and pointed. Her skin tingled as the heat of the oil penetrated the pores already opened and cleansed by the bath. She finally put the oil down and she moved toward the bed with a fierce heat in her belly.

"Hurry," Marianne said.

Sylvie was amused. "You look like you can't wait."

"I can't," Marianne said. She lay down on the bed and spread her legs open, inviting Sylvie, showing Sylvie her sex with the lips unfurled.

"In a moment," Sylvie said. She walked over to

where Marianne had just been standing. She picked up the bottle of oil and oozed it thickly over her flesh. Then she looked at Marianne again and said: "Go on, do it. Masturbate, if you like. Put your fingers inside and do it. You know how much it excites me."

Marianne groaned. She lay flat on her back on the bed, pressing her palms into the mattress. Then she rocked gently to make the bed undulate under her. The bed was suddenly like a living thing that wanted to please her. Her oiled body slid on the sheet as she moved. The air stirred around her, tickling her, teasing her flesh, causing her nipples to tingle again.

"Do it," Sylvie said, her eyes bright, expectant.

Marianne moved her right hand down to her sex. She placed the middle finger on her clitoris and pressed it down. Her labia twitched. She trailed the same finger around the clitoris and along the edge of each lip. Then she placed two fingers on the pink bud, pressing the hard nub against her pubic bone. As her fingers moved with familiarity across her flesh, her sex responded at once. She squirmed her buttocks against the mattress, her anus touching the sheet, puckering, opening and closing as if to catch one of the fingers such a short distance away. She moved her left hand to her breasts to fondle them and tweak each nipple. She moaned as she felt the orgasm about to burst in her sex, and immediately she moved her left hand from her breasts, moved it down her belly and over the side of her hip and around beneath her buttocks. Now a sharp cry of lust escaped her throat as the middle finger of her left pierced her anus as she continued rubbing her clitoris with the other hand. When she felt the intrusion of the finger in her bottom, her sex opened wide, swallowing the two fingers of her right hand as she jammed them into the gaping hole. She moaned and twisted violently on the moving bed as the orgasm erupted.

"Sylvie...oh God, I'm coming...look at me... watch me...I'm coming...I'm coming for you, Sylvie!"

Sylvie had not been idle while Marianne had been masturbating. When the blonde had her body completely oiled, she moved silently to the foot of the bed and she stood there gazing at Marianne's open thighs. She watched as Marianne fingered herself, as both holes opened and closed around Marianne's penetrating fingers. Sylvie's own hand moved to her sex to caress herself as she watched Marianne.

"I see you coming," Sylvie said. "Your sex is wide open and I can see the wetness oozing on your fingers. You're coming, aren't you, darling? I can see it, I can see it."

Sylvie shuddered violently as she came. Her legs shook as she strained against her hand. The orgasm made her weak as she kept her eyes fixed on Marianne's sex, on the wet fingers, the gaping mouth of the vagina, the ring of the anus penetrated by Marianne's finger. Groaning, Sylvie climbed onto the bed and crawled between Marianne's legs. She grabbed Marianne's calves just below the knees and pulled them wider apart. She crawled toward Marianne's sex and pulled Marianne's hands away from the flooded slit. Wild-eyed, her face flushed, Sylvie pushed her mouth against the oozing flesh. She took Marianne's clitoris, captured it with her mouth, sucked it, making it swell even more. She bit it gently and then soothed it with small catlike licks. She sucked it in again hard, and then bit and licked, then sucked even harder. She extended her tongue as far she could and ran it up and down over Marianne's sex. She licked the hot flesh with long laps of her tongue, licked at Marianne's sex-lips and inside her slit, up into the oozing hole and back out again to the clitoris. Marianne gasped, raised her legs up high and pushed her sex at Sylvie's face. She groaned and panted. She came repeatedly, never enough time for one orgasm to stop before the next overtook it. Orgasm after orgasm rolled out of her belly, down her vaginal walls and onto Sylvie's active tongue. Before long she wrapped her legs around Sylvie's head to hold it in place, locking the blonde's head between her thighs. Sylvie never noticed. She was still coming, spasming against the mattress as she sucked at Marianne. Over and over again like Marianne. Sucking Marianne and coming.

Marianne was suddenly exhausted, drowned in pleasure as she relaxed her body. "Keep licking me. It's so good, I can't stop coming."

But Sylvie stopped sucking and shook her head as she tried to get away from Marianne's clenched thighs. She grabbed at Marianne's knees and pulled the brunette's legs apart to free herself.

"I can't breathe," Sylvie said.

Marianne moaned. "Let me suck you now."

Shuddering, Sylvie knelt on the bed and then walked on her knees until she was alongside Marianne at the brunette's shoulders. She bent her body forward and she kissed Marianne's breasts. She swirled her tongue over each rosy-brown nipple. Then she lifted one leg over Marianne, twisted her body around and squatted over Marianne's face. "Here, darling," Sylvie said. She lowered her sex onto Marianne's face, grabbed at Marianne's dark hair to pull the brunette's off the bed. Marianne immediately licked the waiting hole, sucking at it, drinking the juices now pouring from it. She grabbed at Sylvie's buttocks to keep the blonde's sex from slipping away. Sylvie squirmed so much that Marianne had a hard time keeping her tongue on its target. Her nails embedded in the blonde's fleshy backside, Marianne held on as her tongue probed inside Sylvie's vagina. She made her tongue rigid, folding it, then stabbing into Sylvie's sex. Sylvie moaned as she felt the brunette's tongue wriggling like an animal inside her vagina. "Oh yes, oh yes, oh yes," Sylvie said. She sat down on Marianne's mouth, pushed her sex down, forcing herself against the wet source of pleasure. Her sex opened wide, her clitoris twitched and swelled from the heat building in her belly. She cried out, her voice trembling, out of control. When she came, everything inside her turned to liquid and all of it poured onto Marianne's tongue and into Marianne's throat.

Marianne drank from the fountain. She sucked at the flowing sex until she herself had another orgasm from the sheer wildness of it. She allowed her face to be inundated by Sylvie, and the more it happened the more Marianne craved it.

Later, before they made love again, Sylvie said: "I wanted to tell you something."

"What?"

"I may be transferred to Paris soon. If you ever want to leave Robert, you can come to live with me."

"Mmmm."

"I think that would be the happiest moment of my life," Sylvie said.

Marianne nuzzled her face against her friend's breasts. She had no intention of leaving Robert, but she thought maybe it was time she told Robert about Sylvie.

IV.

ANNETTE

Annette Boudin poured herself another glass of red wine and returned to watch the last of a badly-cut old film on the television set in the living room. The cook was gone for the day and nearly all of the evening dinner was already prepared and stored in the expensive automated oven that was the focal point of the Boudin kitchen. The cook had been a necessary luxury from the first days of their marriage, for no matter what the rule was among French women, Annette could barely boil water for instant coffee without ruining it. Charles, of course, never drank the coffee she made; he was much too finicky about his food and drink. But he agreed that whatever Annette lacked in the way of domestic abilities, she made up for it in other aspects, among them her chic appearance and cleverness. Her form was excellent for a forty-year-old woman, even if her dark hair required continual visits to the hairdresser, and in certain places her curves were a bit more evident than they'd been when she and Charles had met ten years ago. It was Annette's second marriage, although when she left her first husband she swore a blood-oath never to let herself be talked into marriage again. Nine years of living with that narcissistic pederast had soured her on men. But Charles Boudin changed her mind. Annette was convinced that Charles had in fact saved her. Charles was a real man, a man with class and breeding and poise, all the things Annette wanted in a man. He was at home anywhere, with any sort of person, whether the workers at his factory or the various business executives he knew. And there was something else about Charles. Annette sighed with pleasure as she sipped her wine and thought about him. Charles was every bit as bent as she was, allowing her various minor amusements with young men who caught her fancy, just as she allowed him to chase every skirt who entered the shoe factory.

These days, however, Annette was not as happy as she thought she ought to be. The young men at her disposal were not many, not in Dampierre at any rate. It seemed there were hardly any handsome young men around, at least not any that she could risk toying with. She had one requirement, a single demand that had kept her secret passions private, unknown to everyone except Charles. She insisted her lovers be married, always married, because married men were not as likely to go shooting off their mouths in some crowded cafe after a few drinks. Not when they had their own reputations and sweet little brides to worry about. And so far things had worked beautifully for Annette. No scandals. She felt warm now as she thought fondly of all the firm young masculine bodies she'd had her fun with, sometimes with Charles watching through the one-way glass disguised as a mirror between the master bedroom and the walk-in closet. That little innovation had been her own idea and it worked divinely. Whoever was behind the glass had a marvelous view of the bed and everything that happened on it. Occasionally she'd entertained a handsome young factory worker while Charles watched them from the dressing room. Later, after Annette's young lover had left, Charles would emerge from the dressing room to complete her sexual exhaustion by inserting his penis in her deluged sex and stroking her until she had still another orgasm. Formidable! The memory of those feverish occasions always brought a heat to her belly. Now she thought of masturbating, wondered if she ought to do it in order to relax a bit. She had no qualms about doing it, but she disliked being interrupted while she was at it. If Charles came home while she was in the midst of it, she might not get to finish it properly and then she'd be on edge the entire evening. Well, never mind that. She needed it, didn't she? She could already feel her breasts tingling as she thought about it. Without any further delay, she left the living room and she climbed the stairs to the bedroom. Now that she was about to do it, she was thankful the servants were out, thankful she had the complete privacy she liked when she played her little games with herself. Charles had watched her masturbate on many occasions, but he knew nothing about her private games, her secret amusements. In the bedroom, she closed the door and she quickly stripped off her clothes. She put on a silk robe and she walked into the bathroom to find an aspirin in the medicine cabinet. This was part of the ritual: an aspirin before she started anything. She had no idea why she needed the aspirin, but it was something she'd been doing for years. After she swallowed the aspirin with some water, she left the bathroom and she entered the bedroom again. In front of the full-length mirror, she pulled the sash at her waist and allowed her robe to rustle to the floor. It fell slowly, the silk slithering down her skin, down her hips and thighs and legs to the carpet. She stepped out of the robe, kicked it aside and turned her gaze to the mirror.

Like a whore, she thought. She thought she looked like a whore these days, her body more ripe-looking than ten years ago. She wriggled her shoulders and watched her heavy breasts sway from side to side like the nichons of one of those whores in Pigalle. Well, go on, dress for it, she thought. Black stockings on the whore's legs. She found the stockings and garters in a drawer and she sat on the edge of the bed to pull them on. After she had the stockings tight on her legs, she brought a pair of black high-heeled pumps out of the closet and she stepped into them. Yes, that was better. Now when she looked at herself in the mirror, the black stockings set off the dark triangle at the joining of her thighs. Standing before the mirror, she swayed her hips from side to side as she lightly ran her fingers through the fur on her mound. A whore's tits, she thought. Look at the big *nichons*. She moved her shoulders again to watch her breasts bounce. She was still attractive, wasn't she? She was still alluring enough to bring out the lust in a man.

She slipped a hand between her thighs, her fingers this time probing into the slit to find the wetness. As she expected, her sex was oozing, the hot juices now streaming out on her fingers. Charles hardly ever sucked it anymore, and the trouble with those factory boys was they never liked it in the first place. She had to coax them, and when they finally agreed it was usually dull. She liked it done with gusto, the mouth making noises as it pulled the sap out of her. A shudder of delight ran through her as she thought about having a mouth down there now, any mouth, even a woman, or maybe preferably a woman since they were usually more expert than a man. Like that whore that time in Paris who picked her up in the metro and sucked her into exhaustion in a hotel room. The whore had given her a business card afterward. Did you like my tongue, madame? She said Annette could have two girls next time and maybe she could suck one of them while the other sucked her. Would she like that?

Annette shuddered now as she remembered it. She raised her hand to her lips and she licked her fingers clean of her juices. She thought the taste was sweet, almost syrupy. Then her sex demanded her fingers again and she moved to the bed. After she stretched out on her back, her hands immediately covered her breasts. She trapped the nipples between her fingers, kneading and pulling at them until it became painful. She groaned, turned over on her belly and pressed the mound of her sex against the mattress, up and down, up and down, as though she had a body beneath hers, as though she were a man doing it to a woman. One of her hands burrowed between her body and the bed and groped for the sex between her legs. She slid her legs wide open, trembling as her fingers found the wet opening of her vagina. What was she now, a man or a woman? She could feel the spike of her clitoris as she probed between the fat lips of her sex. Groaning again, she pushed her middle finger deep inside the hole and held it there, the digit captured, imprisoned in the hot cave, the feel of it inside her body providing her a transient relief. But in a moment the fire in her sex raged even hotter, demanding more of an incursion. She inserted another finger, drawing her knees up so that now she was in a kneeling position, her buttocks raised, naked, as though she were waiting for a lover to take her from behind. Her head pressed into the pillow, her body trembled as she drove her fingers relentlessly in and out of her sex. Now she desperately wanted Charles to be there to do it to her, to take her, to fill her sex with his masculine force. She wanted him thrusting at her, his organ sliding in her sex and ramming her insides. She gasped repeatedly now, each gasp a response to a thrust of her fingers in her sex. It was no good. The fingers were inadequate, not thick enough, not long enough, not brutal enough. In desperation, she moved her free hand behind her swaying buttocks, searched the wet crevice, found her anus and then rammed a finger deep inside it. She cried out as she felt the penetration into the tight channel. Then again she began thrusting her fingers in her sex, the finger in her rectum now moving in concert with the fingers in her vagina. This was better, more definite, both holes grasping at something. Her dangling breasts swayed and slapped together as her body gyrated. She felt the orgasm approaching. She hung a moment on the edge, her sex and anus twitching, and then suddenly she exploded as the pleasure convulsed in her belly.

She finished it rapidly, both hands moving with precision, the warm juices gushing from her sex to cover her fingers. She grunted now, imagining a lover finishing inside her, the sperm squirting deep in her channel as he possessed her completely.

She remained on her hands and knees long after the waves of pleasure had passed, unwilling to withdraw her fingers, panting into the pillow as the final tingling subsided.

It's enough, she thought. After a final twisting of the finger inside the rubbery ring of her anus, she pulled her hands away from her body and she lay flat on the mattress. Enough, enough, she thought. With a groan, she eased off the bed to find the bathroom.

An hour later she was dressed and downstairs in the living room again. She finished the last of her wine and she rose wearily to fix another. She hated when the servants were off and she had no one to look after her. She wondered where Charles was. It was nearly five o'clock and on Saturdays he was usually home by now.

As though on cue, she suddenly heard the tires of a car squealing as they negotiated the winding driveway that led to the Boudin house. She pulled the drapery back far enough to see the dark blue front of her husband's Mercedes. Within a few moments, Charles entered the house and came directly to the living room.

"Well, I'm home," he said.

Annette smirked. "Hello, darling. I thought you were lost to me."

"Something came up at the factory."

"Your baton, Charles?"

He chuckled. "As always, you're astute."

"Who was it this time? One of those cows in the packing room?"

Charles sighed. "Not a cow at all. It was Juliette's sister-in-law. I've hired the girl as my personal secretary."

Annette put her wine down and groaned. "Oh dear."

"You don't approve?"

"I don't approve of every slut in Dampierre knowing about my husband's mistress."

"Darling, the girl will be as discreet as Juliette was. It's in her interest too, isn't it?"

"Juliette is a stupid cow. And what's the name of the new one?"

"Léonie Vogelin."

Annette smirked again. "Was it good, darling?"

"She's like a goddess," Charles said, smacking his lips then blowing a kiss at Annette. "Red hair and breasts like cantaloupes. And the derriere, dear God."

"Red hair?"

"Natural, my love.

And so the teasing conversation continued, Annette probing for details and Charles supplying them without hesitation. Annette learned of everything that had happened in the factory office, and before long she found herself completely aroused as she imagined Charles and the redhead. Before long Annette approached Charles, reached between his legs and tugged playfully at his penis through the front of his trousers. The organ was soft, but as she pinched it gently she could feel the beginning of an awakening. Her fingers caressed the shaft and then stroked the rounded curves of his testicles.

"Are you finished for the day?"

Charles smiled at her. "I could be coaxed I suppose."

"Does she have a husband?"

"She's unmarried."

"A brother then?"

"Poor Annette."

"You won't say poor Annette the next time I have one of the factory boys in the bedroom, will you? Eh, Charles? Why don't you bring one home for me and I'll do the rest while you watch us? Wouldn't you like that?"

She laughed as she felt his penis twitch beneath her fingertips. She knew how much Charles loved to play the voyeur, how much he adored seeing her speared by one of those lusty leather workers with a large member and the vigorous thrusting of a sweating stallion. The more vigorous the connection, the more Charles enjoyed watching it.

"I'll try to arrange something soon," Charles said, pulling away from her and walking to the bar to pour himself some wine. "It's always difficult to avoid the gossip, isn't it?"

After he poured his wine he had some of it and then he went to the sofa and he sat on the edge of the cushion. Anne's eyes sparkled as he removed his shoes and trousers and then opened the fly of his boxer shorts. He pulled the half-erect length of his blue-veined penis out of his undershorts so that it dangled between his hairy legs. "Come on then," he said. "Charm the snake if you can."

Aroused as always by the sight of his thick organ, Annette put down her glass and walked across the rug to join him. She knelt between his legs, gazed at the twitching penis and then at his face. "You're a filthy lecher, aren't you? They ought to arrest you for debauching the girls of the town."

"Take it in your mouth."

"How do you know I want to?"

"I know my Annette."

Yes, he did know her. She was well aware that he knew everything about her. He knew how much she loved to suck a penis, how much she adored the taste of sperm in her mouth. She unsnapped the fly of his undershorts to give herself more complete access to the meaty thickness of his penis. She felt him tremble as her fingers pulled and tugged at the rubbery organ. She leaned close to it, breathing over the purplish knob held between her two fingers.

"I can smell her," Annette said.

"She's a clean girl."

"You're a pig, Charles."

"I suppose that's why you adore me."

Yes, he was right. He knew all about her, didn't he? Meanwhile she could smell the girl and now she wanted to taste her. Charles knew about that too, all about Annette's more than occasional hunger to suck at the sex of a lusty girl. She liked them best when they were peasant girls, but it really didn't matter. When she wanted it badly enough, any girl would do. Now she took the entire purplish knob in her mouth, her tongue swirling once around it slowly, relishing the taste of it, aroused as she felt his penis shudder and jerk within the warm confines of her mouth. In a few moments she had the penis long and hard and throbbing.

Charles started talking about Léonie again. He teased Annette with his words. He grunted as she licked and caressed the fleshy stiffness of his organ. He told Annette that Léonie was a tall girl. He described her legs, her breasts, her buttocks. Annette made sounds of approval around the shaft of his penis as she listened to him. Her lips made a tighter ring now as she rocked against his loins until the hairs around the base of his member tickled her nose. Her chin rested lightly on the twin orbs of his testicles, his fat balls already emptied once today and now no doubt full again for Annette. She adored the male substance, the taste of it, the slippery feel of it on the back of her tongue.

Charles watched Annette, as he always did, with a degree of wonder. He'd been through his share of women, some of them prettier and most of them younger than Annette. But not one of those faceless girls could match Annette when it came to sucking his baton. She was always masterful, with a glorious application of artistry, her attractive lips like an open flower pulling at his stalk. She sucked his penis with such an obvious hunger it amazed him. She sucked as though all she cared for was to have her belly filled with his liquor.

He watched her now as she brought his bloated testicles out of the gap in his shorts and cradled them with her fingers. She sucked voraciously at his penis with her lips and tongue. He groaned as he felt the exquisite vacuum of her throat, the muscles churning and drawing his member to get the hot liquid of his sperm out of his swollen testicles. His eyes bulged with excitement as he watched the shaft of his penis slip wetly from her pink lips, centimeter by centimeter out of her mouth until only the rim of his glans was still held captive. Her tongue played wickedly with the tiny slit, and then again she engulfed the member and buried her nose in the matted thickness of his pubic hair. He grabbed her head and gripped it tightly, positioning her mouth the way he wanted it. He moved her head back and forth as she grunted and squealed with enthusiasm. Her head shook from side to side as she sucked and licked at the underside of his penis to bring him to a crisis.

Before long Charles groaned and Annette could feel the sudden lurch of his testicles as his orgasm began. Her lips went into a rapturous dance of wild sucking, her cheeks hollowing to take the sperm she could feel surging up from his testicles. The glans swelled in her mouth as he began spurting. She swallowed repeatedly as the gushing heat filled her mouth and gathered at the back of her tongue.

When she had the last spurt of semen, she allowed his penis to slither from her lips like a heavy noodle. She licked her lips clean, then licked his glans, bathing it with her tongue until every trace of sperm was removed. Then, and only then, did she rise to lie trembling on the sofa beside Charles.

"My God, you're a mystery," Charles said with a groan.

"Why?"

"The way you suck at it."

"I thought you liked it."

"I adore it."

"How many times did you come with her?"

"Only once."

"No wonder you're so full."

She leaned back against the cushion, drew up her legs and pulled down her panties. Charles turned on the sofa, his eyes on her white thighs above the tops of her dark stockings. He slid a hand between her thighs until his fingers touched the wet swamp of her sex. The outer lips gaped, the inner lips swollen and protruding. Annette groaned as his fingertip stroked the shaft of her clitoris.

"Yes, do that!" she said. "Rub it for me! Rub it and make me come!" She closed her eyes and tossed her head back on the sofa. Her legs moved apart until they were almost at right angles to her body. Charles pushed a pair of stiffened fingers into the red mouth of her vagina and began simulating the movements of a penis. Annette shuddered, her face flushed, her belly heaving, her wet sex making liquid sounds as the strong fingers pistoned in and out of the opening. She came twice before she finally pushed his hand away and pouted at him. "Will you find someone for me?"

Charles looked at the slime glistening on his fingers. "I'll try to arrange something soon."

V.

A JOB IN PARIS

Thanks to the Widow Borel, Tony Sadou was now a waiter in her restaurant outside Dampierre. He was the youngest of the waiters, and some of the others teased him because it was apparent he was now Germaine Borel's favorite. The waiters asked him if the widow had him in her bed, but he always refused to tell them anything. He would merely smile and walk away, do his work and think about his plans. Tony's family had moved north from Marseilles when he was a baby, and even if his family was still poor he intended to make something of himself. He hated working in a factory like his father and brothers did. The restaurant was more pleasant, especially now that he was no longer a lowly busboy and he knew how to please the owner. Tony had learned a long time ago that certain older women found him irresistible, women of forty or even fifty who were strongly attracted to his southern looks and temperament, but eventually more than anything else to the masculine attributes that he carried between his legs. They adored the size of his member, and their adoration always excited him tremendously. These days he hardly ever looked at younger women, and silly inexperienced girls were of no interest to him at all. He saw Germaine Borel no more than once a week because it seemed that was sufficient for her. Their lovemaking in her house had become routine, with Germaine doing much sucking of his penis and then taking him to her bedroom where she had him mount her and do the usual thing as vigorously as possible. Tony always enjoyed it with her, but he'd found another woman in Dampierre to occupy his time when Germaine did not summon him. Tony hoped that Ernestine Kleber might eventually be even more helpful to him than Germaine had been. Ernestine's husband owned a successful trucking company in Paris, and Tony thought that maybe before long he could ask Ernestine to speak to her husband about a job for him. Meanwhile he saw Ernestine whenever she wanted him, which was usually two or three times a week when her husband travelled to one place or another on business. Tony would then go to the Kleber house after he finished work at the restaurant, and he and Ernestine would pass a few feverish hours together. She was about the same age as Germaine, with carefully groomed blond hair and a youthful body always heavily perfumed. Tony had come to adore Ernestine's perfume, and whenever he had the scent in his nose it always aroused him.

It was on a Monday that Tony decided the next time he saw Ernestine he would ask her to speak to her husband about him. Yes, why not now? Tony thought. Was it really necessary to wait any longer? He felt confident Ernestine would help him. He hoped she would telephone him at the restaurant that day, but she didn't. Instead it wasn't until Wednesday that he spoke to her. She sounded happy when she called, saying she'd be pleased to have him come to the house this evening if had the time for it. "You do have the time, don't you?"

Tony assured her he always had the time for her.

"You know I do." He promised to be at the house at five o'clock, which was two hours earlier than usual, and then after that he went to Germaine and he convinced her to allow him to leave the restaurant early.

"I'll make up the time tomorrow," Tony said.

Germaine patted his cheek and told him she didn't mind it. "Don't get into any trouble with one of your girls."

Germaine knew nothing about Ernestine Kleber, and she thought the only other women he knew were girls his own age. He suspected Germaine would be furious if she learned another woman her own age enjoyed his amorous attentions. They're all crazy, Tony thought. Germaine cared nothing about the girls his own age, but only about the older women.

At five o'clock he rushed from the restaurant and he rode his bicycle at top speed to the Kleber house. Ernestine greeted him at the door and kissed him warmly. "My sweet Romeo," she said. She told him the servants were gone, and then she led him to the living room where she served him a sandwich and a glass of red wine. "You look hungry," she said. "The bitch ought to let you eat more at the restaurant."

The "bitch" was Germaine Borel, whom Ernestine knew and whom she disliked intensely. But Ernestine had no idea of his affair with Germaine; he was certain she'd throw him out if she ever learned of it.

After the sandwich and the wine were finished, Ernestine sat on the sofa beside him and she began the usual affectionate kissing and fondling designed to prepare them for the bedroom. Tony wondered when he ought to ask her about the job with her husband's firm. Now or later? He decided later would be more sensible; later, after their lovemaking was finished, Ernestine would no doubt be more receptive to any request he made. Meanwhile he enjoyed her kisses and her perfume, and before long the careful stroking of her fingers across the front of his trousers produced the huge erection she wanted and it was time to adjourn to the bedroom. "My dear Romeo is eager for it," she said with a teasing smile. Then she rose, and without another word she left him, the scent of her perfume lingering in the air to tantalize him.

Tony followed her, and when he entered the room he found her standing by the foot of the bed waiting for him. He took off his jacket and shirt and kicked off his shoes. Then he walked over to her and they embraced. Her head tilted upwards, her mouth open and waiting for his lips. Her tongue came alive in his mouth as he felt her breasts press against his naked chest. She did not have Germaine Borel's enormous breasts, but what she had was substantial enough. He ran his hands up and down her back, feeling her spine and her round buttocks through her skirt. Then he stepped back and he slowly undid the buttons on her blouse and pulled it loose. She shrugged her shoulders and the blouse fell to the floor. Her breasts threatened to spill out over the tops of her brassiere cups as he reached around in back and undid the clasp to free them.

"You seem pensive," she said, turning her back to him as she dropped the brassiere.

"But I'm not," Tony replied.

"You're thinking about something, eh? Why don't you tell me?"

He insisted it was nothing, and in a moment he moved behind her to cup and fondle her breasts from the rear. At the same time he pressed his hardening penis into the crack between her buttocks and moved his hips from side to side to make her feel it better. Ernestine murmured, leaning back against him as she reached behind her with one hand to find his penis and squeeze it through his trousers. "Finish undressing me," she said.

Tony pulled down the zipper at the side of her skirt, and in a moment she wiggled her buttocks as he pulled both the skirt and her panties down her legs so she could step out of them.

Her buttocks never failed to excite him. He would rather play with Germaine's breasts than with Ernestine's, but he found Ernestine's almost spherical backside infinitely more tempting. Part of the reason was that the more attention he paid to Ernestine's backside, the more it seemed to arouse her, and he'd learned that having her fully aroused would ultimately bring him the most pleasure.

He sat on the edge of the bed and he gently pulled her forward to kiss her belly. Then he used one hand to caress her belly while the other hand moved to the patch of auburn hair covering her sex. He rubbed the hairy mound above her sex, deliberately teasing her, his mouth again pressing wet kisses on her belly as she stroked his head and moaned softly. In a moment he slid one hand around to fondle her buttocks, his fingers eventually probing between the full cheeks to stroke the groove.

Her hand continuing to caress his head, she wiggled her hips from side to side and groaned. "Yes, darling..."

Now his middle finger pushed against the tight ring of her anus and he slowly entered her. Ernestine sucked in her breath sharply, moaning with pleasure as the finger filled the passage already lubricated with petroleum jelly before he arrived.

"Gently," she said. This admonition always occurred at the same moment, although of course after the many times he had done this to her there was no need to tell him what she liked. He kept one hand on the mound of her sex as he slowly moved the finger in her backside. Now his fingers penetrated between the fleshy sex-lips to stroke the damp groove. In a moment he entered the other hole, the vaginal orifice, with the middle finger of his right hand. She held his head tightly against her belly as he slowly worked the fingers in the two passages.

After a while she moved her hands from his head and she took hold of her breasts. She closed her eyes and groaned repeatedly as the boy carefully stroked her with his fingers. She rocked backwards and forwards, the tension and pressure building in her body. Tony applied himself with all the skill he had, his mind in a daze of lust, his penis aching to burst from his trousers. Then Ernestine signalled she was about to reach a crisis and she leaned forward, her breasts swinging, her body trembling as she gasped repeatedly.

The hot juices from her sex dripped over Tony's hand as he continued to move both fingers. Both passages were completely open and wet now, the orgasm still shaking her body. A farm woman who had taken him as a lover when he was sixteen had shown him how to do this one day. Ernestine had been ravished the first time he had done it to her. So far the Widow Borel refused it; he'd coaxed her more than once, but she wouldn't allow it. She said it was disgusting to have a finger in her backside. In the front yes, but not in her backside.

Ernestine adored it and she allowed all of it. He dug into her with his fingers, finishing the orgasm the way she liked it to be finished. When he sensed she was through, he pulled both fingers out and he rose. He quickly dropped his pants, his penis snapping forward like a huge club. Ernestine gazed at it with hot eyes, and then she sank down to the bed and leaned forward to take both his testicles and his organ in her hands. He watched as she licked the knob and rubbed his testicles before she started sucking him. Then she moved her head forward and she took as much of his penis inside her mouth as she could manage. She moved backward only to begin another push forward. She closed her eyes as she sucked at the member with a deliberate concentration. The flat of her tongue stroked the underside of his penis, her hands caressing his thighs and the small of his back before they settled on his buttocks. Now, instead of moving her head, she pushed and pulled his hips to keep his organ moving in her mouth. Tony did what she wanted, his hips gently thrusting as he possessed her mouth completely. Amused, he wondered what her husband might think if he were suddenly to walk in on them. Did she do this with her husband? He had no idea what the man even looked like. He thought maybe afterward he would ask her to show him a photograph of Monsieur Kleber.

Now Ernestine removed her mouth from his penis, lifted his scrotum and began kissing it. She licked at the hairy bag, extending her tongue, her fingers rolling the eggs inside the sac. Then she pulled away from him and she fell slowly backwards onto the middle of the bed. She spread her legs and raised them high in the air. Her arms outstretched, she smiled at him. "Come, darling. Come to me now."

After mounting the bed, Tony climbed over her. Ernestine took hold of his penis with both hands and eagerly pulled it toward the entrance of her waiting sex. He pushed forward, entering her slowly, his eyes fixed on the lips of her sex grasping at his thickness.

Her passage was narrower than Germaine's, tight enough so that he felt his foreskin stripped backward from the knob of his penis. In a moment he was all the way inside her, buried to the balls, Ernestine groaning and heaving against him. She wrapped her legs around his waist and started wiggling her buttocks in a mad dance. He reared back and slammed forward again, grunting as he felt the hot grip of her sheath.

He was soon thrusting hard, not holding back because he knew she liked his movements to be vigorous. Germaine was the same: the more violently he pounded her, the more she enjoyed it. Now Ernestine clung to him, raising her mouth to kiss and bite his neck and shoulders. She bucked her sex up into his penis as he slammed it into her, rocking herself up and down on the bed. His testicles slapped against her buttocks as he raised himself up on his hands to penetrate her more deeply. Ernestine soon cried out as she started coming. Tony continued thrusting, looking down at her, watching the jiggling of her breasts, the large pink nipples. Then he felt her passage vibrating and throbbing as it gripped his penis, and the new sensation brought him to a crisis. Ernestine grunted, heaving herself upwards as she realized he was about to come. His testicles seemed suddenly to go numb a moment before he shot a long stream of hot sperm into the depths of her sex. He cried out as it happened again. And again and again. She held onto his buttocks now, urging him to continue spurting. But finally it was over and he lay down on her soft body as she stroked his head and kissed him.

"My Romeo," she said with a soft laugh. "My darling Romeo. Let's go downstairs again and we'll have some more wine."

She left the bed and she brought one of her husband's robes to him. She had never done this before and Tony was thrilled by the idea of wearing something that belonged to Monsieur Kleber. After she donned her own robe, they walked down the stairs together to the large living room.

"I'd rather have champagne than ordinary wine," she said. "Will you join me?"

He nodded, and then when she brought the bottle to him he opened it and poured the champagne into two glasses. They toasted each other, and as they did so he realized he'd never liked champagne that much. He'd much rather have ordinary red wine than champagne, but he was afraid if he told her that she would think him a bumpkin. As she turned and walked away from him toward the bar, he gazed at her and recalled what they had done together, what he had done to her with his fingers. She was barelegged, her legs showing under the short robe, the full calves and the pink heels of her small feet in chic silver slippers. She looked completely poised, self-assured, and now it was hard for him to imagine that just a short while ago he'd actually had one of his fingers in her backside. He had a sudden urge to laugh, but he restrained himself. Don't spoil it, he thought. You know how these women can be. She might get annoyed at him and refuse to see him again. No, that was impossible. She had told him often how much she adored him. He was certain Ernestine craved his embraces even more than Germaine did.

When she returned from the bar, she came close to him and smiled. "Are you rested enough now?"

"I don't know."

"Well, let me see then." She slipped her hand inside his robe to take hold of his testicles and then his penis. She pulled the member out of the folds of the robe to look at it, her fingers stroking it gently. "Oh, you'll be ready again in no time," she said.

Cupping his balls, she said: "I'm going to have more out of these, won't I, cheri?"

As they always did, her skillful fingers soon restored his vigor completely. She continued stroking his penis until it swelled to a full erection, and then she pulled her hand away and said: "Upstairs, my Romeo. Put the champagne bottle in the kitchen first, won't you?" Then she turned and left him, and as he watched her disappear up the staircase to prepare for their second bout, it occurred to him that now she was treating him like a servant. How strange she was! How strange they all were, Ernestine and Germaine and all the others he'd known, these middle-aged women with their soft curves and imperial attitudes. Why was he attracted to them? He tried to fathom it, but he found himself confused. Rather than dwell on it, he took the empty champagne bottle into the kitchen and he tossed it into the garbage bin. Then he left the kitchen and he climbed the stairs, his penis as stiff as ever, wanting her again, determined to have his pleasure with her as a compensation for the sudden misery he felt. He usually felt enormously proud to have these women in bed, but suddenly now the pride was gone and all he wanted was to take her and finish his pleasure.

When he entered her bedroom, he found her lying naked on the bed with her legs wide apart. She smiled at him as he walked toward her and sat on the edge of the bed beside her. Their eyes met, and then he looked at her belly, at her sex exposed by her open legs. He put his hand on the mound, and then he ran his middle finger between the lips to feel the wetness. The misery he'd felt before was gone now; she was a woman like any other woman and she wanted him. He began moving his finger up and down the length of her slit, probing deeper each time until she spread her legs wider. With his other hand he fondled her breasts, and now he bent his head to lick her nipples. His hand kept up a steady motion in her sex, up and down, teasing her, building her excitement and desire. He sucked on her nipples and bit them gently. Ernestine responded by sighing and arching her chest upwards, her hand now fondling his head. Her sex became wetter and wetter under his fingers, and soon he used his hand with more authority, pushing the fingers inside as far as they would go, two fingers and then three fingers, her juices streaming over his hand.

Finally she gasped: "No more!"

His hand stopped moving. "What do you want?"

Her answer was to pull at the belt of the robe he wore, her husband's robe, to get his body uncovered. He rose and dropped the robe, and then he climbed over her with his swollen penis bobbing from side to side like a blind serpent. She gazed at it and wet her lips, and for a moment he thought she'd suck it. But instead she pulled her knees up and she said she wanted it inside her. "Look how big you are. Your zob is like a fat sausage."

"Is your husband's as big as this?"

For a moment she seemed shocked that he'd mentioned her husband. Then she laughed. "Don't talk about my husband now. Come on, put it inside me!"

But when he moved between her thighs, he teased her first by rubbing the knob of his penis up and down the length of her slit.

She caressed his flanks and tried to pull him down into her, but he resisted, teasing her further, waiting for the right moment to enter her. He felt sure of himself now, sure of his muscular body, sure of his rock-hard penis that she desired so much. Then he found the entrance to her sex and he entered her, held his position a moment and then pushed himself deep inside her as far as he could go. He jarred her body when his pelvis hit hers, their pubic hairs grinding together. He held himself there, grinding against her as she winced and strained herself upwards. He reared back and plunged inside her again, thrusting now, thrusting hard, knowing that because this was the second time he could last as long as he liked. He propped himself on his hands to get a better angle of penetration and to be able to watch himself moving in and out of her. Then he watched her face, feasting his eyes on the pleasure in it. She now matched him thrust for thrust, bucking her sex upwards as he drove downwards into her, her throat making a sound of pleasure with each thrust. She raised her legs high in the air and managed to keep her buttocks down. She grunted loudly and dug her fingernails into his shoulders.

Suddenly she stopped moving and she pushed him away from her. "Wait," she said.

Puzzled, he pulled out of her, pulled his penis free of her sex and sat back on his heels. "What is it?"

With a wild look in her eyes, she twisted her legs away and rolled over to kneel on the mattress with her buttocks facing him. "In the other place," she said. "Do it in there."

He looked at it, at the glorious buttocks, the deep groove between them, the tiny knot of her anus. They had done it only once before and now he was thrilled that she wanted it again. A quiver of excitement passed up his spine as he remembered how good it was.

Kneeling behind her, he put his hands on her buttocks and spread them apart. Her anus was now completely revealed and he could see that again she had already lubricated herself. None of the other women he'd known ever did that; it was something peculiar to Ernestine.

"Remember to be careful," she said with a whimper. "You're so big..."

He continuing gazing at the oiled brown ring, and then he placed the knob of his penis against it and slowly pushed himself inside her. She groaned as she felt the invasion. In a moment he had all of his organ in her backside, his testicles pressed against her sex, his hips jerking from side to side as he gasped at the pleasure of it. When he began stroking himself in and out of her, she cried out and started coming immediately. The madness continued until finally he could hold out no longer and he had to come also, his body shaking and a rasping cry escaping his lips as he squirted inside her backside.

He lay on top of her awhile, his belly pressed against her buttocks, and when at last he pulled out of her his testicles hung limp and empty in their sac. Ernestine immediately left the bed to use the bathroom, and when she returned she bent over him and she kissed his lips. "You like that, don't you, darling?"

"Yes," he said.

"And I do, too."

"Doesn't it hurt?"

"Only a little at first. And afterward it's heavenly."

"I want to ask you something about your husband."

She looked astonished. "My husband? Why should we talk about my husband now?"

"No, it's about something else. Do you think he could find me a job with his firm?"

Astonished again, she stared at him and said nothing. Then she smiled and she took hold of his limp penis with her fingers, inspected it and pinched it as if to test whether it could come alive again. "We'll see about that," she said. "I'll give it some thought and we'll see."

Tony reached out his hand to stroke one of her drooping breasts. He was certain now that before long he'd have a job in Paris.

VI.

THE MANNEQUIN

Undoubtedly the grandest house in Dampierre was located on the Jallez estate. Louis Jallez was well-known on the Paris Bourse and a prominent figure in all financial circles. At seventy he was still active in business affairs, but perhaps with not as much energy as in former times. Ten years ago, after a lifetime as a bachelor, he'd married a young fashion model, and to everyone's surprise the marriage had now survived a decade of domesticity. Claire Jallez was now thirty-four and seemingly devoted to her aging husband. Perhaps the absence of children made the disparity in their ages less burdensome. Louis allowed Claire a handsome allowance and enough freedom to make her the envy of many other women of her class. In recent years, Louis was often not in Dampierre or Paris at all, but basking in the sun in Monte Carlo where he had many friends among French and British royalty.

Claire, meanwhile, was a complete Parisian and inseparable from the capital. She was a tall woman with a slender body and thin long-fingered hands, a wide mouth usually painted a bright red, and dark blond hair flowing in waves, more on her right side than on her left due to the asymmetric coiffure she favored these days. She had an angular face still unlined and with only a hint of maturity at the corners of her mouth. When Louis first met her, he was sixty years old and immediately vanquished by her youth and sensuality. For Claire, however, the attraction was the Louis Jallez fortune and a life of complete leisure. She might have easily acquired a younger husband of the same means, but when she learned Louis promised complete devotion and almost unlimited freedom to live her own life, she chose him instead. They were married in a tiny church in the south of France, passed a long honeymoon cruising the Mediterranean on a chartered yacht, and eventually returned to the enormous Jallez house in Dampierre to begin their married life. At first their intimate relations were ordinary. Louis would hint in the afternoon, either by telephone from Paris or in person, that in the evening he would want to make love to Claire. She would prepare herself accordingly, and in the early evening they would retire to her bedroom where Louis would busy himself for twenty minutes or so with his face between her thighs. The position was always the same, Claire on her back with her legs raised high in the air, and Louis flat on his belly with his mouth pressed firmly against her sex. Claire would shudder briefly during each orgasm, and on those days when her pleasure failed to arrive, she would make a pretense to keep Louis happy. After the sucking was finished, Louis would move to his knees and mount her with her long legs over his shoulders and his rigid organ sliding vigorously in and out of her sex. After a dozen or so strokes, he would empty himself inside her grasping passage and then roll away from her to sleep. Claire would wait a moment or two before leaving the bed for the bathroom, and by the time she reached the bidet she was usually already thinking of her plans for the evening.

This routine continued without much variation during the first year of their marriage. Then one evening Louis suggested that Claire model some underthings he'd bought for her in Paris. He'd never asked her to do this before and she was taken by surprise, but she'd been a mannequin after all and it was difficult to refuse him. Besides, she always enjoyed exhibiting her body, even to Louis. That evening she paraded before him in her bedroom wearing the lingerie he'd purchased for her in the Rue St. Honoré. It was obvious that Louis enjoyed it immensely, and afterward he was particularly ardent with her on the bed. A week later her performance was repeated, this time with a display so teasing that Louis brought his organ out of his trousers and immediately stroked himself to a crisis. Claire learned that from the first moment he'd seen her on the runway at the fashion-house where she'd worked, his interest in her had always been voyeuristic. Since she herself enjoyed showing herself to him, this became the new focus of their sexual life. Gradually their intimate hours assumed a new routine, with Louis masturbating while Claire exposed and paraded her charms. Only later would they couple on the bed. By the tenth year of marriage, with Louis now seventy years old, they were no longer even coupling in the ordinary way. After the usual erotic display by Claire, both were now satisfied to have Louis do no more than devote himself orally to Claire's sex. Afterward Claire would sit with her sex exposed and watch while Louis quickly brought himself to a climax with his hand. When his emission was finished, Claire would help him with a small towel, after which Louis would lie down on the bed to sleep and Claire would leave for the bathroom.

Claire enjoyed the new routine. She enjoyed exhibiting herself and she enjoyed provoking Louis' excitement by displaying her body. His oral caresses no longer produced any orgasms, but she'd learned to pretend well enough so that Louis never realized it. She masturbated in private to keep her nerves at rest, and when she felt the need for a more intense sexual experience she always managed to find it somewhere. She'd learned that if an attractive woman knew the right places in Paris, it was not difficult at all to arrange her amusements. What she adored was being made love to by two or three men at once, anonymous young men with muscular bodies and virile members, preferably Mediterranean in their looks. At first she visited discreet houses in Paris where such young men are provided to wealthy women, but as Louis approached seventy and passed more and more time away from her in the south, she often arranged a small diversion for herself in the Jallez house. For these entertainments she recruited young men in the cafes, sometimes in Paris and sometimes in Versailles or Chartres. It was easy enough to pick them up, and she found the amateurs were usually better lovers than the young men provided by the houses in Paris. The amateurs were less jaded and less cynical, and if they occasionally lacked technique they never lacked enthusiasm.

One afternoon when Louis was at the villa in the south, two young men Claire had met the day before in Paris arrived at the Jallez house. She'd sent the servants away, and all she thought of now was the pleasure she'd have during the next few hours with these two attractive specimens. "I remember only one name," she said with a smile as she served them champagne in the large drawing room.

"Which name?" one of them said. They were both in their twenties, with dark hair and dark eyes and sun-bronzed skin. She thought they might be part Arab, but she wasn't certain. Except for one having a broader chin than the other, she could hardly tell them apart.

"One of you is Angelo."

They both smiled, their white teeth gleaming at her. "I'm Angelo," the one with the broad chin said.

"And I'm Luc," the other said.

"Luc and Angelo," Claire repeated. She found herself amused by them, and perhaps a bit drunk from the champagne she'd already had before they arrived. She felt a tingling in her belly as she imagined herself with them. They looked marvelous, capable of giving a woman an enormous amount of pleasure without any awkward entanglements. How wonderful it was to be free of Louis like this!

She told them they looked enough alike to be brothers, and they said yes, some people did think that. She put a music tape on the stereo, and then she brought another bottle of champagne and she asked them to open it. Did they like champagne? "You don't need to drink it if you don't want to," she said. But they assured her the champagne was fine. And indeed it was out of her husband's wine cellar and no doubt better champagne than what they were accustomed to. The young men sat back and relaxed, their eyes on her long legs. As she expected, when she told them she'd once been a high-fashion model, they both seemed impressed. She wondered about them, about their lives and what sort of work they did. They could be baggage-handlers at Orly for all she knew. But she didn't care about that one way or the other; she cared about other things and the work they did was irrelevant. She talked to them about her former life as a model and then about various clubs in Paris. One of the clubs she mentioned was an expensive strip-tease club. They hadn't been there, but they'd been to other clubs of the same kind.

"I suppose every man likes a strip-tease," she said.

Angelo, the one with the broad chin, smiled at her. "So why don't you show us?"

Claire looked at them coyly. "Me? I wouldn't know how."

"Every woman knows how," Luc said. "Why don't you try it?"

She felt a quiver of excitement as she pretended to think about it. The fact was she always did it this way, first the conversation about night clubs and dancing and strip-tease, and then her own little performance that never failed to produce the frenzy she wanted. She imagined them naked, their organs erect and pointed at the ceiling, their testicles bloated with sperm. What excited her more than anything was the idea of having their eyes on her as she exhibited herself.

"All right," she said as she rose. "But I warn you I'm not a professional."

The sun was down, the room already in shadows. She turned up the music a bit, her supple body shimmering under the silk dress as she glided softly across the floor. She kept the slit in the dress away from them; she'd opened the hook that held the slit together and it now ran all the way up her right thigh. She knew very well the idea was to prolong the tease as much as possible; the men she'd known before Louis had taken her to enough of those clubs and she knew all about it. She swayed her body to the rhythm of the music, and then she slowly turned toward them and she allowed her right leg to emerge free of the dress. She gathered the dress with one hand and pressed the front of it between her legs, giving Luc and Angelo a glimpse of the black lace that adorned the bottom edge of her brief panties. Holding the dress tightly in front, she turned her back to them and swayed her hips to the music again. She flexed her backside, the firm cheeks rippling sensuously under the sheer material.

She heard them muttering to each other, and then one of them urged her to take something off.

Instead, as the music temporarily stopped, she faced them again and she smiled. "For a proper strip-tease, one must have patience." She walked over to the table where she'd left her champagne and she sipped from the glass.

As the music started again, she put one foot on the low table in front of them and she allowed the dress to fall away from the upper part of her thigh. With her leg extended, she leaned forward to stroke her fingertips along her calf and over her thigh as she slowly moved her backside to the music. She ran her tongue over her lips as she looked at them. They seemed mesmerized now, both men gazing at her exposed leg with an evident excitement. She thought Luc had an erection, but she wasn't certain.

She danced away from them, and then a dozen feet away she faced them again and moved her body from side to side. Then she turned her back again, and this time she reached behind her to pull at the long zipper. Slowly, she unzipped the dress to expose the skin of her back. Turning to face them again, she eased the dress off her shoulders to expose the tight-fitting lace brassiere that cupped her breasts. She dropped the dress further, exposing her torso and then the upper part of her hips. She halted the descent of the dress just above her mound, allowing them to concentrate on her breasts and belly, thrusting her hips forward with each beat of the music. In a moment she made the dress slip further down, exposing all of her panties and the elastic tops of her long stockings, down, down, until the dress dropped at her ankles and she stepped out of it.

After that she walked toward them and she made Angelo rise. She unbuttoned his shirt and she ran her slender hands over his chest. "Do I excite you?"

"You're a marvel," he muttered.

She laughed and stepped back as he tried to get his hands on her. "Not yet," she said.

The music had stopped, and now as it began again

she again undulated her hips. Her charms were still covered by her brassiere and panties, but she knew her long slim legs and the curves of her backside were enough to excite them intensely. The brief panties barely covered her sex hair, and as she leaned back slightly with her feet wide apart, their eyes were fixed on her nylon-covered mound.

She turned her back again, and now she pulled the thin material of her panties into the crack of her backside, pulled it lewdly between her buttocks to expose the cheeks completely. She heard them muttering again as she weaved her hips from side to side and flexed the muscles of her buttocks in a tantalizing display.

Then she unsnapped her brassiere and turned around. Both men were on their feet, and as they watched her she allowed the brassiere to dip below her nipples. Luc freed his penis from his trousers and immediately it rose straight along his flat belly. Her pulse racing as she gazed at the long organ, Claire danced toward him and blew a kiss in the direction of the dark member. Then she danced back to the center of the room, and there she allowed the brassiere to fall and leave her breasts completely exposed. Her nipples were stiff, standing straight out from her breasts as they bobbed and jerked with the movements of her body. She tossed the brassiere away and turned to watch Angelo pull his penis from his trousers, a lance as long as Luc's, but with a larger knob. He'd already removed his shirt, and now he quickly slipped out of the rest of his clothes before settling back in the chair to watch Claire.

She moved again, and the faster she moved the more her panties rubbed against her sex and inside the crack between her buttocks. The friction maddened her and she writhed her body with more vigor. Then the music slowed briefly, and she slid her panties down her legs to reveal the dark blond thicket that guarded her sex.

Both men were naked now, their hands on their stiff members as she teased them with her body. The drumbeat quickened, and Claire moved more wildly with the music, shaking her breasts and thrusting her hips back and forth as though she were coupling with an invisible lover. Then, as the music slowed, she turned and she planted her feet wide apart with her back to the men. Leaning forward, she flexed her backside muscles as her hips wiggled to the music. Bending further, she reached behind her to grasp her buttocks and pulled them wide apart.

She heard one of them groan. Angelo said something about nearly shooting off, and the idea that a view of her anus would force him to a crisis excited her tremendously.

She turned around and slid her hands over her breasts and then down the bare expanse of her belly to the mound of her sex. Now her body began to rock violently as the music came at a fever pitch. Before long she finished the dance with a sequence of movements that bounced her breasts up and down on her chest as the two men watched her with hot eyes. She was wild now, wild with excitement as she danced naked in front of them, enchanted by the lust in their eyes. Luc's long penis stood erect next to his belly as slumped back in his chair and gazed at her. She walked over to him and put one foot on his penis and pressed the sole of her high-heeled sandal tightly against his body. Slowly, she began to massage his pulsing organ with her shoe. With her leg raised in this position, Luc could stare directly at her wet sex. She smiled at him, moved her foot to the cushion beside his knee and reached down to open the pink lips.

"Is it pretty?" she said.

He groaned. "You could make a man crazy."

She laughed softly, pulling the swollen folds apart to expose her clitoris. Carefully, she slid back the protective skin from the tiny nub and pinched the shaft with her fingertips. The already enlarged clitoris now swelled even more, her fingers stretching her sex to give them a good look at her clitoris while she used the other hand to probe and jerk the mouth of her vagina.

The men groaned together and suddenly they were upon her. She felt Angelo's arms around her and his penis pressing between her buttocks as he fondled her breasts. Luc had his face pressed against her belly, his lips kissing her navel while she ran her fingers through his hair and pulled him more tightly against her. He licked her skin and stroked her thighs as she undulated between them. Before long, Luc's face was planted squarely between her legs, and as she spread her thighs he found her warm sex with his tongue. She thrilled at the daring of his tongue as his lips squeezed her swollen clitoris. Behind her, Angelo was now on his knees and licking every centimeter of her buttocks. He licked her skin near the top of her crevice and then, spreading her buttocks wide, he rubbed his wet tongue down the length of the groove of her backside.

A shudder passed through her body. She stood with her legs wide apart, supported by her two lovers, her anus twitching with pleasure as Angelo reamed it with his hot tongue and pinched the soft flesh of her backside between his fingers while Luc's equally hot tongue squirmed in her sex. An orgasm surged through her sex without warning, her clitoris twitching and her anus contracting around Angelo's tongue. As the climax rushed through her body, she felt herself grow faint with pleasure. "Oh God!" she moaned. Her knees gave out, and Angelo caught her as she fell backward into his arms. He eased her down on the floor with her back against the couch, and when she opened her eyes she found him straddling her body with his turgid penis only centimeters from her face. She reached for the member eagerly and slipped the knob between her parted lips. She licked the hot tip of the organ before Angelo rammed it deep inside her mouth. She pushed him back, and when his penis withdrew she lapped at it with her swirling tongue. With only the smooth knob of his penis in her mouth, she grasped his long shaft and jerked the skin back and forth as she sucked him. She cupped his balls in her free hand, and before long she sensed the eggs were about to release their contents. Sucking at the tip with more force, she jerked the shaft faster and faster. Angelo lurched forward as the hot sperm burst from his penis to drench her mouth. She sucked and swallowed, sucked and swallowed, the warm juice flowing over her tongue until finally she released him and he pulled his spent organ from her lips.

"Go on," Angelo said to Luc. "It's your turn."

Luc looked down at her. "Where?"

Instead of answering, she licked her lips as she looked up at his organ long and curved like a scimitar. In a moment he assumed the position Angelo had taken, straddling her body with his penis shaking in front of her face. She teased his penis with a few flicks of her tongue, and then she slid underneath him so that she was now lying flat on the floor. As he lowered his body, she grabbed his member and pressed the tip against the underside of her breast. His rigid organ felt marvelous against her soft flesh as she slid the loose skin back and forth over the shaft. Still stroking him gently, she pressed the purplish knob against her nipple. She tingled as the wetness from the opening moistened her stiffened nipple and made it slippery. The juice that seeped from the organ made her breasts wet as she continued to fondle it. Sensing that Luc was unable to last much longer, she placed his penis between her breasts and pressed it tightly against her skin. "Go on," she whispered. He groaned as he began thrusting, sliding his swollen member back and forth in the valley between her breasts. She kneaded and squeezed her flesh as she urged him to release the sperm in his reservoirs. She squirmed from side to side, pulling his swollen penis with her as she moved and rubbed the sensitive skin. Luc groaned, his body jerking, and then a moment later the hot sperm gushed out of the tip of his member. Claire tilted her head forward to get the next salvo on her lips. She licked his sperm from her red lips as the rest of his emission splashed against her throat and the top of her chest and trickled down between her breasts.

Later she rose and she took a long sip from the fresh drink that Angelo had poured for her. She picked up her panties and she wiped the sperm from her breasts as she continued to sip the champagne. Angelo was now sitting on the couch, his limp penis resting between his muscular thighs. Far from exhausted, Claire strolled over to him and she sat on his lap. Without hesitation, she pulled his soft penis up between her thighs and rubbed it against her sex.

"Have I exhausted you?"

He chuckled. "No, of course not."

"I didn't think so." She pressed her thighs together and squeezed the rubbery shaft. "No one has really had me yet."

Angelo snorted. "We'll have you soon enough." He playfully squeezed her backside, and the gradually stiffening penis between her thighs assured her it was true. She squirmed her thighs as she fingered and massaged the soft canal that ran down the length of his member. She brushed the knob against her soft sex hair, slowly easing the short foreskin over the purplish crown and then drawing it down again. Angelo nibbled at one of her breasts and took the succulent nipple between his teeth. Claire felt the passion begin to rise higher again as her sex twitched in response to his mouth on her breast.

Now he slid one hand underneath her and he ran his middle finger along the tender flesh between the globes of her backside. He toyed with her anus a moment, and then he trailed his finger lightly back and forth along her crevice again.

Although Claire adored the way Angelo was touching her, the tantalizing stroking of her backside made it impossible to sit still. She wiggled her hips and flexed her thighs around his organ. As she continued to move her buttocks, Angelo probed her anus with his finger. He pushed the finger inside the hot opening and he began twisting it against her soft flesh. She groaned as she pumped her hips slowly. She looked at Luc and she noticed his penis had risen again. When she beckoned to him, he came forward immediately. With Angelo's finger still deep in her backside, she reached for Luc's penis and felt it grow to its full size as he bent over and kissed her lips. Their tongues met and they kissed deeply. In a moment Luc made her rise, and as she left Angelo's lap he eased his finger out of her anus.

She went down on the Chinese rug with both of them, Luc kissing her mouth while Angelo worked his head between her legs from the rear to tongue her moist sex. She opened her sex to Angelo, spreading her thighs to admit his tongue. But Angelo pulled away from her and he began stroking her sex with his fingers. Then he slid his stiff penis between her legs from the rear, bathing it in the juices that flowed from her opening. When his penis was wet, he pulled back and rubbed his glans against her tight anus. She groaned as she felt it. She flinched as the tip of his penis stretched the round circle of muscle and then slipped partway inside her.

Now she lay on her right side and she lifted her left leg over Luc to open her rear hole to Angelo's probing penis. She moaned as he eased the organ inside her yielding backside, as the rigid member stretched the soft anal passage. Then she felt Luc's penis pressing against her wet sex-lips, and as Angelo's powerful penis pushed her forward, she felt Luc's organ begin to slide through the slippery opening of her sex. Soon her heaving body felt stuffed with the constantly moving organs of her two lovers. She moaned and panted in sheer delight as they pumped their members with a skillful rhythm. Her two channels filled, she bound them together with only a thin membrane separating their thrusting members. She was near her peak now, groaning as Angelo spliced his way between her parted buttocks. Her sex churned under the pressure of Luc's penis as it slammed deep inside her vagina.

Dear God, yes! she thought, and the next moment she thrashed uncontrollably as the orgasm gripped her like a vise. Her climax overwhelmed her, forcing her to bite her lip to keep from blacking out. When the spasms that shook her body finally began to subside, her head cleared and she realized that both men were still pumping their members in and out of her body. With a cry of joy, she begged them to finish, and in a few moments she had her wish, the two male bodies grinding against hers, each man grunting as the boiling sperm poured out of him and into one of her channels.

Later, as they lay on the floor together, she sucked each of them to another crisis and took their sperm in her throat. After that she made them dress and she sent them away knowing she would never see them again. In the evening she telephoned Louis at the villa in the south and she talked to him endearingly about his health and how much she missed his presence in the big house.

VII.

THE WOMAN ON THE BUS

Every weekday morning Armand Bastide rode the bus from Dampierre to Chartres where he worked in the office of a small government tourist agency, and every weekday afternoon at six o'clock he rode the bus back from Chartres to Dampierre to spend the evening and the night with his wife and children. Armand was thirty-six, the father of four children, and the husband of a wife who after ten years of marriage cared only about the children and the cleanliness of the small house, often more about the latter than the former. Unwilling to burden himself with complications, Armand had resigned himself to an uneventful life with only small pleasures and predictable changes. That was one reason he found the problem of the woman on the bus so unsettling. The other reason was his fear that his wife would discover his new preoccupation and proceed to make his days and nights miserable.

The woman on the bus was about thirty, and when Armand first noticed her he guessed that like himself she was employed in Chartres. It seemed that she was on the bus every morning at the same time, and then again in the evening at the same time, and before long Armand began to look forward to her company. He never spoke to her, but he always gazed at her, and eventually she became aware of his gaze and it appeared to him that she encouraged it. Not that encouragement was necessary, since gazing at her was always quite pleasant. She was a blonde with ivory skin, bright blue eyes and a pair of full lips made for feverish kisses. She always wore a pale shade of lipstick to make her lips look cool and untouchable, as if she realized her lips were too lush, too pouting to be considered modest. Her body was fully curved, with graceful legs and round buttocks and firm thighs that rippled beneath her dresses. Her throat was cream-colored and smooth, and she had a way of holding her head just so that made it seem she was challenging the men who looked at her to do something. She had high, firm-looking breasts, and from the beginning when Armand looked at her, he always imagined how her breasts would feel in his large palms.

It took Armand some time to become aware of the blond woman's interest in him. For nearly a month he stared at her every morning and every evening on the bus. In the morning in Chartres she left the bus before he did, and in the evening in Dampierre she remained on the bus while he climbed out. When he boarded the back of the bus each morning, the first thing he did was look at the front of the bus to see her sitting in her usual seat. After that he moved forward to find a seat close enough to look at her.

One day the woman began staring at Armand almost as much as he stared at her, and the next day he thought she gave him a slight nod of recognition. And then on another day, she appeared to look back at him as she stepped off the bus in Chartres.

Armand began thinking about her, first during the dull days in the government tourist office, and then in the evenings at home, and then at all hours day and night, weekdays and weekends. The young woman gradually became an obsession, and

Armand realized that unless he could somehow make her acquaintance his life would remain forever unsettled.

So one day when the young woman left the bus at her usual stop in Chartres, Armand left the bus at the same time and he followed her. At a small office building in the center of Chartres, the woman turned in front of the entrance and she seemed instantly shocked to see Armand standing only a short distance away. She said nothing and she entered the building, and soon after that Armand found a taxi and went to his job.

The next day Armand did the same thing: he left the bus in Chartres when the blond woman did, and then he followed her to her place of employment. She looked back at him once, and it was obvious that she recognized him. This time when she reached the entrance of the building where she was employed, she stopped and walked back to approach him.

"You've been following me," she said.

Armand nodded. "Yes."

"Wait for me here at noon."

And with that she left him and entered the building.

Armand stood there a moment, and then he turned and hailed a taxi. He would need to make some minor arrangement at the office, but he should have no difficulty managing the meeting. Shortly before noon that day he returned to the front of the building the blond woman had entered that morning, and in a few minutes she came out and took his arm. "I can't spend more than an hour with you," she said. "We can go to a hotel if you like."

Armand took her to a small hotel near the Chartres railroad station. He learned her name was Mathilde Ruard and that she lived with her husband on the south side of Dampierre near the shoe factory. They had recently arrived from Brittany, which was why he'd never met her as a girl. In Chartres she was employed as a clerk in an insurance office. Once inside the hotel room, she offered no resistance when Armand took her in his arms and drew her body close to his. She placed her hands on his shoulders, feeling the muscles under his shirt. Then she smiled softly and she moved her hips against his with a pressure that excited him. "I won't let you do everything," she said. And then she explained that she would not violate her marriage vows completely, but only up to a certain point. Armand could have her on the bed, but only if he made love to her in a certain way. Then she hinted that what she wanted was a lovemaking that involved only the use of their mouths.

Surprised, but also tremendously excited by her, Armand instantly agreed. He tightened his hold on her as the feel of her hips sent his heart racing. Now he felt the pressure of her thighs and nearly the whole length of her legs. Her hand slid up to his face and then around his neck. Her lovely face came closer, the provocative lips pouting at him, the bright eyes softening. When they kissed, her lips on his were warm and giving, and the wet tongue that slipped into his mouth probed deeply and without reservation. Through his shirt he felt the hard points of her nipples as her full breasts flattened against his chest. He moved his hands down to her bottom, clasping the firm buttocks with his fingers and pulling them toward him. His desire was intense as he crushed her against him, and she also was breathing heavily into his mouth, squirming her hips into his as she attempted to catch the masculine bulge between her thighs.

She moved her head back after a while, her eyes closed but her mouth remaining open. He bent and kissed her neck, sucking at the skin until an angry red mark appeared. She gasped and pulled his head to her breasts. "The bed, darling."

When he released her, she turned toward the bed.

But then he caught her again from behind, squeezing her breasts and kissing her neck again. She brushed her buttocks across his loins, pressing back at him, leaning her head back, her eyes closed. Without altering her position, she unzipped her skirt at the side and then allowed it to slip to the floor. Underneath she wore white panties, and now he could feel the full outline of her backside through his trousers, the firm globes pressing against his penis. She pulled his hands away from her breasts and unbuttoned her blouse and slipped it off. In a moment he held her waist with one hand while he unclasped the brassiere with the other hand. The brassiere fell away, and suddenly the upper part of her torso was naked.

The bulge in Armand's trousers was enormous. He desperately needed to sink his lance into the soft grip of a woman's sex, but of course that was prohibited. Now Mathilde's hand moved behind her, searching for his penis. She found it and fondled it through the trousers, her fingers stroking it, gripping it, measuring its length. His breathing rapid and heavy, Armand clasped her naked breasts from behind. He could see them over her shoulder, full round breasts crowned with pink berries. The feel of her elastic flesh brought him an intense excitement. Then he dropped his hands from her breasts, pressing his hips at her, wriggling at the touch of her fingers on his penis. He slid his hands down over her ribs and the soft curve of her belly and under the waistband of her panties. In a moment he had his fingertips touching the curled hair that covered her mound.

Mathilde turned in his arms. Her face flushed, her fingers fumbled at his fly of his trousers. She found the zipper and pulled it downward, then slipped her fingers into the opening to pull at the long spear of flesh and bring it out. The breath caught in Armand's throat as her fingers stroked the length of his organ. He edged her toward the bed, and with a soft moan she swayed in front of him and collapsed onto the mattress.

Quickly Armand slipped out of his shoes and then pulled off his trousers and shorts. Mathilde lay face down, her sides heaving as if in a faint while he frantically removed his socks and shirt. His penis was fully erect, swollen, demanding immediate relief. Mathilde lay as if unable to move, and now he knelt over her to peel her panties off her backside. His belly churned with passion as the curved globes of her buttocks were revealed to his eyes. He pulled the panties down her thighs, then over her shapely calves and off her feet. Except for the beige stockings held up by elastic at their tops, Mathilde was now completely naked.

When Armand covered her, his body burning, Mathilde immediately began struggling under him. She squirmed and whimpered, pleading with him. "Please, you promised!"

Yes, he had promised. For another moment or two he ground his loins against her backside, pressing himself against her with hot passion. He kissed her neck and bit it, and then finally he slid his body to the side before he began kissing her again. This time his mouth moved down her back and over her buttocks and thighs. She moaned softly as he drew her thighs apart and then made her rise on her knees. She knelt with her head and shoulders down, her eyes closed, her face flushed. A soft cry escaped her throat as he stroked her buttocks. "Please, you mustn't..."

Armand sighed. "Yes, I know."

He lay at an angle underneath her with his head between her thighs and his eyes on her sex, on the pink folds that glistened with her syrup. Then he raised his head, placed his mouth against the moist sex-lips and pushed his tongue firmly between them. A gush of fluid immediately covered his tongue. She tasted sweet and slightly salty at the same time, and in a moment he began moving his tongue in the groove to lap at the warm juices.

As Armand began to lick her, the breath shot out of Mathilde in a gasp and she jerked away an instant, only to ram her hips backward immediately to cover his mouth again. Now his nose was against her backside and her sex was opened wide to him. She cried out as his tongue moved again. He found the hard little clitoris and licked it. He worked his lips closer and began to suck it as her buttocks swayed around him like a pair of squirming pillows.

Then Mathilde shifted her body on the bed, moving over him without dislodging her sex from his mouth, and suddenly he felt her hands on his penis and then her wet tongue. He felt her tongue licking the length of his organ, and then the hot presence of her mouth as her lips closed over the tip. She took the entire penis, engulfed it down to the root, pulled back to the glans and then engulfed it again. Her body rocked with each movement of her head, her sex pushing at his face and then withdrawing, and soon Armand groaned against her sex as his loins convulsed. As he spurted into Mathilde's mouth, he felt a new gush of syrup stream over his tongue. They clasped at each other's bodies, their mouths working, sucking, drawing out the fluids of their passion until finally they rolled apart gasping like two fish suddenly brought to land.

After a while he tried to kiss her, but she wouldn't have it. "Please don't," she said softly. "I can't stay with you any longer." And after that she hurried to get dressed again, glancing at him occasionally with a look of mild surprise that he made no effort to put his clothes on.

"I'll wait," he said. Then he added: "When will I see you again?"

"I don't know."
"Tomorrow."
"No, not tomorrow."
"Then the day after tomorrow."
"The day after tomorrow is Saturday. I can't see you on Saturday."
"Then Monday."
"I told you I don't know."
Not knowing what else to say, Armand said nothing. He reasoned he would see her on the bus in the morning, and then he would persuade her to go with him again to a room. How could she deny it when they'd already been together? But he'd known enough women to realize Mathilde was a puzzle. He watched her finish dressing, and then he watched as she applied some lipstick to her lips. At the door she turned and smiled at him. "Goodby, Armand."
He lay there alone awhile, and then he dressed and he went to his job.
The next day he sat beside her on the bus and they talked, but she refused to meet him in Chartres again. "No, it's impossible."
"Monday then."
"I don't know."
In Chartres he watched her leave the bus. In the afternoon they sat together on the bus again, but this time she would hardly talk. Again he mentioned Monday, but she said nothing.
"You exasperate me," he said.
"I'm sorry," she said quietly.
He was afraid to say anything, afraid he would spoil it for good. The fact was she excited him tremendously and he was afraid to lose her. She'd brought an intense excitement into his life and he dreaded the thought of losing it.

He passed the weekend thinking of only one thing: Mathilde.

On Monday when he met her on the bus, she seemed different, more buoyant. When again he suggested they meet in Chartres, this time she agreed. "Yes, why not? Wait for me at the same place."

At noon they had a simple lunch first, and then they went to the same hotel and the same room. After some brief kisses, Mathilde quickly removed her dress and lay down on the bed. She wore white lace underwear today, with grey stockings and a white suspender belt. Showing no coyness at all, she opened her legs to display the gusset of her panties drawn tight against the bulge of her sex-lips. He could see the wetness, the matted blond hairs fringing the pink groove.

Without undressing, he climbed onto the bed. He pulled her panties away quickly, and she parted her legs again. Now his gaze fixed on the rosy gash awash with syrup. He bent closer, caught the outer flanges of her sex with his thumbs and spread the fruit wide open. The inner slit flared, pulsating, a wet red mouth. He gazed at the dark red of the opening denied to his penis but not to his tongue. Above the slit, at the top of the wet groove, her clitoris appeared erect. When he extended a finger and touched it, Mathilde closed her eyes and shuddered. "Yes, there!" she said. "Do it, won't you? Suck me now before I..."

He fell to the feast offered by her gaping sex. His lips sank into the warm center, his tongue striking at the inner hole, entering its elastic rim and extending deeply into the channel. She squealed and circled her sex against his face, smearing her syrup over his mouth and chin. He wallowed in it, luxuriating in the sticky wetness and musky smell. His tongue struck in and out of the wet opening with a lizard-like fluttering movement. Now it lapped upward, along the groove to her clitoris, the tip of his tongue rubbing the erect bud. Mathilde jerked and bumped her sex against him. She cried out as she scissored her thighs against the sides of his head. "Yes, yes! Don't stop!"

He used his tongue like a brush, bold sweeping strokes up and down, bending and twirling her clitoris, swabbing the mouth of her channel, sliding down to the soft crease between her buttocks. He backed up and pushed her buttocks apart, and immediately Mathilde tilted her crotch upward to give him access to her anus. He licked around it, around and around, then centered on the elastic ring of muscle and pushed his tongue inside it, sinking his tongue into the orifice, fluttering it rapidly, slowly, rapidly again, his wide-open lips fastened to the soft flesh surrounding her rear crevice. Then he pulled his tongue out of her anus completely and he used only his lips to suck at it.

Mathilde groaned, a deep groan of delirium as she bucked her backside against his mouth. For an instant his mouth was dislodged, but then he found the place he wanted again and returned to his sucking and tonguing. Then suddenly he shifted his mouth from her anus to her sex and he surrounded her clitoris and sucked it hard. She came instantly, crying out her joy, both hands grasping his head as her buttocks squirmed on the mattress, and then a moment later collapsing under him with a final shudder.

When she opened her eyes and looked at him again, she blushed. "Your wife is a fortunate woman."

He was seated in a chair facing her as he untied his shoes. "I never do that to my wife."

"Then I feel sorry for her. Let me see what you have there now and I'll make it good for you."

This time he removed only his trousers and shorts, and then he went to her and she sat up on the bed and took his penis in her mouth. She held his testicles in one hand while she stroked his organ with the other hand, and although he wanted it to last a long time it ended too quickly for him. He had a violent release, his passion inflamed by the previous lovemaking, his body jerking as he spurted in her sucking mouth.

Afterward she wiped her lips with a tissue and she smiled. "You have healthy sperm."

"Why don't we do it the ordinary way next time?"

She looked fearfully at him. "No, I forbid it! I'm sorry, I must go now."

"Don't be annoyed."

"I'm not annoyed, I'm just in a hurry to leave."

But he thought she looked angry because he'd said he wanted to make love to her in the ordinary way. He wondered what she did with her husband, what they did and how they did it and how often. What a strange woman she was!

They saw each two or three times a week for nearly two months. Each time they did the same thing: first Armand would suck her sex until she had an orgasm, and then she would take his penis in her mouth and suck and stroke it until he had his own pleasure. What they had done the first time, the two of them naked on the bed together and sucking each other at the same time, was never repeated. Armand saw no point in it since being like that with her only inflamed him and made him want to get inside her. Mathilde seemed satisfied with what they did instead, the lovemaking while they were half dressed, the wet sucking of her sex and the final taking of his product in her mouth.

Then one day Armand decided he'd had enough; it was too much, too frustrating, he couldn't bear it any longer. He had to couple with her in the ordinary way or he'd go mad. When they met at noon in front of the building where she was employed, he said nothing to her about his decision. She took his arm as usual and they walked to the little cafe where they usually had their simple lunch. Afterward they went to the same hotel near the railroad station, the old concierge smiling at them because he knew them now as lovers, giving them the key to their usual room.

Inside the room, Armand took Mathilde in his arms, kissed her and began pulling her skirt up to her waist. But suddenly, as if she realized that today his intention was different, she pulled away from him and gave him a suspicious glance. "Please, Armand, let me get undressed..."

As he looked at her, he was more certain than ever that he had to have her completely. He watched her walk to the bed, her hips swaying and the firm globes of her buttocks revealed by the tight dress. He went after her, and at the edge of the bed he stopped her and with her back to him he held her arms in his hands.

"What is it?" she said, her voice uncertain. "What are you doing?"

"I want you the ordinary way."

"Armand, please..."

As he pushed her forward, she instinctively braced her body on the bed. He had one arm about her slender waist, the other hand high up on her back at the base of her neck. He pushed her forward even further, forcing her to kneel on the bed with her head down.

She tried to struggle, this time in earnest, but Armand knew what he wanted and he was determined to have it. He grabbed a handful of the dress at the small of her back and pulled at it until he exposed her thighs and then the curves of her buttocks encased in her thin panties. In a moment he had the panties down, and although she struggled again he quickly pulled them off her thighs and legs and tossed them away. She struggled with him, but she said nothing; she struggled in silence. She sucked in her breath as he stroked and pinched her naked buttocks, and then again as he opened her sex from behind to look at it.

"Were you a virgin when you married?"

"Yes, of course!" she said.

"Then I'm only the second man to have you."

And then he unzipped his trousers and he brought his penis out, and when she understood what was about to happen she moaned with dismay. "Armand…"

He ignored her pleading. He gazed at her sex, at the plump little bush pouting at him, the curled blond hair, the long pink lips slightly gaping as they waited for him. He stepped forward and eased the knob of his penis between the lips, rubbing himself up and down in the wet groove.

"Don't move," he said.

"Armand…"

"I said don't move."

She whimpered, but she stopped moving. He bent his knees for the proper alignment, and then as he jabbed forward the broad glans of his member pressed her sex-lips flat. Then a moment later the red mouth yielded and Mathilde groaned as the knob of his penis lodged inside the opening of her passage.

"Oh God!" she said.

"Now you can move."

"No!"

"As you wish."

He could feel her vaginal muscles contracting around his penis. He could feel the glistening droplets of her syrup rolling down the insides of her white thighs. He dug his fingers into her hips and pushed forward, then leaned back to watch as the entire length of his penis was engulfed by the narrow channel of her sex. The image of her delicate sex stretched around the girth of his penis inflamed his senses. He adored it almost as much as he adored the feel of it. He enjoyed it even more as she started to squirm and wriggle her hips, not to escape, but to suck more of his organ inside her body. With an abrupt lurch, he buried the remaining length of his penis inside her passage and she momentarily buckled as she felt it.

"Oh God!" she said.

But she was already beginning to rotate her hips and he could see her tight little sex grasping at him with each internal contraction. He pulled his penis back halfway and then drove it inside her again with enough force to make her body shake. Again and again he rammed his organ inside her depths, slamming his hips against her, reveling in the feel of her cool backside against his belly. Already, he could feel his testicles tightening as the juice swirled inside him in preparation for the crisis.

Mathilde responded completely now. She arched her backside toward him, sobbing with each strong thrust of his organ in her passage. Her hips moved up and down and side to side, pushing back to meet his attack, then sliding forward with the impact of his ramming. And with each penetration of his penis, with each surge of his loins, her breath exploded in a whimpering cry of delight.

Then he stopped suddenly and he forced her legs wider apart. Now his penis was jammed inside her at an awkward angle. Now when he pushed in, the top of his organ rubbed against the upper limits of the opening where it folded into the short stretch of skin between her sex and anus. His eyes fixed on the small anus as he imagined what it would look like with his penis crammed into it. From the way she responded to his tongue, he had no doubt she would adore having his penis there too. But not now. Not this time. Now he put a hand high up on her back and he pushed her upper torso down until she folded her arms and rested her head on them.

"Armand..."

Her sex contracted on him powerfully, the muscles at the entrance of her opening clamping down on his penis as though she were a virgin. He knew she was coming now, knew it even before he saw her hands jerking on the sheet. Watching her come was all the impetus he needed for his own climax, and the next moment he grunted like a rutting animal as he crashed his loins forward and exploded inside her.

"Armand..."

He felt the knob of his penis press against the opening of her cervix.

"Armand..."

She came again. He could see her backside clenching and unclenching, feel her hips jerking out of time with his own, follow the way her round thighs trembled and her knees weakened. Her belly heaved and tightened as she felt the jets of sperm squirting inside her.

"Oh, Armand!"

It seemed to him as though his orgasm lasted forever, but finally the spasms slowed, became irregular and stopped. His penis began to shrink inside her as she trembled in the last throes of another climax.

"Oh, Armand..."

As he withdrew his penis from her stretched opening, her hand moved to her sex and she took her clitoris between her thumb and two fingers and jerked at it until a final shuddering caused her to collapse on the bed.

He began dressing before she rolled over on her back. When she saw him half-dressed, his trousers and shorts not yet covering him, she called out to him. "Wait..."

"What is it?"

"I don't hate you."

Armand approached the bed. "I suppose not."

She looked at him a long moment. "When will I see you again?"

"I don't know," Armand said.

"Armand..."

He said nothing and she sat up on the edge of the bed to look at him again as he stood close to her. When her eyes rested on his dangling penis, he jerked his loins forward and she smiled.

"Yes," she said.

Lifting his member with two fingers, she took the glans in her mouth and she started sucking it. Armand stroked her head as he gazed at the open window on the other side of the room, the white curtain fluttering in the breeze, the roofs of Chartres. They would need to find a room somewhere, maybe not far from where she worked so they could save time. A small room and a kitchen so they could have their lunch in privacy when they wanted it. In the winter there was no amusement in sitting inside a crowded cafe. It was summer now, but he imagined in winter he would adore her even more.

VIII.

THE END OF AN AFFAIR

Louise Alban lived with her husband in a large white house near the Dampierre monastery. She was neat, trim, and looked ten years younger than her true age, which was forty-four. She had long black hair that she kept tied in a chignon, and deep brown eyes. Her two children were grown, her son now an instructor in philosophy at the Sorbonne and her daughter studying medicine at the University of Montpelier. At the moment Louise was in Paris, which she visited often, lying on a bed in a hotel room, massaging her lover Henri Bacq's head as he nuzzled and kissed her sex while she still wore her black lace panties. The nylon gusset that covered her sex was only a few centimeters wide and elastic enough for Henri to hold it to one side as he ran his stiffened tongue up and down Louise's hairy grotto. As he smacked brief kisses over the puffed lips, Louise took pleasure in the feel of his warm breath on her prominent clitoris.

Louise's brassiere was as flimsy as her panties, and now she slid her left hand up to it and she brought her right breast out of its confining lace cup. She squeezed the globe, rubbing the large nipple with her fingertips and quivering with excitement. Again she moved her legs on the bed, and each time she moved them faithful Henri was right there with his tongue and his lips to take full advantage of what was exposed to him.

Outside the window of the hotel room, the traffic bustled on the Boulevard Haussmann. The window curtain provided some privacy, but the shutters and the window itself were open and the noise of the traffic was clearly audible in the room.

Louise now lifted one leg high in the air, and immediately Henri's tongue fluttered down past her sex to the exquisitely sensitive stretch between her sex and her anus. Henri loved to kiss and lick her there. He loved to kiss and lick her anywhere she might crave it. Louise often thought of Henri as a pig, and he therefore made an excellent lover for her since the more like a pig a man behaved in bed the more pleasure she had from it. Still dressed in his business suit and tie, Henri had now been feasting on her for nearly twenty minutes.

Outside on the boulevard a truck sounded its horn, a bus answered with its own horn, the traffic flowed and the pedestrians continued to walk past the shops and cafes. Inside the hotel room, Louise now shuddered and slowly rolled over on the bed.

His face flushed and hair tousled, Henri drew back on his knees to watch every move Louise made. His hard penis tented the front of his trousers. He sighed through his wet lips as he gazed at her. She was something to look at under any circumstances, but especially now. He reached down to rub his penis through his trousers as her full buttocks came into view.

Louise had the firm buttocks of a girl, the large globes almost spherical in shape, perfectly matched, the split between them dark and enticing. She was completely aware of the way this part of her anatomy attracted certain men and she enjoyed flaunting her beauty. All that covered her buttocks now was the single black strip that went round her jutting hips, and the second black strip that vanished into the crack between the globes. Henri thought her buttocks were perfect in every respect, firm and resilient, but still pliable enough to quiver as she now gracefully repositioned herself on the bed.

"My God, you're superb!" he murmured as Louise leisurely drew her knees up under her and squirmed her fine, plump buttocks from side to side.

Louise felt a quiver of pleasure as she anticipated Henri's kisses. She had learned early in their affair about Henri's main weakness: his need to pay a slavish homage to her body in ways that most other men declined. She adored the lewdness of his lovemaking, and it was in fact the only reason she'd kept him as a lover. Out of bed he was a complete bore, often silly, a typical boulevardier who fancied himself a sophisticate. Louise had been wondering for some time if she ought to find some excuse to break off her affair with Henri, end the business once and for all, find someone else perhaps, or maybe avoid a lover for a time altogether. But at this moment she wanted Henri; he was like a drug and she needed him.

She continued squirming and shifting her hips, and now she reached behind her to run her hands up the backs of her thighs and the globes of her buttocks. In a moment she smiled against the pillow as she felt Henri's warm breath join her hands in caressing her presented derriere.

"Louise, let me kiss you."

"Don't be so impatient," she replied, and she went on with her teasing, even if she herself seethed with impatience.

"Please!" he repeated. "The taste of your sex made me half out of my mind! Let me kiss your bottom now!"

She clucked and sighed in mock exasperation with him, hooked her fingers in the string between her buttocks, and drew it aside. " All right, do it then." She heard him groan with satisfaction, and an instant later warm chills ran up and down her spine as Henri's hands reverently closed on her hips and he began nuzzling and licking his way through the groove between her buttocks.

"You have the most beautiful cul in the world," Henri muttered, hotly panting his way up and down through the groove, kissing and fondling the quivering globes, dropping his tongue down to her sex to taste her running syrup.

Louise listened to the traffic on the Boulevard Haussmann, the sounds of Paris at six o'clock in the evening. She wondered how many other married women were at this moment receiving the kisses of secret lovers who provided them with thrills they never had from their husbands. Certainly her own husband would never do what Henri was now doing. She couldn't imagine it. She would find it ludicrous if he ever attempted it and she would definitely refuse him. But Henri was something else; Henri was another circumstance completely. She adored the way Henri kissed her buttocks, the way he worshipped the secret recesses of her body. Having Henri on his knees behind her like this provided her with a marvel of thrills.

"Kiss me everywhere," she murmured, and Henri happily complied, crouching lower to send his panting hot breath and the tip of his tongue to the fullness of her sex and the juices welling up inside it. He inhaled deeply, breathing in the warm fragrance of the cleft. Then he moved his lips again, tickled and delved with the tip of his tongue around her anus, licked and lapped it while she squirmed on the bed and moaned.

Now Henri drew back a moment and he gazed through glazed eyes at Louise's anus, at the tight knot twitching with life. Then he extended his tongue and he touched the dark ring with it, wriggled and burrowed his tongue into the sphincter to feel the hot clasp of the muscle.

Louise shuddered with delight as she felt it. This was what she adored, the animality of it, the perfect pleasure of the tongue in that unlikely place, the tongue like a small snake wriggling inside her tight opening, the lewdness of it, Henri like a pig behind her, snorting at her, sucking everything no matter where his mouth happened to be. Or course she liked the other things also, the ordinary things: the licking of her sex, the sucking of her clitoris, the penis inside her vagina, the male thrusting to the final explosion. But she could get the ordinary things from her husband, even a good sucking of her clitoris when he was in the mood for it. But this sort of thing brought her the most intense excitement, an irritation of her senses that always left her breathless and totally vanquished. She squirmed and mashed her breasts against the bedspread, squirmed her buttocks in Henri's hands as the long wedge of his tongue slipped in and out through the ring of her anus. She supposed that if she wanted it, he would do this for hours, cement his mouth to her backside and lose himself completely. She could feel the wetness, his saliva dripping all over the groove between her buttocks. Then he pulled his tongue out of the orifice and he began kissing her buttocks again, mumbling about them, groaning his eagerness to put his penis in there. She wanted it now anyway. When her anus was wet and open like this, it was glorious to have it filled with something, to feel the invasion of the male organ in there.

"Go on, do it," she said.

"Louise, I adore you. Why don't you leave your husband and stay with me?"

"You know that's impossible."

"I dream of it constantly."

"Henri, if you intend to do anything, do it now."

She wriggled her hips, thinking of his penis. His organ was perfect for it, not thick enough to cause her any real pain, and the knob of a small size. He continued preparing her with a finger now, a finger that screwed and wormed in and out through the tight ring. Then he pulled the finger out and she felt him get off the bed. She heard the rustle of his clothes as he quickly undressed, her excitement at a peak as she waited for him. In a few moments he was kneeling behind her again, muttering, his hands fondling her buttocks, then his face pushing between her buttocks as he lapped and licked at her anus again.

She groaned, wriggling her buttocks in his face. "Do it, Henri!

"Yes, yes! I'm sorry."

He pulled his face away from her buttocks, and before long she felt the rubbery knob of his penis pushing at her anus. She trembled, shifted her knees a bit, then clenched her teeth as the stiff organ slowly entered her body.

They both groaned. Henri's hands continually stroked her buttocks as he filled the tight passage. As Louise felt the hot penis in her backside, a shudder of intense pleasure passed up and down her spine. She wanted it desperately now, all the force of it, the complete invasion, the possession of body. Dear God, what a frenzy! she thought. The feel of it was marvelous, her passage attuned to it after all the years with various lovers. Even with her husband on occasion, although with him the preparation was never adequate and more clinical than provocative. But this was lovely! Henri at his charming best. She imagined she could feel every ridge and vein of his penis. It was certainly almost as good as having it in her vagina, just as having a tongue back there was almost as good as having her clitoris sucked. She moaned with abandon as the sliding friction increased in her anus, as Henri's hands pulled and pushed at her gyrating hips. He was thrusting repeatedly now, a smooth thrusting whose pace increased as he approached his climax. She wanted it. She wanted the feel of his hot sperm gushing inside her passage. She twisted and turned her hips, urging him to reach his crisis. When he finally started coming, she used the muscles of her backside to milk his penis, quick jerking movements of her hips and belly. She felt the twitching of his penis each time it squirted inside her. She imagined the heat of the sperm spreading out through her bowels to her breasts and her sex and then to her brain. She wallowed in it, wallowed in the sensations, milking the penis with her backside even after the spurting dwindled to a mere oozing and Henri sighed and relaxed his hold on her hips. Her peak had passed also, and as usual it wasn't quite enough. But it would do for now; maybe later when she was alone...

She quivered again, squeezing Henri's deflated organ once more as he withdrew it from her body.

"An enchantment," Henri said.

Louise groaned as she rolled over on her back. For a moment she remained motionless, and then she lazily lifted her bottom and pulled off the bikini panties that were now irrelevant. Henri remained on his knees, gazing with adoration at her, his wet penis drooping. She hugged her breasts and said, "That was lovely, Henri."

Henri tore his gaze from her face and looked down at her belly. Her sex-lips were swollen, open like pink petals, the dark hair on each side of the gap wet with her juices. He licked his lips and said, "Is there anything else at all I can do for you, my love?"

Louise idly fondled one of her breasts. If she wanted it, he would now suck her off again. Maybe it would be even more delicious than before, but she was suddenly satiated. She'd had enough of him today. She extended a hand to him and said: "No, it's enough. Help me into the bathroom."

He smiled at her, assisted her off the bed and walked behind her with his eyes on her buttocks. Inside the bathroom, she gave him what she knew he wanted so much: she allowed him to watch her on the bidet. She sat down, turned on the water and washed herself as Henri craned his neck and looked down at her spread thighs and buttocks. Of course it excited her, it always did. What a pig he was! When she urinated into the bidet, she heard his grunt of satisfaction.

"Louise, come home with me now. Stay with me this evening."

"Don't be absurd." She had no idea what sort of home he had. Was it an apartment or a house? They always met in a cafe before moving on to a hotel.

When she rose from the bidet, he fell to his knees, tore a tissue from the roll and began wiping her sex. She allowed him this, opening her legs as he gently blotted the moisture from her sex-lips. Then she turned around and bent over, leaned her hands against the commode and shuddered with pleasure as he blotted the tissue up and down between her buttocks, drying her completely and then kissing her.

"No, Henri, it's enough. Don't start anything now." She turned around again and coaxed him out of the room to have some privacy. Later, when she came out of the bathroom, she found him dressed and waiting for her.

"I'll help you dress," he said.

She sighed as she pulled on her tights. "Darling, I don't need any help."

"I'll help you anyway."

"Henri, why don't you go now? I think I'll telephone my son and have him meet me somewhere."

"I'll wait for you."

She could see he already wanted her again. His eyes were bright as he watched her step into her skirt. For a man of fifty he could be in remarkable form on occasion.

"I don't think we'll be seeing each other again," she said.

Staring at her, he said nothing. The shock was too great.

Then he said: "What do you mean?"

Louise shrugged. "It can't go on forever, can it? My husband is becoming suspicious and you know how I hate complications. I told you that at the beginning. Anyway, I think it's time to finish it, Henri."

He groaned. "I can't live without you."

"That's ridiculous."

"It's true."

"It's ridiculous."

And so it went. He begged her not end the affair, but she insisted it was finished. Everything had an end, didn't it? Then he wanted to make love to her one last time, but she refused it, doubting he could manage it but not telling him that, telling him only that now that she was dressed she wouldn't think of it. She made him leave the room before she did. She remained behind, waiting, not wanting to meet him again outside the hotel or anywhere else. Once it was finished with a man, she liked the ending to be complete, without ambiguity. She hoped he wouldn't be foolish enough to telephone her in Dampierre. No, not Henri. The nice thing about Henri was that he was a discreet gentleman. Except, of course, when he was behind her with his face against her buttocks. She quivered as she remembered it. She finally rose, checked to see that she had everything, and left the room.

IX.

A DIFFICULT CHOICE

In the last century Dampierre had been noted for its many aristocratic families, descendants of the old Versailles court, but in recent times nearly all these noble families had abandoned Dampierre for other parts of France. One of the estates that remained was the old de Chantac acreage, the chateau now falling to pieces and inhabited by the last of the de Chantac line, the young Countess Marie de Chantac. She was still a beauty at thirty-six, but she'd had two disastrous marriages, both childless, and it seemed she had no intention to produce a son to inherit what was left of the family estates. Marie did the best she could for the upkeep of the chateau and the land surrounding it, but she spent more of her time in St. Tropez than in Paris or Dampierre. Wherever she lived, she liked large dogs and good furniture. She was racy, good-looking, and with a tall girlish figure kept in form by much strenuous tennis. She was known in the Dampierre region as a woman who drove a fast car with dogs looking out of the windows. She actually loved horses more than dogs, and one of the reasons she returned to the family chateau each year was to ride the de Chantac horses in the surrounding forest. But as soon as the warm weather arrived, she would return to St. Tropez where she had a small villa adjacent to one of the nude beaches. She liked her sexual pleasures, but she also liked her dignity, and so she avoided the orgies in St. Tropez and she led a quiet life in the midst of the mayhem. Years ago she had tried loving women for a short time, but she became bored with it and she returned to bedding men. Her first husband managed to get himself drunk enough to drown in a bathtub in Cannes, and her second husband drove a million-franc racing car off the Corniche in Monaco and plunged into the sea. Marie thought it peculiar that the death of both her husbands had been connected in some way to water. She never considered herself a tragic widow because each of her marriages was about to end in divorce shortly before fate intervened. Marie, in fact, considered her marriages to have been ridiculous. She told her intimate friends that she had yet to meet a man who knew what a woman's sex was about. She was cynical about men and she was particularly cynical about people who had a great deal of money. She hated the stupid aristocracy, but she never minded using her lineage to accomplish her purposes. Her current quandary involved the choosing of a new husband. Did she want one? She had two suitors, one an enormously rich man of fifty, and the other a man ten years younger whose major assets dangled between his legs. She therefore defined her problem as choosing between fullness in the bank or fullness in the testicles. Which was more important? Did she dare attempt a marriage again?

One day when Marie was staying at the chateau in Dampierre, she went out riding in the surrounding forest. She rode her favorite mare, enjoying the horse, the fresh air, the old trees, and the occasional fox that scampered through the brush in fright whenever she approached. There was a quiet spot near a stream that she remembered, and today she guided the horse there along a narrow and seldom used trail. When she arrived at a place where she could see the water, she stopped and dismounted. She tethered the horse to a tree, and she was about to step forward closer to the stream bank when she heard a strange noise.

It was not the ordinary noise of the flowing stream, but the noise of a disturbance of some kind. Curious, and a bit afraid in the shadows of the old forest, Marie moved forward as quietly as possible. This time she could distinctly hear the sound of splashing in the stream. She moved cautiously to a clump of trees that seemed the last barrier between herself and the sound. Yes, she'd been correct about the splashing. Beyond the trees the splashing sound was distinct. She nervously pulled back a large branch and peered through to the other side. What she saw in the water at once shocked her.

In a shallow and quiet portion of the stream a naked man stood washing himself. His back was turned to Marie, and she watched the muscles in his buttocks ripple with every movement. Marie quivered, and before long one of her hands slipped down between her legs while the other hand slowly rubbed her breasts through her blouse. When the man turned around and faced her direction, Marie's excitement increased significantly. He was a burly man and he was perfectly built, with broad shoulders sweeping down to a narrow waist and a forest of black hair on his chest and around his genitals. He stood quietly in the water, soaping himself, running his hands over his chest and thighs. The level of the water was hardly beyond his knees, so that his long penis, with its pendulous sacs, was in full view.

Marie gazed at the man, fascinated by the sex, by

the way it hung there, by the swinging of his genitals when his body moved. Of course she had seen naked men many times before, but somehow this was different. It occurred to her this was the first time she had ever looked at a naked man without him knowing she was looked at him. The idea of a secret observation excited her intensely, but it was merely nakedness after all, and before long she relaxed again. She pulled her hand away from her thighs and breasts and she simply enjoyed the perfectly natural sight of a nude bather. She'd seen so many of them in St. Tropez, but of course there the men always wore a cache-sexe to hide their genitals. This was more fitting, she thought. She found the dangling penis and testicles exciting to look at, but even this excitement gradually faded.

Then the man in the river did something unexpected, and Marie's excitement suddenly returned in a rush. At first she thought he was merely washing his penis. But before long, as his hands manipulated the dangling member, a huge erection appeared and it was obvious there was more than washing involved.

Marie watched in fascination. She felt so tightly constricted now that it became almost impossible for her to breathe. She could not take her eyes away from the man as he spread his legs, pointed his huge penis toward the sky, and ran his hand back and forth along the erect shaft. With every stroke of his hand, Marie's heart pounded furiously, her body aching with tension as she wondered if she ought to turn away and allow the man his privacy. She had watched men masturbate before, but never without their knowing it. Did she dare to watch this? She asked herself why not? If this man wanted privacy, he ought to be doing this somewhere else than on the grounds of the de Chantac estate. Who was he anyway?

Maybe some worker from the town enjoying the isolation of the forest. Well then, she could enjoy him also. She was amused now as she watched his bloated testicles jerking under his pumping hand. He was well-made, this one, the sex large enough to be intriguing, the dark forest of hair around his genitals giving him a definite look of virility.

The man continued to stroke himself, pumping his sex faster and faster, almost beating it with his fist. He was moving violently now, jerking his buttocks forcefully. Every stroke now was accompanied by a loud moan. The moans became shorter and more intense, until finally in one vigorous spasm of stroking he shot his white essence into the stream.

Marie gasped as she caught the glint of the sperm arcing out of the upright penis. For ten seconds or so his organ spurted again and again. Marie continued to watch him as he finished milking his already deflated organ.

Finally she turned and she crept quietly back to the mare and mounted her. With hardly any noise, the horse and its rider eased through the shadows of the forest and away from the stream.

Oh dear, Marie thought with amusement. It always excited her so when she saw them spouting like that, the white sperm erupting from the tip of a swollen penis. She tried to remember the men she'd seen. Only the second of her two husbands. Once a lover in Cannes. Another lover in Paris. She'd seen a stallion milked of sperm once and that had excited her beyond measure. You're a lecherous woman, she thought. Yes, she was, wasn't she?

When she arrived at the chateau, she went immediately to her bedroom and she locked the door. Then she stripped her clothes off and she threw herself on the bed to relieve the ache in her sex with her fingers. Once. Twice. Three times. Each orgasm brought a soft cry out of her throat as her body heaved on the bed. After that she walked naked into the shower to clean the sweat off her skin, and it was there under the spray of lukewarm water that she decided she could no longer put off a decision about her third marriage. Emile or Paul? The bank account or the testicles? Now fresh from the scene in the forest, she favored the testicles; but would she still favor them in a year's time? In a year's time a luxurious life with Emile might appeal to her immensely. Dear God, how difficult the choice was!

The next morning she arranged to visit Emile at his apartment in Paris. As usual, he was eager to have her visit him, and when she arrived he had champagne and caviar served in a drawing room that overlooked the Seine and the Louvre on the other side of the river.

"What a magnificent view," Marie said.

"But you've seen it many times."

"Yes, but it's never enough."

Emile chuckled, his eyes on her sleek nylon-covered legs. He was a dapper little man with a curled moustache and soft hands. He'd made millions from a dozen emerald mines in South America, a fortune so great he often claimed he had no idea how much money he had. But Marie never believed that; she suspected Emile counted his money very carefully. Although she had occasionally allowed him to make love to her, the event had never yet proved to be remarkable. Today however, her passion fueled by the incident in the forest at Dampierre, she felt quite ready for Emile's caresses.

As they stood at the window sipping their champagne and nibbling at the caviar, Emile talked of an impending trip to Egypt.

Marie raised an eyebrow. "Emile, you're not going away again?"

"Just a few days. It's a hotel venture in Cairo, and I want to look at the site before I agree to it. I should be back by the middle of next week unless it's more complicated than I think."

"You ought to relax more."

"Why don't you marry me and we'll spend our honeymoon in the midst of the pyramids."

"With all those mummies?"

"Then we'll go to Rome instead and drink wine in the Borghese gardens. Marry me, Marie."

"Oh Emile, you know how uncertain I am. Do you really think we'd be happy together?"

"I'm sure of it."

"Let me think about it while you're in Egypt."

"I'll have a dreary time in Cairo without you." With that he put his arms around her and kissed her.

Marie opened her mouth and their tongues collided and swirled around each other like two dripping serpents, and soon Emile's passionate kiss stoked the fire already smoldering in Marie's vitals. She broke the kiss and said: "I should give you something to make you remember me while you're in Egypt." And the next moment she placed her hand on the now growing bulge in his trousers, rubbing it up and down, enjoying the feel of his awakening penis beneath her hand. Despite his age, Emile never failed to respond to her. The shaft was as hard as a rock in no time, and with deft fingers she loosened his belt and then unzipped his fly. She quickly pulled the front of his underwear down to reveal his rearing member. Not an unattractive one, she thought; a pleasant handful for a woman, the knob bulbous enough to be inviting and the shaft behind it deliciously corrugated. She pumped her hand up and down on the stalk to inflate it even further. Emile babbled his appreciation of her efforts as she tugged his trousers and underwear down to his ankles at the same time. "That's much better," she said.

"Darling, we're at the window," he said.

"It's only the Seine. And if they see us from the Louvre, it will increase their appreciation of the exhibits."

After that she removed all of her own clothing while Emile finished undressing himself. Her breasts swayed in front of her, her nipples like hard little pebbles, the areolas already puffed with desire.

Emile led her into an adjoining bedroom, and Marie lay back on the bed and told him to do it between her breasts first. She squeezed her nipples with her fingertips, exciting him further as he walked toward her with his swollen penis bobbing like a conductor's baton. Her mouth watered as she thought of his organ gliding between her breasts and touching her chin. As he straddled her body, she pushed her breasts together to form a cavern between them, a warm groove inviting his organ to travel through it and into her mouth beyond it. The opening at the tip of his penis now leaked enough fluid to lubricate its passage. Emile shifted forward, his hairy testicles tickling her diaphragm as he pushed his penis into the deep valley between her breasts.

"Marie, darling..."

"Further, my pet. I want to lick the tip, too."

Emile pushed forward, and immediately her tongue caressed the purple knob, rolling over the smooth skin and tasting the fluid at the tip. Marie adored the taste and feel of a penis in her mouth and it always produced a sharp excitement in her belly. She thought of the man in the stream, that lovely organ he had pointing at the sky as it erupted in a fountain of sperm. She slid her hands around to hold Emile's buttocks as she watched his belly move backward and forward. He moved his organ between her breasts as if he had it in her sex, and it was obvious he was enjoying himself immensely. She kept her mouth open and wet each time he pulled out of it, but the emptiness lasted only a moment as he quickly pushed his organ between her lips again.

Before long he appeared on the verge of a crisis, and Marie quickly decided she'd rather have the ejaculation in her belly. Emile never produced enough to make the watching of it worthwhile, and at the moment she felt a need to have that hungry hole down there stuffed to capacity.

When Emile pulled his penis out of her mouth again, she said: "In my minou, darling. Do it there, won't you?"

Of course he immediately obliged her. With no hesitation, he moved his penis down her body, over her taut belly and into the hairy gap between her thighs. She pulled her knees back to offer him full access, watching the excitement straining his face as he rubbed the knob of his organ between her labia. In a moment he found the opening and plunged forward with a groan of delight.

In harmony with her lean outward appearance, Marie had an exceedingly narrow channel, an elastic passage able to grip even the smallest penis. She now gripped Emile with her internal muscles, more to increase her own pleasure than his. A German lesbian had once shown her how to practice the movements on her own fingers, and Marie was now quite adept at it. As Emile's organ plunged into the depths of her vagina, she could tell by his face that he felt her muscles contracting around his flesh.

She smiled up at him. "Do you like it, darling?"

He groaned. "You're a wonder!"

"It's as if I'm sucking you with my *minou*."

"Marry me, Marie..."

"I told you I'll think about it while you're in Egypt."

Again she gazed at his belly and at her pubic mound below it and the stretched glistening lips of her sex. He stroked his penis in and out of her opening. Marie was thrilled by it, aroused by the wet conjunction, her body responding in high key to Emile's lovemaking. She thought of his testicles ready to explode their contents and she slid a hand down to find them and squeeze the eggs. Then she tickled the sensitive region between Emile's testicles and his anus, and immediately the result she wanted was produced. Emile made a croaking sound in his throat and spurted at once deep inside her vagina. Marie writhed and moaned as she came, holding his testicles with her fingers to feel the exciting jerking of the reservoirs.

Afterward, as his sperm oozed out of her sex, Emile thrilled her again by gallantly licking the combination of his product and her feminine juices. Marie writhed on the mattress, her hands on Emile's head as she enjoyed his talented tongue. Eventually she urged him to move his body so that his penis, now sticky with slime, was in easy reach of her mouth. First she held the member high and licked at the drained testicles underneath, running her tongue around them and then taking both eggs in her mouth at once to suck on them. Meanwhile, her hand pumped his penis with the vain hope that it might be revived. Unfortunately, Emile was now exhausted, and after his tongue had given her sex a thorough cleaning, he pulled away from her and sighed. "Dear Marie, I'm afraid you've vanquished me."

Later, as she sat alone in a taxi crossing the Pont Royal, Marie thought of how fond she was of Emile. Was it wrong to accept his love knowing she could not return it in full measure and that her real interest was his immense fortune? Many marriages had succeeded with far less to sustain them. Oh dear, what a quandary! she thought. A shiver of pleasure passed through her as she remembered his agile tongue licking at her drenched grotto. Which nose would she rather have in her pubic bush, Emile's or Paul's?

So she thought of Paul Dupuy now, lusty Paul whose masculine attributes made Emile seem like an amateur. If only Paul had Emile's fortune! With Paul there was never a need to leave the bed unsatisfied. She'd wanted Emile to take her again, but he hadn't the vigor for it. Even a shooting of sperm in her mouth while she fingered herself would have sufficed her. Her sex beginning to tingle again, she fixed her thoughts on Paul. What time was it? Yes, it might still be possible. At the Place des Pyramides, she made the driver stop at a cafe and she hurried to a telephone. Paul was happy to hear her voice, and overjoyed when she offered to visit him at his studio in the Rue St. Augustin. "I'll expect you at once!" he said, and the urgency in his voice made Marie quiver with anticipation. Twenty minutes later she was beside Paul in his bed, both already stripped in preparation for the amorous activities. He stroked one of her full breasts, his fingers toying with the fat nipple. Marie smiled at him, cupping her breast with her hand as she moved to rub the nipple against his lips. "Do you like this one, darling? This one or the other one?"

"I adore them both," Paul said. "The two fruits of Venus."

"My *nichons*."

"Exquisite."

"And also this handsome asparagus that will soon spear me."

She slipped a hand around the shaft of his rampant penis and squeezed it gently. The impressive organ jumped in her grip like a living thing. Her fingers moving with precision, she stroked his foreskin back and forth over the glistening tip of his swollen knob. Now she moved down on the bed a bit, bent over his penis and began licking it with her tongue. At the same time she kneaded his testicles with her fingers and looked at his face. "Is it good?" she asked.

"I think I'm about to come," he groaned.

Marie immediately pulled her hands and mouth away from his penis. "That will never do!" she said. Despite his impressive attributes, Paul was often too hasty as a lover. She left his genitals and moved back beside him and kissed him. She told him to play with her first, to excite her until she was ready to come also. He kissed her, thrusting his tongue inside her mouth, rubbing it against hers as he stroked her breasts. Then she urged him to use his mouth on her breasts, to do that while he fondled her sex with his hand. As he slid his hand between her thighs, she moved them wide apart. He tickled the lips of her sex and eventually found her clitoris and teased it with his fingers.

"Ah, that's better," Marie said with a moan. She stuffed her breast into his mouth with one hand and dug her nails into his neck and shoulders with the other hand. She whispered in his ear, urging him to pinch her clitoris with his fingers, and then to push two other fingers inside her. Sex juice gushed over the pink flesh of her vulva as his fingers slid in and out of her body. After a while Marie suggested that she lie on her side while he take her from behind. In a few moments they had their bodies arranged, Paul spearing her from the rear while she pulled one of her buttocks upward with her hand. His penis slid easily between the wet walls of her vaginal passage, and immediately she contracted her muscles to grip the member. He slipped one arm under her and the other arm around her to grasp her breasts. He thrust his penis deeply inside her sex, heaving his hips as the sperm gathered in his testicles.

Marie had known how it would be with him, and she was now busy fingering her sex to hasten her climax. She started coming, and then in a moment she felt Paul coming also. She writhed her buttocks against his thrusting hips as she pictured the hot sperm gushing inside her.

He's not so bad, she thought. He was always fast, but her compensation was that he could go on and on. He had such an attractive large penis, and a big heavy scrotum that always excited her when she fondled it. She could teach him everything, couldn't she? She arched her back with pleasure as she felt his muscular organ sliding back and forth in their copious juices.

When he finally pulled his penis out of her, she rolled over to fondle him with her hand. Leaning over his belly, holding his penis gently, she began licking it clean with her tongue. Paul grunted with pleasure as he watched her. She licked his penis clean, and before long it showed the first signs of revival. Now she washed his testicles with her tongue, licking the fat bag as she held it up with her fingers.

Finally she rolled over on her back and she held her knees apart with her hands. "Do it to me again, darling. And then afterward we can suck each other awhile as an apéritif for the evening. You'll take me to dinner, won't you? Come, darling, do it to me now."

She moaned with satisfaction as he climbed over her and entered her again, this time with his body on top of hers, his strong organ lurching inside her and shaking her belly with each thrust. She reached underneath to find the huge testicles and hold them. Again she thought what a pity it was he lacked Emile's money. With Emile she could indulge her love for horses by owning an entire racing stable. What a burden it was to decide between them! Next month, she thought. By the end of next month she would definitely make her decision. Meanwhile she gripped Paul's testicles more firmly as she sensed he was about to empty his reservoirs. Magnificent! she thought. The eggs were so huge in her hand! And the next moment she cried out with him as the finale arrived, her mind in a whirl of pleasure that went on and on.

X.

AN UNEXPECTED RETURN

Robert Lamarche knew his wife Marianne well enough to understand how easy it was for her to develop the most intense passions. At one time her passion might be clothes, but then after seemingly endless trips to the salons in Paris she would tire of clothes and the world of fashion and she would absorb herself in something else, maybe African art or classical films or the latest fad in political causes. These days Marianne's passion seemed to be her friend Sylvie. The two women were constantly together ever since Sylvie had moved from Lyon to Paris. Robert had met the blond Sylvie and had been quite impressed with her energy and beauty, and not unsurprised to learn of her success in her business career. She was a type, Sylvie was, and after Robert made her acquaintance it wasn't long before he realized the friendship between his wife and this slender blond woman might be more than it seemed on the surface. Robert eventually concluded that Marianne and Sylvie were most probably engaged in a lesbian affair of an intense character.

He said nothing to Marianne about it. What purpose would that serve? He had no desire to cause a furious conflict between himself and Marianne if it could be avoided. Since Marianne and Sylvie had known each other since adolescence, he reasoned the affair had probably continued for years and years. But Marianne had married him, hadn't she? And she certainly did not act or talk like a lesbian. And she certainly had given no indication that she wanted to end the marriage. So the only aspect of any consequence that remained was whether he had any reason for jealousy.

Ah, jealousy! If Sylvie was an actual threat, if she actually wanted to take Marianne away from him, then he supposed he had a right to be jealous of the affair between the two women, a jealousy based on a fear of losing Marianne. But suppose Sylvie had no such intention, what then? Would his jealousy be reasonable? Was he that selfish concerning Marianne's affections? He thought it might be different if Marianne were involved with a man; but somehow the fact that Sylvie was a woman made jealousy seem ridiculous. Then a small voice in his mind warned him: Be careful, you fool, a lesbian can be more dangerous than a male lover. Yes, he knew that. But each time he imagined Marianne and Sylvie in each other's arms, it was not jealousy he felt but excitement. He felt an intense excitement as he pictured them together kissing and fondling on a bed, their bodies exposed, their hands occupied with the most precise caresses. And when he thought of them like that, his mind always focussed on Sylvie's naked, blond body. More and more he began to imagine himself with Sylvie, the blond lesbian responding to him, yielding to him in a torrid embrace...

Sylvie visited them often in Dampierre. Marianne seemed grateful that Robert had so easily accepted her friendship with Sylvie, and the two women spent more and more time together. During the week, Marianne often travelled to Paris to have lunch or dinner with Sylvie, and on weekends Sylvie often came to Dampierre to pass the time with Marianne and Robert. Marianne and Robert never discussed Marianne's true relationship with Sylvie; the game was to pretend the friendship was merely ordinary.

Then one day everything changed. Robert had planned a day-long business trip to Luxembourg, when at the last moment the plans were changed and instead he arrived home in the early afternoon. He found Sylvie's car in the driveway, and as soon as he entered the house he suddenly suspected the two women were occupied with each other in a way that was far from innocent. For a moment he thought of warning them, but a strong impulse to surprise them together overcame him. He listened carefully and deduced they were in the guest bedroom, the room that Sylvie sometimes occupied when she visited them for the weekend. He crept silently along the short corridor, and sure enough the door of the guest room was wide open and no matter what he expected he was still shocked by the scene.

They were both on the bed, Sylvie kneeling and wearing only panties, and Marianne similarly undressed and behind Sylvie with her face pressed against Sylvie's nylon-covered buttocks and her throat making guttural sounds of lust.

Robert had never thought of them like that. He'd imagined lesbian caresses that were tender, gentle, almost chaste. This was something else. Marianne now had her face pulled back only a centimeter or two from Sylvie's backside and her mouth moved to kiss one of the buttocks where it was exposed below the edge of Sylvie's underpants.

His heart pounding, Robert heard Marianne murmuring endearments. His wife's hands were on the blonde's buttocks, kneading the globes, fondling them. She pursed her lips and brought them into contact with Sylvie's curves, planting wet kisses on the jutting derriere. Sylvie moaned as she pushed herself backward into Marianne's face. Then the blonde pulled at her panties with her hands, stretched them even more tightly into her sex lips and the crease of her backside. Marianne slid her arms around her friend's thighs and held her tightly, caressing her shapely hips as she repeatedly kissed her round buttocks. The audible smacks of Marianne's lips on Sylvie's flesh reached Robert's ears clearly and made him delirious with excitement. Unable to stop himself, he groaned aloud.

Abruptly, Marianne pulled away from Sylvie and whirled off the bed. "Robert!"

Sylvie quickly snatched up a dressing gown and struggled to put it on. As her arms twisted behind her back, Robert thrilled at the sight of her naked breasts jiggling like two ripe pears. He saw the stiff nipples and wondered if Marianne had teased them and rubbed them. He suddenly had an intense desire to have Sylvie, to possess her.

Marianne groaned. "Robert..."

"The trip was canceled," he said.

"We didn't expect you..."

"Yes, I gather that."

Then Marianne smiled, a clever smile as an overture to the next declaration. "We were trying on underwear. Sylvie needed some panties and I..." Staring at him, her rapid breathing causing her naked breasts to rise and fall, she suddenly stopped talking as she realized her story was preposterous. Then her eyes dropped to the evident bulge in the front of Robert's trousers and her lips curled with amusement as she realized his sexual excitement. "I suppose you can see Sylvie and I are more than just friends."

"Yes."
"And you're not offended?"
"No, I don't think so."
A shudder seemed to pass through Marianne. She slid a hand between her thighs, and then inside the front of her panties, the fingers visible through the sheer nylon as they probed the top of her slit. Her eyes vacant, she said: "What an absurdity."
Behind her on the bed, Sylvie chuckled. "You're both absurd. Marianne, stop masturbating."
"I'm not masturbating, I'm only touching myself."
Robert wondered if they were both drunk. Meanwhile his erection was so enormous he thought it would burst through his trousers. He wondered what he ought to do now. What does the model husband do when he finds his wife in bed with her lesbian lover? Yes, Sylvie was right, they were both absurd.
Her fingers still toying with her sex, Marianne looked at him again and said: "Are you sure you're not angry?"
"Quite sure."
Sylvie now leaned forward to stroke Marianne's shoulder. "He means it," the blonde said. She whispered in Marianne's ear and a flush came to Marianne's face. Now Marianne pulled her hand out of her panties and she leaned back against Sylvie.
"I don't know," Marianne said.
Suddenly uneasy, Robert made as if to turn away. "I think I'll leave the house awhile."
"No, wait..."
"What is it?"
Marianne shrugged. "Why don't you watch us together? We're not children, are we? Since you already know about us, why not?"
Robert felt his heart pounding again as he stared

at her. It occurred to him she hadn't just decided this, she'd thought about it for some time. She wanted it; no doubt Sylvie wanted it too. And as for himself...It was madness, wasn't it? Maybe they were all mad.

"All right," he said, and he walked over to a chair and he sat down. "Why not?"

A sigh escaped Marianne's lips and she abruptly pulled away from Sylvie and left the bed. Barefooted, she walked to the dressing table and she opened Sylvie's purse and extracted a tube of lipstick. Robert watched her breasts dangle as she leaned toward the mirror to paint her lips.

"How long have you known?" Marianne said.

"A long time."

"It's very good with us, Sylvie and me."

He looked at Sylvie. "Maybe Sylvie doesn't want me to be here."

Her back resting against the headboard, her robe closed and her arms folded across her chest, Sylvie shrugged. "Men always have this fascination for lesbians, no? If you want to see how it's done, I don't care. Marianne is all I care about."

Robert felt an annoyance with her. "Listen, I've seen how it's done, I've seen films..."

"But not with your wife in the films."

"No."

He expected her to say that maybe he would learn something, but she didn't. Instead she rose from the bed, and without warning she slipped out of the robe and dropped it onto a chair. Then she looked at him with her hands cupping her small breasts. "Do you like me?"

"Yes."

She smiled. "I do it with men sometimes. I'm not exactly what you think I am." Then she walked around the bed and she and Marianne closed their arms around each other.

He felt the heat in the room and he wanted to remove his jacket, but he was afraid to change his position on the chair. Suppose he moved and everything crumbled into nothingness? They were pressed against each other, the two bodies, female flesh against female flesh, murmuring together. They kissed. He could see their mouths in a kiss as they slipped their arms around each other's waists. Breasts pushed against breasts as their hands roamed. It occurred to him that Sylvie was now tasting her own lipstick on Marianne's lips. His wife's lips. What a madness! he thought. Marianne's somewhat larger breasts pushed against Sylvie's breasts. Hips pushed against hips as the two bellies collided. They turned a bit, and now Sylvie had all of her back toward him and he saw hardly anything of Marianne. They moved against each other, a slow practiced grinding as Marianne's hands now slid down Sylvie's back and inside her panties to grasp her buttocks. He watched intently as Marianne's hands caused Sylvie's panties to ride down a bit, and then still further to reveal most of the globes, the firm-looking buttocks. Were they firm? Marianne knew; her hands cupped the globes, stroking them, gliding over the rounds. He thought he would spend inside his trousers as he watched Marianne pull Sylvie's buttocks apart and then push them closed again. Then Marianne dipped her knees slightly to pull Sylvie's bikini panties down over the cheeks. Now Robert could see Sylvie's backside in all its beauty.

Marianne rose again and smiled at Robert over Sylvie's shoulder. Now she had a wicked gleam in her eyes. "Doesn't she have a beautiful derriere, darling? And the jewel in front is precious too. Shall I take her to bed and show you how we make love to each other? Shall I do that, darling?"

Robert nodded. He suddenly wondered if Marianne hated him. Maybe she did. Maybe he was wrong to think her affair with Sylvie was harmless. But he was hypnotized by them. They couldn't have planned his early return, but they certainly seemed to welcome it. He felt confused, but he didn't care. Any explanations would have to come later. Right now he could think of only one thing. His penis was so rigid in his trousers it could no longer bear the confinement. He rose and he began undressing, watching them as he did so. Neither woman paid any attention to him as they moved to the bed with their arms around each other's waists. He removed his trousers completely, and then he slid his shorts to his ankles and stepped out of them. What a relief as his penis at last bound free. He stripped off his jacket and tie and shirt and now he was naked. He shivered, not from a chill but from sexual excitement, an excitement more intense than he'd felt in years, an excitement so strong it made him feel a peculiar numbness.

He sat down again and he watched them. They were already locked in an embrace, straining their soft bodies together. Marianne stroked Sylvie's hip and pushed her thighs open. She made Sylvie lie with her legs splayed, then quickly tugged Sylvie's flimsy panties all the way down and dragged them over her ankles. Then Marianne returned to her former position beside Sylvie's slender body. "She's so beautiful, isn't she, Robert?"

He nodded. He had his fingers curled around his stiff penis, merely holding it, still too self-conscious to masturbate openly. "She's quite beautiful," he said.

Then he noticed Sylvie gazing intently at his penis and he squeezed the base with his fingers to make swell up more.

Sylvie chuckled. "Look how excited he is."

"Yes," Marianne said. Her hand moved to the blond tuft of Sylvie's pubic hair. She slipped her fingers between Sylvie's thighs and into the open sex.

Robert quivered as he watched his wife play with Sylvie as if Sylvie were a delicate instrument. Was Sylvie always the passive one? He guessed not. He'd never known Sylvie to be passive about anything. Even now she opened her legs wider as she gazed at him directly, maybe taunting him as her sex was deftly penetrated by Marianne's fingers. Marianne slowly pulled the inner lips apart. While Marianne did this, Sylvie moved a hand to Marianne's buttocks. She kneaded the rounded cheeks, pinching large, soft folds of flesh between her fingers, then slowly allowing the flesh to escape. She whispered something to Marianne, and Marianne moaned in response and languorously opened her legs. As he held his inflamed penis tightly in his hand, Robert watched Sylvie's fingers sink into his wife's open sex. The fingers pushed into the soft mouth and vanished, buried completely inside the passage. Sylvie looked at him, her eyes bright with victory as she began a slow thrusting of her fingers in and out of Marianne's gaping sex.

Robert squeezed his penis tightly. Then at last he began to stroke it slowly, only a light stroking to relieve some of the ache in his organ. When Sylvie's eyes met his, he felt a twinge of embarrassment but he went on with it. Slowly, he thought. There were too many delights yet to be enjoyed.

The women on the bed kissed again. They were now totally absorbed in each other and paid no attention to him. Their passion mounted, their lust grew wilder. One of Marianne's hands groped desperately for Sylvie's breasts. She found and squeezed a mound of flesh with her fingers. Moaning, Sylvie grasped one of Marianne's breasts with a similar fury. They began a simultaneous thrusting motion with their hips, driving their sexes against the fingers that penetrated them. Marianne gasped suddenly as she started to come. Sylvie's fingers rammed faster, pushing and thrusting into Marianne's wet opening. Marianne threw her head back, her mouth gaping as she cried out. Then Sylvie closed her eyes and visibly shuddered as her own climax occurred. Marianne rolled over on top of Sylvie and began thrusting at her like a man. Sylvie wailed, groaned, their bodies clashing as they came together.

When they broke apart, Marianne looked at Robert. Her face flushed, she raised an arm and gestured to him. "Come here, Robert."

He rose from the chair, and as he walked toward her, Marianne moved off the bed and into his arms. Her body, still wet from the heat of Sylvie's lust, pressed hard against his. Her breasts were like twin cushions on his bare chest. His senses reeling, his penis a surging shaft of desire, he kissed her. Even without the closeness of Marianne's body he would have been unable to contain his lust, but with his wife's naked flesh rubbing against his own, his need for release overwhelmed him. He locked his arms around Marianne's back and fell with her onto the bed beside Sylvie. His legs pushed between Marianne's thighs, forcing them open. The panties were still twisted around her sex, gathered in a tight bundle across her thighs. He pushed them aside, making room for his penis to thrust beneath the wet gusset. He began sliding the hard length of his penis in and out of her sex.

Marianne groaned. "My panties, darling. I'll take them off." She gasped, writhing the mouth of her sex over the knob of the driving organ. But he was already inside her, driving thickly up her belly, her passage stretched around the girth of his shaft. She moaned as she felt it. She tried to draw back, but he held her fast as he continued thrusting. She clutched at his shoulders, her fingernails raking his skin. "Robert, wait..."

He heard her gasp something about Sylvie and he stopped thrusting. When he turned his head to look at Sylvie, he found the blonde gazing at them. She lay on her side facing them, her eyes bright and unblinking as she stared at their connected bodies. He released one of Marianne's breasts and he reached out a hand to Sylvie. She hesitantly moved nearer. She trembled as his fingers came to rest on her hip, but she offered no resistance. He began stroking her, urging her body closer to them. In a moment Sylvie's buttocks were within reach of his hand and he slipped his arm around her waist and pulled her close against himself and Marianne. Sylvie closed her eyes and trembled as he ran his fingers into the deep crease of her backside, his palm fondling one buttock and then squeezing.

Sylvie said: "What do you want?"

And Robert said: "I don't know."

"Finish inside her while I hold both of you."

Marianne moaned. "Yes!"

He began thrusting inside Marianne again, and soon he could feel Sylvie's hand wandering over his buttocks and down to his testicles and his sliding penis and Marianne's wet opening. The feel of Sylvie's fluttering fingers was too much to bear, and after a few more thrusts he cried out as he emptied himself inside Marianne's body.

Later, when his vigor was restored, he mounted Sylvie and she clasped her arms and legs around his body to hold him. Marianne lay beside them, kissing them both, stroking their bodies, murmuring her excitement.

"Now everything will be different," Marianne said. "Now everything between us will be different, won't it? Dear God, I adore it!"

XI.

THE LOVERS

Gabrielle Montier was a blond girl of twenty-six, married two years and with no children. She'd been pregnant at the time of her marriage, but shortly afterward she lost the baby, a great calamity for her since the only reason she'd married the father was to solve the problem of the pregnancy. Now she was bored with her marriage, beginning to hate her young husband Bernard, wanting a child but not wanting Bernard's child. How long could the marriage last under those conditions? For the time being divorce seemed out of the question. Neither family would approve and there was hardly enough money to maintain their home, let alone pay for her divorce. So Gabrielle suffered with her condition, resigned herself to it, told herself it was after all not unusual for people to be married to each other when they ought not to be married to each other. The young men in Dampierre looked at her with interest in their eyes, but they knew she was married to Bernard and they had no stomach for difficulties. Bernard had many friends in town, and anyhow no one had any idea that Gabrielle was unhappy because she did her best to appear the opposite. But she did enjoy it when they looked at her, when she felt their eyes on her body, on her breasts that she thought were much too heavy and drooping for the slender frame she had, hardly any hips at all, only the aggressive breasts. Her legs were shapely and she liked to wear shoes with thin high heels and a dress short enough to show her calves. Her husband never seemed to appreciate her sexuality, but she had fantasies that other young men did, even if none of them had ever been her lovers. There was one young man in the town who had been her lover when she was only sixteen, but Pierre Laubie had his own wife and family now and they hadn't spoken to each other in years.

Gabrielle worked at the Boudin shoe factory as an inventory clerk. She'd been thinking of attending an evening school to become a secretary, hoping that with such training she might find a job in Paris and persuade Bernard to leave Dampierre. She'd come to hate Dampierre because so far the town hadn't brought her much in the way of happiness. Paris was something else. In Paris a person could hope for things and find a new life.

But then Gabrielle learned a life could change in Dampierre as well. One afternoon she came out of the gate of the shoe factory and she found Pierre Laubie leaning against the fender of an automobile. Although she hadn't seen him in ages, she recognized him immediately, and when he waved an arm at her she knew immediately that Pierre had been waiting for her in particular.

After they exchanged greetings, she said: "What are you doing here?"

Pierre smiled. "What do you think?"

"You know I'm married, don't you?"

"And so am I. Come have a coffee with me."

"Is this your car?"

"Yes, of course. Come on, get in."

After a moment of hesitation, she climbed into the

tiny Renault. The day was Thursday, and on Thursdays Bernard was never home until late in the evening. Besides, she didn't care. She could talk to an old friend, couldn't she? But as soon as she and Pierre were in a cafe and started talking, she realized he was after something else than just a friendly chat.

"Listen, maybe I'd better go home," she said.

"We've been here only ten minutes."

"I'm married, Pierre."

He shrugged. "To me that doesn't matter. I think about you all the time."

Gabrielle felt the sudden pounding of her heart. "You do?"

"I swear it."

She blushed when she saw the way he looked at her breasts. Yes, maybe he did think about her occasionally. They'd been young then, almost children, but the memory was still strong for her.

"What's your wife like?" Gabrielle said. He'd married a girl from Chartres and Gabrielle had never met her.

"She's a wife," Pierre said. "We've been married six years and she's a wife. And your husband?"

"My husband is a husband."

Pierre chuckled. "Yes, of course. Why don't we make a picnic tomorrow? Maybe you can be sick at the factory, eh?"

Gabrielle resisted the idea at first, but eventually she yielded. Yes, why not? The more she talked to Pierre, the more she liked him again. He made her forget her troubles at home, her stupid life with Bernard and her boring marriage. She told Pierre she would pretend to be sick at the factory and he could wait for her outside the gate before noon.

Pierre was happy. "We'll go to Sceaux," he said. "I know a place where they have wild roses."

And so late the next morning, Gabrielle reported to her supervisor that she was ill and she left the factory and climbed into Pierre's car. She felt marvelous, and as they drove off they laughed together as they talked about old times, the boys and girls they had known and what they were like now. Gabrielle was thrilled when Pierre put his hand on her knee and squeezed it. But when he moved the hand to her thigh, she gently pushed it away. "Not in the car," she said.

"You excite me even more than you did years ago."

"We were children."

"Let me touch your breasts."

"Pierre, please..."

"They're larger than before."

Gabrielle was amused. "Well, what do you think? I'm a woman now."

When they arrived at Sceaux, Pierre drove directly to a secluded part of the park where there were indeed wild roses growing among the tall pines. They found a place safe enough from prying eyes and they spread out the blanket and had their picnic, the cold meat and the cheese and the red wine that Pierre had brought in a large basket. Gabrielle was on edge because she had no interest in the food or the wine but only in what would happen afterward. She wondered if Pierre understood how much she needed to be close to him, to make love to him. Would she regret it afterward?

Before she could think any further about it, Pierre reached over and pulled her into his arms. Everything between them had occurred so fast, yet it seemed perfect and genuine. It was almost as if fate had brought them together again, the present moment decided many years before. Their mouths brushed lightly at first, and then Gabrielle's lips parted and Pierre ran his hot tongue inside her mouth, coiling and lashing, entwining with her own. Her wet lips fluttered against his, and her arms encircled his body to draw him tightly against her. He began moving his tongue in and out of her mouth, thrusting it between her lips in an unmistakable simulation of a penis thrusting in a vagina. Gabrielle melted completely under the assault. Her own tongue glided against his, sweeping and thrashing. Understanding that her need was just as great as his, Pierre broke off the kiss and nudged her onto the blanket that lay before them. Lying on her back, rolling her head from side to side and sighing deeply, Gabrielle allowed him to do what he wished with her.

When he kissed her again, she moaned softly and arched her back to press her breasts against his chest. She could feel the bulge between his legs pressing against her thigh, his penis rising, jolting to full erection in a series of jerks until, standing like a heated crowbar between them, its hard outline burned against her. She squirmed toward it, molding herself to the contours of the organ, pressing hard against it as if to push him into her loins through the layers of their clothing.

He wanted her breasts now. He fumbled with her blouse until he had her chest exposed. She had deliberately worn a brassiere that opened in front, and in a moment he had it unhooked and her breasts revealed to his eyes, the nipples stiff with her excitement. Her hand reached behind his head to draw his face down to the globes. She rubbed the mounds against his face, whimpering when she felt his lips. "Yes, my breasts!" she gasped. "Kiss them, darling. Make it good for me."

Pierre steadied her, his hands gripping her hips as

he began kissing her breasts. His tongue slipped out, traced a path into the deep valley between the globes, then circled, climbed in a spiral up one heavy globe toward the top. She trembled violently as his eager lips closed over her swollen nipple to suck it. He moved from one breast to the other, sucking each stiff nipple in turn. Gabrielle rubbed against him in ecstasy, working her hot breasts against his mouth, her hips squirming in his hands.

As she pushed her breasts against his face, she slid her hands down and fumbled with his belt, unbuckled it, then pulled down his zipper. With trembling hands she managed to push down his trousers and shorts to his thighs. Pierre then pulled away to get them off his legs. In a moment he rejoined her, and now her hands reached for his penis and wrapped around it. It grew even larger in her grip, throbbing with heat against her fingers. But in a moment she reluctantly released the organ as he pulled away from her and moved down her body. He snaked his tongue down along her belly until his mouth nuzzled between her thighs and under her skirt and then against the gusset of her panties. He bit into her like a wild man, filling his mouth with her nylon-covered sex until she groaned and begged him to stop. "Let me get my skirt off," she said.

She swiftly unzipped her skirt and he helped her remove it. Her panties she removed herself, and then her blouse and brassiere. Now she was naked on the blanket and completely exposed to him, and when he pushed her legs apart to look at her sex she quivered when she saw the lust in his eyes.

"I never looked at you when we were young," he said.

"Yes, you did."

"But not like this."

She was suddenly aware of the difference between Pierre and her husband. Bernard was really only a boy masquerading as a man. It was the masquerade that he carried into the bedroom and it always detracted from their lovemaking. But with Pierre she felt at ease completely. She felt at ease and free, unashamed of her lust. With Pierre she could acknowledge that she had a body and that her body could receive and provide pleasure. How easy it was to love someone if the match was proper! With Bernard this experience would be impossible.

As Pierre looked at her sex, she yearned to prove to him how much she wanted his love. With a shudder of abandon she drew her legs up and parted her thighs, spreading them wide to reveal her sex completely. "Pierre..." she whispered. She arched her body, writhing, pushing her belly upward. "Darling..."

He gazed at her sex, and then he reached out and he gently touched her. His fingertips brushed against the lips and then dipped between them and pried them apart. "My God, you're lovely," he said.

Gabrielle trembled, holding her knees back as he looked at her, blushing as she realized no man had ever looked at her this way. She felt his fingers in her sex, the fingertips stirring the wetness. She imagined her clitoris was stiff and protruding, her anus twitching, everything revealed to his eyes.

Finally Pierre leaned forward to put his mouth on her sex. Her thighs caressed his cheeks as her belly heaved against him. He ran his tongue in a long sweep, lashing the full length of her slit, lapping her from anus to clitoris. She went wild when she felt it. She rubbed madly against him, panting, moaning as he swept her repeatedly with those long strokes of his tongue. Then he tilted his head, and fitting his lips to her gap he began thrusting his tongue deep inside her vagina. She groaned as she felt the movements, the wet tongue like an animal in her sex, wriggling, coiling, probing her depths. He used his tongue in her sex as he had before in her mouth, thrusting steadily, his lips sucking and pulling at the folds of her sex and then at the swollen bud of her clitoris.

Before long she began coming, a jolting series of orgasms that made her feverish with lust. The juices flowed freely from her sex, running over his tongue and coating his lips. His mouth left her an instant, dipping down and then sweeping up again, gathering her syrup as it streamed between the globes of her buttocks.

Completely abandoned to him now, she reached down and used her own fingers to spread her sex wide open around his active tongue. He lapped relentlessly at the inner folds, sucking at her like a thirsty animal. She felt a new and deeper sensation and she started bucking wildly, her buttocks squirming against the ground, her sex rippling, closing around his tongue and sucking at his lips.

Then her orgasm reached a peak and she trembled violently, gasping, arching her body and crying out and then finally lying flat on the blanket again.

Pierre continued sucking at her sex another minute or so, long enough to start a new pleasure rising in her belly, and then he straightened up between her legs and he smiled at her. "I think you like to be sucked."

Gabrielle blushed. "Yes, why not? Doesn't your wife like it?"

A cloud passed over Pierre's face. "She's not very amorous."

"And neither is my husband."

Pierre chuckled. "Then I suppose we belong together."

Gabrielle's eyes fixed on his penis. For the first time she became aware how magnificent it was. The straining organ rose tall and powerful above his bloated testicles, twitching and jerking with impatience, the knob a fiery red in the bright sunlight and glistening at the tip. With a cry of delight, she reached out to grasp the rigid member. She wrapped her hand around the base of the shaft and gripped it firmly. The organ jerked at her touch, and she licked her lips as she imagined how marvelous it would feel when she had it stuffed inside her sex. More aggressive now, she pumped her fist up and down, slowly and steadily, watching the knob bulge in response to her caress. Then she loosened her grip and she ran her hand along the member to cap the crown with her fingers. The small slit in the glans gaped open and dripped a clear fluid on her fingertips. Holding the shaft of his penis with one hand, she now cupped his testicles with the other hand and felt the shape and weight of the eggs with her fingers, the orbs sliding in the sac. She heard him grunt with pleasure, his breathing heavy as she continued fondling him. Now as she gazed at the bloated glans, she realized her mouth was watering. Oh God, yes! she thought. She had to have him in her mouth! With Bernard she never liked it; she did it when he wanted it, but she never liked it.

She sat up on the blanket and she looked into Pierre's eyes a long moment. Then she swiftly bent her head to kiss his swollen penis. An instant later her soft lips closed over the knob and she began sucking it.

He groaned. "Gabrielle..."

She pulled her mouth away from his organ. "Lie down," she said. She pushed at him gently until he lay flat on the blanket. Then she crouched beside him and she looked down at his magnificent erection, at the juice now streaming out of the tip. She wanted to engulf the organ, swallow all of it down her throat, gorge herself on his flesh. Instead she merely touched it, her fingertips running lightly along its length, over the fat glans and down along the underside to the sac that held his testicles. She lowered her head again, but not directly toward his penis this time. Her tongue extended and the moist tip lapped at the inside of his thigh, then ran up the crease where his leg joined his torso. The contact brought a growling noise from him, and when she turned her eyes to the side she saw him clench his hands on the blanket beside him. This evidence of his passion excited her tremendously, and she suddenly wondered if his wife ever did this to him. Did she suck his penis like this? No, maybe not. Or maybe without pleasure. Maybe Bernard thought of her the way Pierre thought of his wife: a woman "not very amorous." What a folly! Gabrielle thought. Meanwhile she adored the feel and taste of Pierre's organ in her mouth, the heat of it, the masculine strength. Now she pulled her mouth away from the tip and she licked his testicles. Her tongue lapped with broad flat strokes over the hairy sac. She continued licking it until she had it thoroughly wet with her saliva, and then she moved her mouth to the tip of his penis again and she kissed it. She fluttered her tongue over the swollen knob. Fitting her lips to the underside of his shaft, she ran her mouth slowly up and down the long fat wand. Her mouth moved higher with each sliding caress, her tongue wiggling along the stalk, tickling it, coaxing it to swell even further. Finally she could wait no longer; she had to have it in her mouth. She gave a last teasing lick at the tip of his penis where the clear fluid seeped out, and then she slipped her lips over the bulbous glans and she engulfed it completely.

Pierre groaned as she began to suck. Only the knob was in her mouth, her lips working over it, her tongue sliding under it as her mouth slurped and pulled at his tumescent flesh. He raised his head to watch her suck him, and then he fell back on the blanket again. Her blond hair brushed his thighs, her cheeks hollowing as she sucked vigorously on his thick organ. Now she began to suck deeper, running her mouth up and down on his penis, taking him as deeply as possible before sliding her lips back to the glans again. Each time she had him engulfed completely, his knob lodged partly in her throat; she would hold it a moment, then drew upwards, sucking all the way until only the tip remained collared by her lips. She went down again, rose again, using her mouth with a masturbatory rhythm. Savoring the feel of his throbbing organ, she moved with tantalizing slowness to make it last. As she sucked hungrily, her tongue lashing back and forth beneath his glans, his penis seemed to grow even larger until it stuffed her mouth completely. Her lips stretched around the expanding shaft as the knob pushed at the entrance to her throat. She hesitated an instant, then sucked again, her head sliding up and down, her lips gliding over the girth of the shaft. His penis was now so swollen she found it difficult to move freely. She had to push her head down, forcing the opening of her throat over the tip of the organ. When he felt her throat snapping at his glans, Pierre groaned hoarsely and squirmed on the blanket. She realized he was close to coming, and eager to have him erupt in her throat, she sucked with more deliberation.

But Pierre had other ideas. She felt his hands tangling in her hair, and in spite of her moan of protest, he pulled her head away and his penis slid out of her mouth with a wet noise.

She whimpered. "Please, darling...Let me..."

"No, not now. I need to get inside you."

She felt a keen disappointment at being denied the pleasure of his sperm in her mouth. But disappointment was instantly replaced by avid anticipation to have him inside her, this magnificent erection plunging deep in her sex. She groaned as he made her lie down on the blanket and then rose over her. "Yes!" she cried. "Yes, I want it!"

He mounted her, bracing his knees between her legs and cupping his broad hands under her buttocks, hauling her hips up to meet his own. She arched her back and drew him over her. Then she grasped at her own thighs and pulled her legs back until her knees were pressed against her breasts. In this position, her pink and dripping sex was wide open to him and completely vulnerable.

"Do it," she moaned. "Please..."

He paused a moment to gaze at her gaping sex, and then he brought his penis down until it nudged against the opening. The instant it touched her, she felt as though an electric spark flashed between them to ignite their passions even further.

The head of his penis now nestled between her labia. Rather than enter her at once, he moved his glans up and down at the entrance. Tantalized by this caress, Gabrielle began thrashing wildly beneath him. Her hips squirmed as she rolled her head from side to side. Her breasts heaved as she panted and clawed at his arms and shoulders in a desperate attempt to get his penis inside her. "Please!" she cried.

He thrust forward, pushing only the tip of his organ into her tunnel. The mouth of her vagina clamped around him, gripping his shaft just behind the knob and holding it. As her sex clutched at him with its internal muscles, his penis slowly pushed into her passage. Centimeter by centimeter, her vagina sucked at his member until finally he rammed his hips forward and penetrated her completely.

She cried out with pleasure as the thick penis exquisitely filled her. Their pubic bones ground together as he tried to jam his penis inside her even further. Then he paused again as she squirmed. As his belly rubbed against hers, she could feel his bloated testicles pressed against her buttocks. His fingers dug into the globes now, lifting her, holding her there as he penetrated her completely.

She cried out again, clawed at his flanks, her thighs closed over his hips, rippling, urging him to start moving. Her heels drummed against his buttocks.

Pierre could no longer resist her writhing body. He drew back slowly until only the head of his penis remained lodged in her sex, and then he plunged forward to push the full length of his organ inside her. He pulled back and thrust forward again, and Gabrielle sobbed with pleasure. She soon fell into rhythm with him, pushing her belly down as he thrust forward to impale her, then as he withdrew using her internal muscles to squeeze the length of the retreating shaft.

Now they moved together easily, sharing the tempo, Pierre taking her with long, gliding strokes, increasing the frequency gradually as both their linked bodies surged toward higher and higher peaks of passion. As the sensation intensified, they melted into each other. He rammed his penis in and out as Gabrielle rotated and writhed around the sliding organ. Her sex slurped at it, a flood of juice gushing from her as he pistoned into her, the syrup running down into the crack between her buttocks and soaking the blanket beneath her.

Pierre heaved up, changing the angle of his thrusting so that now his penis rubbed directly over her clitoris with every stroke. This new thrill caused Gabrielle to jerk violently, her mind inflamed and her body completely out of control. He rammed her again and again, plowing into her, his testicles slapping against her sweaty buttocks with each stroke.

Intense waves of rippling sensation coursed through her belly as she came. Her orgasm increased in strength and intensity until the surging waves merged into one extended climax. When she cried out at the very peak, Pierre let himself go and his penis exploded in the depths of her sex.

He jabbed her as he spurted, once, twice, then again. She opened her eyes in time to watch his face as the pleasure convulsed it. She felt the new wetness in her sex, sperm flooding her vagina to mix with her own juices.

Drained, Pierre collapsed over her. Gabrielle continued to writhe gently awhile, and then she ceased moving and she cuddled against him with his softening organ still gripped by her sex.

Later, after they were dressed, Pierre said: "When will I see you again?"

Gabrielle shuddered as she realized how happy she was. “In a few days if you like. But only after work.”

“And after that? Can you manage twice a week?”

“Yes, of course.”

As they walked hand in hand out of the wood, they laughed together when Pierre reminded her the factory people thought she was ill.

“And my husband,” she said. “Bernard will think so too.”

“What will you tell him?”

“I’ll tell him it was a woman’s problem.”

Demon Heat

CONTENTS

Part One

THE QUEEN OF THEBES

Lambert thought the Pharaoh Akhenaten reminded him of a certain stockbroker in New York: sneaky eyes in a rather stupid-looking bony face. Hail the Pharaoh, Lambert thought. Akhenaten was all over the place, his mug on every souvenir ashtray and teapot up and down the filthy Nile.

After ten days in Egypt, Lambert was becoming bored with it. All the days had been dull, of no consequence except for a few interviews with some unimportant people in Cairo. He knew Cairo, knew it well enough to be wary of it, well enough to keep it at arm's length. You could lose yourself in Cairo; the place could swallow you up, close around you and strangle you.

In the meantime he was pushing forty and still wandering into the mud-holes of the world like a dumb rhino.

This morning on the boulevard they call Talaat Harb, he suddenly decided to visit the Museum of Antiquities for the third time. He waved down a taxi and was there in twenty minutes, walking through the huge doors and into the cool hall on the ground floor. As usual the place was crowded, tourists from everywhere milling about, talking, sweating despite the coolness. He had no fixed idea about what he wanted to look at, but he decided to go up to the first floor and wander around the Tutankhamen galleries again. The rooms on the first floor were usually less crowded than those on the ground floor, and occasionally it was possible to have some privacy in one of the rooms, an opportunity to look at the exhibit without the annoyance of someone standing nearby and babbling about it.

The rooms in the galleries were of two kinds: open rooms with only two walls, and closed rooms with four walls and two doors opposite each other, all the rooms arranged in sequence around the central atrium, the rooms filled with literally thousands of objects from the dynasties of ancient Egypt.

When he reached the first floor, Lambert wandered away from the north end toward the Tutankhamen rooms. The open room that contained Tutankhamen's bed had no visitors in it, and Lambert stood there a while looking at the bed, at the sheet gold stretched around the frame, thinking of Tutankhamen in that bed, the bed of a Pharaoh of Egypt.

The sounds of the other people on the floor seemed distant, and finally faded altogether for some reason. The place was so enormous, so cluttered with antiquities, that the acoustics were unpredictable.

The open room that had the gold bed in it was adjacent to another room, a closed room containing even a larger bed, this one surrounded with gold string rather than sheet gold, but still imposing. Lambert had been in these rooms before, but he'd spent more time in the open room than in the closed room, and now as he glanced at the other room he suddenly noticed a woman inside it and he was startled. He was certain she hadn't been there a moment ago.

It could happen like that in museums. You stood alone, isolated in a reverie about some object or artifact, and abruptly someone else was there to disturb the isolation. He was certain that an instant ago the closed room had been empty, but there was the woman looking at him, an attractive dark-haired woman, either an American or a European. He met her glance, and then he turned away to look at Tutankhamen's bed again.

And then another surprise: the woman suddenly entered the room he was in, her high heels making a clicking sound on the marble floor.

She walked into the open room where he stood beside the case that enclosed Tutankhamen's bed and said, "What do you think of it? It's extraordinary, isn't it?"

What he was thinking was that the really extraordinary thing was the way she'd approached him, casually and without artifice, as if their acquaintance was already a matter of course.

She was a tall woman, maybe thirty, with short dark hair, dark eyes, and perfectly shaped dark eyebrows. Her thin triangular face looked young, but somehow she gave the impression of being older than she looked. She wore expensive clothes that seemed to suit her perfectly, and no jewelry except for a black pearl necklace.

The dark eyes stared straight at him.

He nodded. He said yes, the pharaoh's bed was extraordinary, the exhibit was extraordinary, the museum was extraordinary.

She smiled. "And Cairo? Isn't Cairo extraordinary?"

They talked. She said she was an American, but he thought she had a slight foreign accent. They toured five or six of the other rooms together, and by then he was enough taken with her to suggest they have coffee somewhere, maybe in a place near the American Embassy. Then they talked about the Cairo hotels and they discovered they were both staying at the Continental Savoy.

"Then why not the Savoy?" she said. "It's as good as anywhere, isn't it?"

She told him her name was Magda Clare.

"Hungarian?" he said.

She seemed amused. "Something like that."

In the taxi he noticed her legs for the first time, the full calves and slender ankles covered by very sheer brown stockings. He cautioned himself against absurd expectations: she was an American, and travelers of the same nationality did after all talk to each other. He remembered innocent hours passed with American women in various places around the globe. But he felt this was somehow different, somehow unique.

But go easy, he thought.

They talked in the taxi, chatted about Cairo, the traffic, the smog. There was no talk of personal affairs. She seemed totally uninterested in his personal affairs, his business affairs, any of his affairs. She said she was a tourist, and that was all. After she learned he was in Cairo to write an article about an Egyptian political figure, she dropped the subject completely.

The half hour or so they spent in the Savoy coffee shop was unremarkable except for the end of it. At the end of it he suddenly felt a desperate need for her. It came over him without warning, and after that he could think of nothing else.

"You look unhappy," she said.

When he replied, the words came out of his

mouth without his willing them, or at least it felt like that. "Come up to my room with me," he said.

Did he actually say that? It was certainly something like that, the words blurted out, unbidden, unwilled, almost with someone else's voice. Lambert was shocked at his own audacity. He'd known the woman only an hour or so, and it seemed ruder than hell to be making such an obvious proposition to her. She hadn't flirted with him, or anything like that. What right did he have to make assumptions about her?

She looked directly at him, no expression in her dark eyes, her face impassive, and she said: "All right."

Looking beyond her, he could see his own face in a mirror. His face looked gaunt, perturbed. Maybe it was the history; maybe in a country with a 5000-year-old history anything could happen. Was that what it was?

He knew hardly anything about her: he knew her name was Magda Clare and that she said she was American. He guessed her age at thirty-two, and she wore no wedding band, no rings of any kind. And that was all. She did have a slight foreign accent, but it remained unexplained.

When they walked into his room, Lambert felt at a loss because he had absolutely nothing to drink, no alcohol in the room at all. She laughed when he mentioned it, dismissing the idea completely. "This is Egypt," she said.

Yes, of course, this was Egypt.

Then she looked at him and she said: "Why did you ask me here? Do you want to make love to me?"

He stammered something. But she seemed uninterested in what he said, and ignored it. She came into his arms and kissed him, a strange sort of kiss because her lips felt as cold as ice. He was shocked enough by the coldness to pull away from her, and then she kissed him again and this time her lips were hot. Not merely warm, but hot enough to cause a tingling pain in his own lips. Or did he imagine it? He thought the sudden change in the temperature of her lips astounding. Then in a moment he felt a strange and intense lassitude overcome him, so intense that he almost had trouble remaining on his feet.

As they kissed, she moved a hand between their bodies and she lightly rubbed the front of his trousers in a way that brought him an immediate erection. The bold fondling took him by surprise and she was immediately aware of it.

"Don't you want me?" she said.

"Yes."

"Then don't be so shy. Or maybe what I'm doing bothers you. Does it bother you? It doesn't feel like it bothers you. It feels very nice to me. It feels like you have something for me."

She continued the rubbing, but now it was really more a grazing than a rubbing, a tantalizing stroking of her fingertips across the front of his trousers that made his penis feel as though it would burst. He still felt the strange weakness, and when she urged him to lie down on the bed he was happy at the chance and did that at once. But instead of joining him on the bed, she remained standing, gazing at him. He thought she wanted to undress while he watched her, but in a moment she sat on the edge of the bed and she calmly searched for the tab of the zipper at the front of his trousers. When she found the tab, she pulled it all the way down and then slid her hand inside the opening. She brought his penis out, her fingers tugging at it, getting the whole length of it out in the air, carefully, without fumbling.

Her face showed no expression. She did not look at him; she looked at his penis as she slowly stroked it and tickled it with her red fingernails, caressed it as though it were a living thing in itself and something not part of him. She seemed totally uninterested in anything else. Her eyes were bright and she seemed to be cajoling it, working to get the erection at a maximum, the knob and the shaft as fully swollen as possible.

"How long has it been?" she said.

Lambert was taken aback. "What?"

"Since the last time you came."

"I don't know. I guess about a week."

"Good."

When he suggested they get their clothes off, she ignored him. Instead, she dropped her head and she took his penis in her mouth, engulfed it completely, then pulled back to suck at only the knob.

Now, suddenly, he felt the heat of her lips again, an almost scalding heat enveloping him down there as she sucked at his penis, and before very long he groaned and spent with enormous force, his body heaving, his organ shooting a great deal of sperm in her mouth as she continued sucking at the tip. It was the most intense orgasm he'd ever experienced, a great gushing of fluid out of him, a blast of total ecstasy that took him completely by surprise.

"Jesus," he said.

Then, when he glanced down at her face, he had a terrible shock that almost caused him to faint: she was looking up at him, her red lips sucking fiercely at his penis, but her eyes seemed to be clear white and with no pupils. The illusion was horrible, although it lasted only a moment, and then she closed her eyes and opened them again and the dark pupils were back, staring at him, her mouth now sucking slowly and sensuously at the tip of his organ as she finished draining the sperm out of his balls.

She rose up after that, her lips wet, her face for the first time showing a look of satisfaction.

"Are you all right?" she said.

"Yes."

"You're a strong one."

He looked at her. "What do you mean?"

She shook her head. "Never mind." Then she said he might call her in the early evening if he liked. "Before eight," she said. "Maybe you ought to rest until then." And after that she walked out.

He wanted to run after her but he was too weak. Instead he lay there staring at the ceiling with his mind in a whirling confusion, his body still feeling the aftereffects of the orgasm, the total release, the laziness. But the exhaustion of energy was more than he'd ever experienced after a climax, a complete removal of any urge to move a muscle.

He remembered her telling him he ought to rest.

He felt drugged, his soul wiped out.

He wanted her back with him; he desperately wanted her back with him.

At seven in the evening, he called the hotel switchboard and asked for Miss Magda Clare. Room number? He said he had no idea what room, but she was definitely a guest in this hotel.

Whoever it was returned to the phone and said no, he must be mistaken, there was no one by that name registered at all. Had she been registered yesterday? Had she checked out? No, not at all. "Extremely sorry, sir." Lambert was too confused to argue and he hung up. After that he had a light dinner brought up to the room, and passed the rest of the evening making an attempt to read the newspapers.

Absurd, wasn't it?

What happened now? Was he supposed to sleep peacefully after this? He caught sight of his reflection in the mirror and he thought he looked sick.

Next morning.

When he awoke he could think of nothing but the events of yesterday. He lay on the bed and struggled with them, reviewed every detail from the first moment he'd seen Magda in the museum to the last moment when she'd walked out of the room. Had it really happened? He had breakfast brought up to him, and afterward he sat down to work on the article about Salah Hamad. He wanted Magda. If at all possible, he'd find her. He was determined to find her again.

He went first to the hotel desk and he asked them to check the hotel register again. The concierge assured him that no one named Clare was or had been registered at the hotel. When he described Magda to him, the concierge merely shrugged and said he had no idea who she was. Then it occurred to

Lambert he could telephone some other hotels in Cairo, and he returned to his room and did that. He called all the hotels popular with tourists, but none of them had any registration in the name of Clare or Claire or anything similar that he could think of, and for security reasons they refused to suggest the names of people on their lists.

After that he went out again. He took a taxi to the plaza called Midan Tahrir and he wandered around with no particular plan in mind, just looking at people in the cafes, people in the shops, and so on. It was silly, of course; he knew he'd never find her that way.

Later he went to the Museum of Antiquities again. He returned to the first floor and the room where they'd met. It was crowded this time, a dozen or so people milling around Tutankhamen's bed as they listened to a slender blond girl talk to them in Swedish. Lambert left the room immediately, and after that he wandered through the museum for another hour before returning to the Savoy.

Now it seemed ridiculous to think that he'd find Magda again. Cairo, after all, had ten or eleven million people in it. No matter what sort of despair he might feel, there was really no one who could help him.

Four days later. Perfunctory work, a few more interviews, dull days and even duller nights. Every afternoon he returned to the museum, to the same room where the bed of Tutankhamen was displayed. Lambert suspected the guards thought he was up to something, since rather than study the bed all he did was wander in and out of the same room doing nothing. Or maybe they thought he was crazy. But they seemed rather blasé about it, and so far he'd had no trouble with them.

He spent a great deal of time thinking about her, reliving the time with her, regretting very much that he'd never had a chance to make serious love to her. Or to even look at her body. He'd seen nothing of her body, really. He kept thinking of her legs in the taxi from the museum to the Savoy, the way she'd crossed her legs, the brown nylon, the shape of one calf. He thought maybe all this interest in her legs occurred because here in Cairo the women didn't show much of themselves, certainly not the ordinary Egyptian women on the streets. They kept their bodies well-covered, the shoulders and legs never bare, the breasts always hidden by the folds of their cloaks or burnooses or whatever they called them. Some of the women were more modern and they dressed in the Western style, but still with considerable modesty.

It was crazy to think of Magda's legs when he had the more important memory of her mouth sucking at him. But when he thought of her mouth, he also thought of her eyes, that horrible instant when her eyes seemed to be without pupils, and then he found himself too disturbed by all of it and he stopped thinking of anything.

Then Magda Clare came back to him.

He'd been in Cairo nearly three weeks, when one afternoon he returned to the museum once more and saw her. She was on the first floor again, not in the room with Tutankhamen's bed but in one of the rooms close by. At first he wasn't certain it was her, but then she turned and showed her face and a shock of happiness went through him.

When he approached her, she seemed amused to see him. "Jack, it's you."

He'd made up his mind to be angry with her, but now that the moment was here the anger seemed ridiculous. But he did his best to tell her how annoyed he was that she'd left him without the means of contacting her. When she learned how much time he'd spent looking for her, she seemed more amused than ever.

"But you shouldn't have," she said.

"It's better than working."

She smiled, her eyes dropping a moment to the front of his trousers.

She walked with him down the stairs to the ground floor of the museum, and as they approached the main entrance he said: "Let's go to the Savoy."

She laughed. "No, I don't think so."

"Please, Magda..."

She looked at him a long moment. "Do you really want me?"

"Yes."

"You might be sorry, you know."

"I don't care."

Now her eyes looked distant. "I'm remembering how it was with you. You had a great deal of *laban* for me."

"What's that?"

"It's the Egyptian word for milk."

When they arrived at the Savoy, he had some tea and strawberries immediately brought up to the room. Magda still resisted telling him much about herself as they sat opposite each other in the two chairs near the open window. He asked where she was staying in Cairo, but she merely smiled and avoided an answer. Then she noticed his eyes on her legs, and she sat back and casually pulled at her skirt to expose her knees. "Will it excite you to look at me?"

He nodded, feeling a lurch of arousal in his belly.

She exposed her legs without being coquettish about it, her hands pulling her skirt back until the tops of her stockings were revealed.

"Is this enough?"

"It'll do for the time being."

"We won't do any more than last time, you know."

"That's crazy."

She shook her head and made to cover her legs.

He pleaded with her. "No, please..."

"I mean it about not doing any more than we've done."

"You're teasing me."

"No, I'm not teasing you," she said. "Yes, I am teasing you with my legs, but the purpose of that is to get you spunky."

"To get me spunky?"

She laughed. "That's not American, that's British. It means to get your balls full. I'm going to suck you again, and you'll have a great deal of lovely stuff for me, won't you?"

So there it was, the bald expression of what she wanted from him. She wanted his sperm. He'd never in his life had a woman talk about it like that, and he found himself completely confused by it. What she wanted was a great deal of sperm in her mouth when he ejaculated.

"You look astonished," she said.

"I am astonished."

She seemed annoyed. "Don't be a child about this. I thought you liked it enough last time."
"All right, whatever you say."
"That's much better. Now bring it out and let me look at it while I tease you up some more."

He'd heard it said the duet of the snake charmer and the snake was nothing but an allegory for the female and the penis. Like a snake seemingly mesmerized by a snake charmer, his penis seemed mesmerized by Magda. He was already erect when he exposed himself, his penis rearing up and weaving from side to side like a pink reptile. Her eyes brightened when she saw it, and in a moment she rose from the chair and she lifted her skirt high enough to expose everything below her waist.
She wore a garter belt to hold up her stockings, and under that a pair of white lace panties with an opaque gusset. She had flawless legs, the stockings drawn tight on her thighs, the nylon gleaming in the light from the window.
"Does this excite you?" she said.
"Yes."
"Men are so easy, you know. I won't let you look at my cunt because you might become too frisky. But how about my ass? Do you like asses?"
Her panties were cut high on the sides, and when she turned her back to him to show him her ass, most of each buttock was clearly revealed.
Yes, he did like asses. His excitement was now more intense than ever. He took his penis in his hand, curled his fingers around it and squeezed it. Then she turned to face him again, and when she saw his hand on his organ, she hissed at him: "Stop that, you fool! I don't want you coming yet!"

Stunned by the anger in her voice, he pulled his hand away from his penis. The organ twitched, a drop of fluid now appearing at the tip, hanging there a moment and then streaming out on his bloated glans. When Magda saw the seeping, a soft cry came out of her throat and she immediately threw herself on her knees in front of him, closed her mouth over the tip of his penis and sucked it in a frenzy.

Lambert almost bolted off the chair as he felt the heat of her mouth, a blistering heat like the last time, painful enough to disorient him completely. He started coming, spurting in her mouth, the sperm shooting in great jets that apparently delighted Magda. Each jet produced a muffled moan of satisfaction from her throat.

When he looked down at her, he was afraid he'd see those empty white eyes again, the eyes without pupils, but this time her head was bent at such an angle that he couldn't see her eyes at all.

She continued milking his penis with her lips until the end, and then she used her fingers to squeeze whatever remained out of the opening into her mouth. When she finally pulled her face away from the organ, she licked her lips and smiled at him. "Now you've made me happy," she said.

This time he prevented her from leaving him. He had to lie down because he was too weak to sit or stand, but he insisted that she lie with him on the bed.

"You could kill a man like that," he said.

"Yes, it's true."

He'd been jesting, but her reply was apparently serious. He looked at her and felt extremely uneasy. "Has it ever happened?"

She laughed, running her hand over his chest and down to his belly where his fly was still open, his penis dangling like a limp sausage out of the slit. "Now you're afraid of me," she said. "No, I don't want you to be afraid of me. You have a lovely product, not so thick because you're not a boy any more, but the boys don't do it for me. Maybe something is missing with them. And the boys are so bitter and I don't like it when it's bitter. You know, they told me to stay with the boys, but I've discovered they might be wrong."

"What are you talking about?" Lambert said.

"Never mind, you won't understand. I think I'm leaving now."

"No, please..."

"Would you like to travel to Luxor with me? I'm leaving for Luxor tomorrow, and if you like we can go together."

Still too weak to leave the bed, he turned to look at her as she stood near the dressing table. She had no expression on her face, and as she gazed at him her dark eyes seemed to bore right through his skull.

His voice almost a whisper as he looked at her red lips, he nodded. "Yes."

Then he noticed the mirror behind her and he felt a wrench in his heart. She had her back to the mirror, but the mirror showed nothing. Her body had no reflection in the mirror over the dressing table.

She agreed to have dinner with him that evening. She met him in the lobby of the Savoy and they rode a taxi to a restaurant he knew in Hassan Hegazi Street. He thought she looked exquisite, more beautiful than ever in a white dress, white stockings and white high-heeled pumps. She wore a necklace of small Italian beads around her throat, but apart from that no jewelry.

In the restaurant, he tried to find out more about her, and asked questions concerning her personal life.

"I don't even know if you're married," he said.

She seemed amused. "Would it make any difference?"

"No, I suppose not. Where do you live in the States? In New York?"

"Yes, why not? Why not New York?"

He thought the answer strange and he said so. "I get the feeling you don't want to tell me anything about yourself."

Magda smiled. "Aren't you satisfied with what you have? I thought you had a nice time this afternoon. It *was* nice, wasn't it?" Now the smile was teasing him.

"Yes," he said.

"Very spunky. Do you feel all right? How's your health?"

"I feel fine."

"And your health in general?"

"I'm as healthy as a horse."

She looked puzzled. "As a horse?"

"It's only an expression, isn't it? Anyway, I'm healthy, not sick, no insidious diseases if that's what you're worried about. You won't catch anything."

But she seemed to have lost interest in the subject and she said no more about it. He then asked her where she was staying in Cairo and he expressed his annoyance about the way she'd lied to him a week ago about staying at the Savoy.

She nodded. "But now I do have a room at the Savoy."

"You do?"

She agreed that after they returned to the hotel, she would come to him in his room and be with him awhile.

Later, in his room at the Savoy, he sat near the window, looking at the lights of the city as he waited for her. He could think of nothing else except Magda, what she looked like, the things they had done together. She seemed to have cast a spell over him, but he wasn't a man who believed in such things and he told himself it had to be something else. Maybe it was only a special vulnerability he had to a certain type of woman. Then he remembered the moment in the afternoon when he'd failed to see her reflection in the dressing-table mirror. How the hell had that happened? Maybe the angle had been wrong. He went to the bed now, and he lay down on it and looked at the mirror from what he thought was the same position. But he couldn't tell anything one way or the other, and he finally decided it had to be an illusion of some kind, like that moment when he thought she had no pupils in her eyes.

Someone knocked on the door and he leaped off the bed.

Magda came into the room wearing a different outfit, a maroon satin robe, and Lambert felt a quickening of excitement as he realized she was probably naked under it. She wore open sandals with high heels, and when he looked down at her feet he could see her painted toenails.

After the door was closed, she did not resist him when he took her in his arms and kissed her. Once again he experienced the incredible heat of her lips, and as he caught the familiar scent of her perfume he felt himself totally bewitched by her.

As he kissed her, his hands stroking her back and buttocks through her thin robe, Magda rubbed his penis through the front of his trousers and said: "Will it be a big one again?"

"Let's do something different than last time."

"Like what? Do you want to suck me? Yes, why don't you do that? But get your clothes off first."

As he undressed, she slipped out of the maroon robe and she tossed it onto the chair. Except for the shoes, she wore nothing at all, and for the first time ever he saw her completely naked. Her breasts were full and firm, scarlet-tipped, rising proudly from her chest. The dark nipples pointed slightly off-center and tilted upward just a bit. She had a trim waist, a taut flat belly and narrow hips. At the joining of her thighs was a full, bushy mat of dark hair that completely hid the slit of her sex.

When she saw the state of his erection, she smiled and came to him, took his penis and his balls in her hands and carefully fondled them as if to test his tumescence. "Perfect," she said. "All right, suck me off first, if that's what you want."

He went down on his knees in front of her, amazed at himself, amazed at how passive he was with her, how docile. He pressed his mouth against the bush of dark hair, nuzzled into it and probed the slit with his tongue. She had a lovely thick-lipped cunt, scented with some exotic perfume, and as she moved her legs apart to make it easier for him, the wet heat of her sex overwhelmed him. She rocked against his face as he sucked, and as she did so her cunt became hotter, the wetness turning into a lake of juice between her labia. The taste of her was strange, an unusual metallic taste, something he'd never before experienced with a woman.

She continued rocking on his mouth, inundating his face with her juices, but if she had an orgasm he was never aware of it. He thought the abundance of fluid was certainly an indication that she felt pleasure from it, and the opportunity to actually drink the flow from her sex excited him tremendously.

When she finally pulled away from him, both his face and her thighs glistened with her juices. "You're much too messy about it," she said in a dull tone. "Look how much you've wasted."

He was stunned. He felt the flush of embarrassment in his face, cursed himself for it as he remained on his knees in front of her. But instead of rising up and venting his anger at her, he reached out to grab her legs and pull her forward. Before she could prevent it, he began licking the wetness from her thighs, and when she realized what he wanted, she laughed softly and she moved her legs apart to help him. "Yes, do that," she said. "Lick it everywhere like a pussy-cat."

Her taste was now familiar, and he liked it more and more. It seemed less metallic, more like a strange fruit of some kind. He cleaned her thighs as thoroughly as he could, and when he finally rose up he thought his balls would burst if he didn't come soon.

She touched him carefully, avoiding his penis, but curling her hand under his scrotum and weighing his testicles. She led him to the bed and she urged him onto his back, smiled at him as he lay there with his erect penis jutting upward along his belly.

"Try to calm down," she said.

"I can't."

"Yes you can. Use some willpower and calm down. The longer you delay it, the more you'll have for me. Don't you want to make me happy?"

"Yes."

"Cool down and I'll let you suck me again."

He shuddered as he did his best to reduce his excitement. But just looking at her excited him. Everything she did excited him. Even hearing her talk excited him. Whatever it was she had done to him, she'd made him totally hers.

She moved toward the bed now. She climbed onto it, straddling his body with her back to his face. He had a complete view of her rear, the full buttocks, the deep dark split between the globes. She widened her knees and shifted backward, her ass sliding over his chest, pushing back until his vision was obscured as the hairy sex came down on his face.

In this position her cunt was even more overwhelming than before. He had the smell and taste of her again, the strong taste that was so strange to him. She was also very wet again, her juices dripping, streaming out of her lush cunt and into his mouth. She gave a slight wriggle from side to side, as if to settle herself into a firmer position, and then she leaned forward and he suddenly felt the heat of her mouth surround the knob of his penis.

There was no way he could hold back under this double stimulation, and in a few moments he gave it up altogether and he started spurting in her mouth. As had happened before, the orgasm was tremendous, the sperm blasting out of him, each jet a burning salvo through his penis, his hips lifting off the bed as she continued holding the knob in her mouth. She sucked furiously, pulling everything out of him, and then he cried out against her wet cunt as he felt her fingertip pushing at his anus, pushing all the way inside it and pressing against his prostate to empty him completely.

He collapsed with the taste of her cunt in his mouth. He recognized the taste now: her juices had the taste of black olives.

When he opened his eyes again, the room was dark and he realized he'd been asleep for some time. He had no idea how long, and he felt too tired to find his wristwatch. Anyway, what did it matter? Magda certainly wasn't in the bed beside him, so she must have returned to her room. He lay there in the dark thinking about her, about what they had done together. Then he touched his face and he felt the crust of her dried juices. A shudder of delight went through him as he remembered the taste of black olives that came out of her. He closed his eyes, dozing off as he thought about Magda, his mind in a blanket as he finally slept again.

Sometime toward morning he suddenly came awake as he felt the familiar burning heat around his penis. Magda was back, bending over him somewhere in the dark, her mouth sucking at his organ. He felt her fingers tugging at his balls, then another finger probing his anus as she had done the night before. He groaned as he felt the fingers going in, pushing inside his body. probing inside him, finding his prostate and rubbing it.

In a moment he started coming, his body jerking as he spurted in her mouth, his belly heaving as she sucked the sperm out of his balls. He heard a noise, a muffled sound, and he realized it was Magda grunting with pleasure as she took what she wanted from him.

Late in the morning they traveled by plane to Luxor. Lambert felt an extreme lethargy after all the activity of the previous night, the wild sucking and the way Magda had drained him. The orgasms he had with her continued to be the most intense he'd ever known, complete convulsions that made him wonder if it was possible to kill someone with too much sex. Was it possible?

The airplane trip was uneventful, but when they arrived at their hotel in Luxor, Magda came in through the door connecting their rooms and she said: "Let me suck you before we go out again."

He tried to put her off. "After last night, I doubt if I can get to first base."

But she coaxed him, teased him about being exhausted. "Do you want me to go out and find a boy somewhere?"

"I'm pooped."

"Don't worry, I'll revive you. Trust me, lover."

He gave in. He was learning her will was stronger than his. At least now it was. Before he'd met her, he'd always thought of himself as something different than what he was now.

The first thing she did was to bare her breasts, remove her blouse and bra and then approach him where he sat in a chair. Holding a breast in her hand, she pushed the tip at his mouth and started him sucking it. The nipple was warm, and when he felt it expanding in his mouth he was excited by it. He sucked one breast, and then the other breast, and before long he felt his penis twitching in his trousers as it started to extend.

Magda evidently recognized that he was responding to the breast sucking, but she wasn't satisfied. "No, you're not ready yet."

She pulled her breasts away from his face, turned her back to him, lifted her skirt, and pulled her panties down to bare her buttocks. "Kiss it," she said. "It'll make you hot and fill your balls."

As he gazed at her ass, he felt his excitement indeed increasing, his penis becoming more swollen as it lengthened. He understood what was happening to him, what was happening between them, and he was surprised that it didn't bother him at all. It seemed to be something he wanted, this yielding to every demand she made. Maybe it was the way she'd been draining him of sexual energy. But if that was the case, the energy was returning now and he still felt overwhelmed by her.

Once again he did what she wanted. Leaning forward, he started kissing her buttocks, running his mouth over the smooth globes of her ass, licking her skin with his tongue. As he licked his way into the dark crack, she muttered words of encouragement and moved her body against his face.

She'd been accurate about the effect on him. When she finally pulled her ass away, then turned around and made him rise and drop his trousers and shorts, she found him fully primed for her. "Something nice for Magda," she said with a smile, her fingers stroking his balls, lifting them against his hard penis and then dropping them again. "Are you okay?"

"Sure," he said.

"I'll draw you off, and then you can rest for an hour. After that we'll go out on the west road. I want to show you a special place."

"You've been here before?"

Still holding his balls in her hand, she seemed amused. "Yes, of course."

She sat down in the chair, and as he stood in front of her with his trousers and shorts at his ankles, she took his penis in her mouth and she started sucking it. He groaned as he felt the heat of her mouth again, the burning sensation on the knob of his organ. As he looked down at her, he could see her cheeks hollowed by the force of her sucking. She held his balls in one hand, tugging at the bag of his scrotum. When she moved the other hand between his legs, he thought she would put a finger in his ass again, but this time she did something different. She found a spot immediately behind his balls and she rubbed it with considerable pressure. Instead of making him come sooner, it actually slowed him down. With a loud sucking noise, she pulled her mouth off his glans and she looked up at him while her fingertip continued rubbing the magic spot.

"Does this hurt?"

"No, but I've got to come soon."

"Yes, of course. Just a little more and then we'll finish you off."

She covered the knob with her mouth again, and then he felt her finger moving back between his buttocks to find his anus. The fact was he didn't like her finger in there that much, but he had no doubt it helped her get everything out of him.

She was sucking hard now, and in a moment his body jerked and he cried out as he started coming in her mouth. She kept the finger working inside his ass as she took what he had, and when he was finally drained she pulled her mouth off the tip of his penis with a satisfied smack of her lips.

"That was a good one," she said. "Now go lie down and rest."

She seemed rejuvenated, her face with a high color, her dark eyes brighter than ever. He, on the other hand, felt as though he were half-dead. He had barely enough strength left to make it to the bed and rest his bones.

In the afternoon she took him out on the west road to a place called the Valley of Queens. Some years before, Lambert had visited Karnak on the other side of the river and the Valley of Kings to the north, but this was his first visit to this other place. Magda seemed to know a great deal about it. She called it Biban el-Harim, and patiently explained to him that it contained nearly a hundred tombs of queens and princesses and princes of the 19th and 20th dynasties. She took him on a tour of some of the tombs, and then to one in particular that seemed to interest her greatly. She said it was the tomb of Queen Mafernit, one of the wives of Ramses I.

"She was the loveliest woman in Thebes," Magda said. "Ramses wanted her to be a goddess, but I think she failed him."

As she said this, Magda stared fixedly at the edifice of the tomb, and Lambert had the impression she was trembling. But it lasted only a moment, and after that Magda took his arm and led him away.

In the evening after dinner, Lambert realized how tired he was and he told Magda he thought he'd better turn in early.

She gave him a teasing look. "Am I exhausting you, darling?"

"Maybe it's the tombs."
"The tombs?"
"All these Egyptians building tombs for themselves. Did they really think it would work? Did they really think the tombs would give them immortality? They became dust like everyone else, didn't they?"

Magda remained silent a long time. Then she said: "Are you ill?"

"I don't know. I feel a little weak. Maybe I've caught a bug here."

But he knew it wasn't that. If there was anything wrong with him, it was this crazy infatuation he had for Magda. He'd more or less given up the assignment in Cairo; he'd have to cable New York and tell them about that. All he cared about now was the time he spent with Magda. He wanted more of her, but he was also afraid of it. He had no idea why, but he was beginning to be desperately afraid of something happening to him.

He slept alone in his room. Sometime during the night he awakened in the dark and he thought he heard noises from Magda's room through the connecting door. He became curious, then after a while desperate to know what was going on in there. Did she know anyone in Luxor? Or was she merely talking on the telephone? The connecting door had no keyhole, but then he remembered the connecting balcony outside.

He left the bed, slipped his feet into his loafers and quietly opened the glass door to the balcony. Outside, the sky was black with only a few stars and the air was cooler than he expected. Half the balcony was lit up by the light from Magda's room, which meant she hadn't pulled the drapes to cover the glass door. He shivered in his thin pajamas as he moved carefully across the balcony to a place in the shadow from where he could look through the glass door and into Magda's room.

The first thing he saw was that she wasn't alone. She had a man in there, a young man in a uniform of some kind, and after a moment Lambert realized it was one of the hotel porters. They were standing near the bed, Magda wearing a robe and with her arms folded. Then she spoke to the porter, and when Lambert heard her voice he realized the sliding glass door was partly open.

He tried to make out what she was saying, and then he was shocked when it became apparent to him she was speaking Arabic. Fluent Arabic, if he was any judge of it. He knew nothing of the language and he had no idea what she was talking about. The porter nodded and said something in reply and Magda seemed annoyed. She went to the dressing table, opened her purse and removed some paper money from it, Egyptian pound notes. Then she returned to the porter and she handed the money to him, watching him as he folded and stuffed the money in one of his pockets. After that she moved closer to the porter and she placed the flat of her palm directly over the crotch of his trousers.

Lambert was filled with both astonishment and anguish as he watched them. Magda rubbed the front of the porter's trousers with her hand, said something to him in Arabic and then made him sit down on one of the chairs. After he was seated, the porter opened his fly and he brought out a long curved penis. Magda immediately dropped to her knees and took the knob in her mouth to suck it.

Lambert was groaning under his breath now, watching her head move, watching the pleasure on the face of the young porter. Was he feeling the incredible heat of her mouth? Lambert guessed that he was; certainly the expression on the porter's face was one of extreme bliss.

Then the porter lurched in the chair as he started coming. Magda kept her head down, kept his penis in her mouth and swallowed everything as he ejaculated. After that she continued sucking him, never withdrawing her mouth from the organ, and Lambert now had the impression the porter was coming again, even stronger this time, his head thrown back and his mouth open as Magda's voracious mouth sucked the sperm from his balls.

The porter's eyes were wide and his face pale as Magda continued sucking his penis after the second orgasm. He cried out something in Arabic, but he made no attempt to stop her. She continued sucking him until he lurched once again, lifting himself off the chair as he came in her mouth for the third time. Lambert could see her sucking madly at the still erect penis, but he couldn't believe the porter was actually ejaculating so soon after the last time. The porter suddenly fell back in a slump, and soon after that Magda pulled her face away from his lap.

She rose to her feet, and Lambert shuddered as he watched her wipe her mouth with the back of her hand. Then she licked her hand to recover whatever she could of the porter's sperm. After a while she looked at the porter again. He was still slumped in the chair, his eyes closed, no sign of life in him. Magda went to him and she lifted one of his eyelids with her fingers. The porter stirred and muttered something as Magda spoke to him in Arabic. She helped him to his feet, then helped him to the door of the room. In a moment she had him out of the room and the door closed and locked.

It was when she turned back to the room that a sudden chill passed through Lambert. He could see her eyes for the first time, clearly see that she had no pupils in her eyes at all, only the white corneas. Her eyes were exactly the way they'd been that time in Cairo. He steadied himself, afraid he'd faint right there on the balcony.

What did it mean?

He watched her as she walked to the dressing table. She found a brush and she began brushing her hair with it. Now all he could see of her face was what he saw in the mirror, not much of her eyes at all, and it was only when she turned her face at a certain angle that he saw her pupils again. Whatever it was that had happened to her eyes, they now looked normal.

This time, at least, she had a reflection in the mirror. Had he really imagined the absence of a reflection the last time?

As he continued watching her, she unbelted the robe and slipped it off her body. She had her back to him, and he felt a twitch of longing as he admired the perfect curves of her buttocks and thighs.

She turned sideways to the mirror to look at her profile. She ran her hands over her breasts, and then down over her belly and around to her buttocks. She turned her back to the mirror, looked over her shoulder and pulled her buttocks apart with her hands.

Then she faced the mirror again, and this time she leaned forward to kiss her own image. She started licking the glass, and Lambert's skin crawled as he watched the two pink tongues, the real one and the reflected image, duel with each other. Her tongue began to move rapidly from side to side, and suddenly there were four tongues instead of two. Was he imagining it? Then he realized the real tongue had split in two partway down its length. It lasted only a few moments, and then the four tongues became two tongues again.

Magda now moved away from the mirror and she walked over to the bed. She raised her right leg, put her right foot on the edge of the bed, and slid her right hand past her belly to find her sex. Lambert watched her fingers going in, first two fingers, then three fingers, then all of the hand. He muttered a curse as he watched her penetrate her cunt with her hand until she had most of her forearm inside her body. It seemed impossible, but he couldn't deny his eyes. She appeared to be doing something to herself deep inside her belly, struggling with something. He could see her juices running out of the widely stretched opening, wetting her forearm and the insides of her thighs.

Finally she finished whatever she was doing to herself, and she pulled her hand out and she started licking it, cleaning it with the flat of her tongue the way a cat would clean itself. Then she finished cleaning herself and she put her leg down. After that she pulled the covers down on the bed and she climbed under them. A moment later she switched off the lamp and the room became dark.

Shivering in the cold now, Lambert left the balcony and returned to his room. He found one of the easy chairs, slumped into it and groaned with despair.

In the morning Magda came into his room to have breakfast with him. She seemed in good spirits, much happier than the day before. After the breakfast arrived and when they were alone again, she slipped her robe off and said she'd rather be naked.

"You don't mind, do you? You don't mind looking at me?"

He said he didn't mind at all. So now he had her

ripe breasts to look at while she sat across the table from him near the open door to the balcony. Although the memory of last night and his fears about everything were never far from his mind, he soon found himself aroused by her body, particularly by her nipples, which now seemed to be thicker and more extended than ever before. It occurred to him that as the days passed, her body appealed to him more and more, the fleshy parts, the bony parts, the coloring, everything about her was becoming a source of sexual arousal.

She seemed perfectly aware of what was happening, of how excited he was by her breasts, because after a while she took her breasts in her hands and she smiled at him as she teased her nipples with her thumbs. "Am I exciting you, darling? Come, lie down on the bed with me."

There was no way he could resist her. She made him remove his pajamas and lie down on his back. Then she said she felt marvelous this morning and she was going to make him a present of her cunt. She said they would couple for the first time. She would mount him while he lay on his back, but he had to promise her he would tell her when he was ready to come.

"I want your stuff in my mouth," she said. "Do you promise?"

"Yes."

She seemed happy, her fingers tickling his balls and then the underside of his penis. "You look strong again," she said.

After that she mounted him, climbed over him and straddled his body, then squatted down over his penis to take it with her sex. In a moment she had it inside her, her cunt stretching around it, grasping it as she eased herself down on his lap.

He started groaning immediately. The heat, the hot grasp of the passage was enough to bring him to the edge of a climax. Her cunt was as hot as her mouth, and that coupled with the clenching tightness of the sheath made it the most exquisite cunt he'd ever experienced.

She moved slowly and carefully, sliding upward and then easing down again, watching his face as she did it, milking his penis with a skill he'd never imagined.

"I can't go on with it," he said.

"You're ready to come?"

She hurried to pull back, sliding her cunt off his penis, sliding her body back on his legs and then quickly bending forward to take his glans in her mouth. With a hoarse cry, he began shooting in her mouth, the orgasm even more intense than what he'd had with her previously, a total convulsion of his senses, her lips pulling at the tip of his penis in a way that kept the pleasure going for what seemed like an endless time.

Later, as she lay beside him stroking his organ to another erection, she said: "Do you want to stay with me? Maybe we can find a place in Cairo."

He felt a sudden panic and he started trembling. He realized that if he didn't get away from her at once he'd soon be helpless, totally in her power. Whatever she was, whatever thing she was, there would be no way to escape her unless he did it immediately.

"I can't," he said.

He made up some story about his work, about an editor in New York, about a job that had to be finished. She seemed annoyed, but she made no attempt to stop him from leaving. She rose up and said: "Do whatever you like. I'm going out for a while."

He watched her leave, torn apart inside, wondering if his fear of her was completely foolish.

The fear was too strong. He had a need to run, to get out of there without seeing her again.

In the afternoon he took the first plane out of Luxor for Cairo, and at the Cairo airport he quickly found a plane for London and he left Egypt.

On the BOAC plane, the British stewardess looked at him closely and asked him if he suffered from air sickness. "Would you like a tablet, sir?"

"No thanks, I'm fine," Lambert said.

He started trembling again as soon as she left him. He could think of nothing but Magda. When he closed his eyes, he saw Magda's face, the eyes without pupils, her red-lipped mouth.

Was she really finished with him?

Was she laughing at him?

Lambert had friends in London. The Walkers put him up in their Kensington house without any fuss, Tony Walker telling Lambert he was happy to have a man who knew how to drink under his roof, and Sybil Walker saying that as long as he refrained from stepping on the children he was most welcome. Tony worked for the BBC. Lambert had met him in a bordello in Madrid, although Sybil thought the place where they'd met had been more innocent.

Aside from the Walkers, Lambert had other friends in London, and within a week after his arrival most of them knew he was in town and he began to have his mind occupied. That was exactly what he wanted, the chance to forget Egypt and everything that happened to him there. He'd spoken once again to the editor in New York who had given him the

Salah Hamad interview assignment, and after some patient lying on Lambert's part about why he'd had to abort the job, the editor seemed mollified and promised Lambert he'd have something else for him soon. In the meantime Lambert thought he needed a rest, and he decided to do nothing for a while, at least as long as his bank account could withstand it.

He saw people, renewed old London acquaintances. And he went to parties. There was always a party somewhere in Bloomsbury or Mayfair, sometimes with people he knew well and sometimes with people he knew hardly at all. He thought going to parties was a good way to keep his mind off Magda.

One night at a crowded Bloomsbury party, Lambert heard a feminine voice in his ear:

"You look puzzled, Jack."

It was Sheila Paton, a girl he hadn't seen in years. They'd had a brief fling one time, but no more than a single steamy weekend in the country. He vaguely remembered her getting married soon after that.

Now she smiled at him. "Are you puzzled, Jack?"

"I'm always puzzled. I'm puzzled by life. How've you been, anyway?"

"Middling, I'd say."

"Still married?"

She laughed. "It lasted one year and thirteen days. The only thing I regret now is that I never counted the days before I packed and left him. I don't like the number thirteen."

She was a tall girl with green eyes and long red hair, and hips that looked fuller under the dress than he remembered them.

Lambert said. "Think of it as three hundred seventy-eight days."

And Sheila laughed again. "Jack the realist. Are you still writing nasty articles about the British? Or maybe by now you've grown to like us."

He went home with her. He felt no great desire for it, but she seemed to want it and he thought it might do him some good. She'd be his first woman after Magda, and it might be just what he needed to get himself back to normal again.

When they arrived at Sheila's flat in Bedford Way, she lost no time falling into his arms. "I've been needing it," she said. "It gets very lonely sometimes."

She opened her mouth as they kissed, and she murmured with pleasure as he pushed his tongue between her lips.

When they stopped kissing, she said: "We had a lovely time that weekend, didn't we?"

Lambert nodded. "That's the way I remember it."

She brought some Scotch out of a cabinet, and after she poured some of it into two glasses they toasted each other. Then she said she needed to change and she left him. He sat down on the sofa, sipped the Scotch and looked at the cozy little room. She'd had another place when he'd known her years before, not this one. He wondered how old she was. Was she thirty yet? The Scotch was beginning to warm his belly, but he still felt no great enthusiasm for sex. Had Magda ruined him? He had a few moments of apprehension as he thought about it. The time he'd spent with Magda had been so crazy, anything was possible.

Then he heard Sheila come into the room again, and when he looked at her his eyes widened. He'd expected her to come out in a robe, but instead she wore no more than her underthings. The lace-edged black bra and panties barely contained her soft curves of her breasts and buttocks. When she saw the way he looked at her, she smiled at him and did a pirouette. "Interesting?"

Lambert felt his excitement rising. He told her how lovely she looked, and after she sat down on his lap he helped her remove the brassiere. She had long pear-shaped breasts, springy to the touch and warm under his hand. She sighed and kept her arms around his neck as he spread his fingers over one breast and then the other breast. Then a gasp of pleasure came out of her throat as he bent his head to suck at one of the thick nipples.

"Oh Lord, I love that," she said.

He sucked her breasts until her pink nipples were stiff and swollen. She began undressing him, but he suddenly had an urge to do something, and the more he thought of it the more the idea excited him.

"Take the pants off and I'll suck you," he said.

She laughed and blushed at the same time. "I'm not refusing that."

She quickly left his lap to remove her lace panties, and in a moment she looked the way he remembered her, long-boned and lush at the same time, with a flaming bush of red hair that was tufted on her mound and on either side of her slit. He made her lie down on the sofa on her back, and then he raised her legs, opened them and dipped his face down to the tangle of red curls.

She moaned the instant his mouth touched her cunt. He captured the long clitoris with his lips and sucked at it until he was sure she was coming. Then he moved his mouth lower down to get what he wanted, the flow of hot juices out of the opening. She seemed to go wild with excitement again as he noisily sucked the syrup out of her gaping sex. He tried to remember the last time they'd been together, whether he'd had such pleasure doing this to her, but he guessed he hadn't. He'd certainly never before hungered for the fluid that much.

The flow of her juices invigorated him, aroused him to a feverish excitement. When he finally stopped sucking her, she wanted to bring his penis out and do the same to him. But he said no, he wanted her on a bed, and when they hurried to her bedroom he quickly peeled away the rest of his clothes and mounted her immediately.

She cried out as he entered her, raised her legs high and then pulled her knees back against her breasts. He rammed her cunt again and again until at last he exploded inside her passage.

Afterward, as he lay beside Sheila in the dark, he felt a great despair as he realized he still missed Magda's taste on his lips.

One day, while browsing in a dusty Soho bookshop, Lambert laid his eyes on a heavy volume about demons and vampires. The subject had never before been of interest to him, but now he felt a sudden curiosity. Was it the experience in Egypt? He looked at the book, idly turned the pages one after the other, and then he finally bought it and he took it home with him to the Walker house. There, one evening while Tony and Sybil were out to the theater and he stayed in minding a cold, Lambert looked at the book again.

He had no patience to read the book completely, but in the section on vampires he found two sentences that seemed to leap off the page at him:

According to certain legends, however, not all vampires restrict themselves to the ingestion of blood. This more esoteric subject will not be treated here.

From the jacket of the book, Lambert learned the author, Professor Arthur Cordwain, lived in London. Lambert hurried to the telephone book, found the name and made the call. A few minutes later he had an appointment to visit Professor Cordwain at home the following afternoon.

Arthur Cordwain was a small man with a pink bald head and a fringe of white hair around his ears. His back bent, he shuffled down the hall as he led Lambert to his sitting room.

"I don't have many visitors," Professor Cordwain said in a thin voice. "I'm afraid you'll find the tea cold and the place a bit dusty."

Lambert assured him none of that mattered. After they sat down in the sitting room, an old woman with a sour face served tea in a cracked teapot. As Professor had predicted, the tea was barely hot.

"She's a witch," Professor Cordwain whispered after the old woman left. "But a man my age needs a housekeeper." Then his voice became louder. "Now tell me what you're after, young fellow. You're American, aren't you? Had an American colleague once, but he died during the Blitz. Block of granite fell on his head during one of the raids."

Lambert recounted how he'd been looking at Professor Cordwain's book and how the two sentences had piqued his curiosity. "That's my interest," Lambert said.

"Writing something, are you?"

"Yes, sort of."

Professor Cordwain smiled and sat back in his chair. "It's a pity that most people know damned little about vampires. They're most fascinating, you know. Most fascinating." And with that Professor Cordwain began an account of vampirism, his thin voice rising and falling, his eyes popping with excitement as he talked about his obsession. Lambert learned that according to the most popular legend, vampires were the ghosts of heretics and criminals, returned from the grave in the guise of a monstrous bat to suck the blood of sleeping people who usually became vampires themselves. Two famous supposed vampires were Vlad V of Wallachia in the 15th century, and the Countess Bathóri in the 17th century. The Countess was arrested for murdering young girls and washing in their blood to keep her skin in a youthful condition.

"But those are the common European legends," Professor Cordwain said. "Other legends exist in the Orient and the Near East." And then he spoke of legends that had vampires feeding on victims without actually draining their blood. Instead, these vampires drained the life force by ingesting the sexual fluids.

Professor Cordwain chuckled. "Rather shocking, isn't it?"

"Yes," Lambert said.

"These are the Lucullian vampires."

"Lucullian?"

"After Lucullus, the Roman Emperor with a reputation as a glutton. But as far as I can tell, the legend itself originated in Ancient Egypt. The first of these Lucullian vampires was apparently Egyptian and not Roman. I suppose it's possible the Slavonic vampires of Hungary and Rumania were descendants of the Lucullian vampires of Egypt."

Lambert was stunned. He was silent a long moment, and then he said: "Did they sometimes have eyes without pupils?"

Professor Cordwain waved his hand. "Yes, yes,

that's quite common among all the vampires. Eyes without pupils and an absence of a reflected image. Not at all times, you see, but only at particular moments. And of course the Lucullians are pre-Christian and they have no fear of the Cross. Fascinating, isn't it?"

"Yes."

"There's one other significant note about the Lucullians."

"What's that?"

"I've never been able to find any method of killing them. None of the legends say anything at all about that." Professor Cordwain rubbed his hands as he smiled at Lambert.

When Tony Walker was sent to Belfast on assignment, Lambert found himself alone for the first time with Sybil. It had never occurred to Lambert to make a pass at her, so when Sybil gave the proof she wouldn't mind it if he did, he was taken by surprise.

What happened was that one evening, after the children were asleep, they started drinking in the sitting room, talking about themselves and about what they wanted out of life. The nanny who looked after the children had the day and the night off, and Sybil seemed to be enjoying a sense of freedom as she soaked up one gin tonic after another.

"I'm getting blotto," she said.

"Don't worry, I'll tuck you in," Lambert teased.

Sybil teased him right back. "Would you?"

Then after a while she rose up and she left him for five minutes or so, and when she returned Lambert had the shock of his life as Sybil walked into the sitting room stark naked.

Casually walking over to the bar to fix herself another drink, she said: "Are you going to make me an indecent offer."

She turned and gazed at him with one hip thrust out, smiling and then lifting her glass to sip her gin.

She was a full-fleshed woman, broad hips and long legs with plenty of calf, shapely breasts that drooped a bit, and a thrusting mound covered with a dark bush of hair. Lambert immediately rose up to take her in his arms and kiss her. Her lips were warm, and her breasts and belly felt marvelous as they pushed against him.

"I do like you," she said in a throaty voice.

"I'm thinking about Tony."

"Please don't. This is my doing, not his. You're not disloyal to him if it's me who's pulling you into bed."

Lambert wasn't sure he understood the logic of that, but he let it pass. In the meantime he had his hands all over her body, and there was no question that she excited him. But what he really wanted from her was something special, and when he told her about it she seemed amused.

"That's lovely," she said.

"You don't mind?"

"Trust me."

He followed her into the bedroom, his eyes on her swinging hips and full round buttocks. Poor Tony, he thought. But Tony, after all, might at that moment be busy with an Irish girl in Belfast.

Inside the bedroom, Lambert quickly undressed while Sybil watched him. When he was naked, she gazed with sultry eyes at his upright penis and patted the bed beside her. "Hurry, love."

He lay down on his back beside her, and she immediately swung her body around and straddled him facing his feet. He took her broad hips in his hands and pulled her backward until her cunt came over his mouth.

She groaned as she pressed her crotch against his face. "Oh, you beautiful man," she said. "Do it to me. Suck it all you want, lovey."

He buried himself in her ripe sex. What he wanted more than anything was the juice, but it took some time before there was enough of it to make him happy.

Meanwhile, Sybil had leaned forward to take his penis in her mouth, and she was now making noises of pleasure as she slurped over it with her tongue and lips. Lambert was surprised at how little he cared about what she was doing. All that concerned him was getting her cunt running so that he could drink from it.

At last Sybil's juices became plentiful enough, not merely a slick coating inside her slit, but a thick liquid that ran into his mouth with a delicious abundance. He thought of Magda, of the taste of Magda's running sex. Maybe this wasn't as good, but it was close enough. And as he thought of Magda's cunt, his excitement quickly peaked and he came in Sybil's mouth. She ground her sex more firmly down on his face as she took the squirts of sperm, and when she started coming again Lambert had a second mouthful of her lovely syrup.

Later Sybil told Lambert he'd given her one of the best nights of her life. But Lambert was now uneasy as he realized how crazy it was to want Sybil's juices that much.

Was it Magda's doing?

Was something frightful happening to him?

He finally left London and he returned to New York.

He no longer played the game of attempting to forget Magda, attempting to forget her existence, attempting to forget their days together in Egypt. His hunger for Magda was greater than ever. He thought about her constantly, noticed every woman who resembled her.

In New York he began an affair with a dull little housewife only because the woman reminded him of Magda. He became tremendously excited whenever the woman sucked him, because then, with his penis in her mouth, she looked more like Magda than ever.

Then one day, while searching for a telephone number in the phone directory, Lambert idly looked at the listing of CLARE. He felt a sudden shock when he found the name Magda Clare listed at an address on West End Avenue. Was it possible that it was her? He dialed the number immediately, and in a moment he felt a sudden happiness when he heard her voice.

"This is Jack Lambert," he said.

She was the same, the same pale, almost translucent skin, the same lovely red mouth, the same dark eyes that pierced directly into his soul.

"I think I frightened you in Luxor," she said. She poured some Scotch into a glass and brought it to him. "Did I frighten you?"

"Yes."

After that there was no more talk of Luxor. He did everything she wanted. She teased him by delaying it, but before long she had his penis and balls out of his trousers, her fingertips tickling the sac of his scrotum and the shaft of his organ. She smiled at him, kissed his mouth, fluttered her tongue between his lips as she gently stroked the fullness of his balls.

"Don't move," she said. "I want to get into something sexy."

He waited for her. He stood there in the center of the room with his drink in his hand and his penis and balls exposed through the open fly of his trousers. The blinds were not completely closed, and he wondered if anyone out there could see him. What would they think? Would they think it odd to see a man standing there with a drink in his hand and his penis and testicles exposed? He thought of closing the blinds, but he resisted the impulse; it was Magda's house and not his.

Then Magda returned and he no longer cared about the blinds or the window.

She wore a black leather corset that began just below her breasts and ended just above the neatly clipped triangle of dark hair. He thought her breasts and hips looked fuller than before, but he wasn't certain. The black corset had long garter straps, and these held up sheer black stockings with opaque black bands at the tops. On her feet she wore black patent leather pumps with high pointed heels.

"Do you like it?" she said.

"You're exquisite."

"Lie down on the carpet, won't you?"

He did that immediately, stretched himself out full length on the carpet and waited for her. She smiled down at him, then turned to face his feet and straddled his body with her legs. In a moment her body came down, her buttocks dropping as she squatted over his face, the two globes coming closer and closer until finally the hairy crack of her sex pressed against his mouth and he began a noisy searching with his tongue and lips.

She made a mewling sound, pushed herself down a bit more, and then leaned forward to take the bulb of his penis in her mouth.

He cried out against her cunt as he felt the intense

heat of her mouth suddenly enfold his organ. It took only a few moments before he began spurting, and when he did he felt the same incredible bliss he'd had with her before in Egypt.

Afterward she asked him if this time he would stay with her.

He felt himself on the edge of trembling, but he controlled it. "Yes," he said.

"That makes me happy."

"Will I become like you?"

She smiled at him and touched his cheek with her fingertips. "Are you afraid, darling?"

Part Two

FROM THE JOURNAL OF JACK LAMBERT

...to express something to me. She said she had shopping to do, maybe two or three hours of it, and then she'd return. After she left, I went to the window and I watched the street as best I could to see her come out the front entrance. She came out with the doorman beside her, and then he stepped out into the street to wave down a taxi for her. He held the door as she climbed into the cab, and then she was gone, the taxi heading south.

After that I returned to my chair in the living room to finish reading the newspaper. But soon I had to put the newspaper down because I had no further interest in it. It's always like that when she leaves me alone. I can't seem to concentrate on anything when she's gone, and of course when she's with me again my mind is completely occupied with her, and what we say to each other, and what we do together, and so on.

I sat in the chair for about an hour. I had the television on, but I paid hardly any attention to it. I like this

East Side apartment better than her old West Side apartment or my own apartment in the Village. For one thing the building service is much better and the street in front of the entrance is always clean. I don't go out of the apartment that much, but when I do go out with Magda it's more pleasant to have a clean sidewalk in front of the building.

My physical condition continues to slowly deteriorate, but I have the impression now that it's levelling off. Magda says the weakness won't persist, and that it's merely a matter of my body making an adjustment to things. Since it's almost three months that we've been together now, I suppose the idea that a plateau has been reached might be accurate. In any case, she continues to drain me two or three times a day, depending on her mood and on her assessment of my physical condition. She does her best to keep me primed, of course, and that part of it is always exciting. The most extraordinary thing is that it's never possible to predict her behavior in advance, predict what she'll do or what she won't do. This morning, for example, before she decided she wanted to do some shopping in the afternoon, she called me into her bedroom and she asked me to lick her sex. Usually when I do this she makes me stop as soon as her juices become abundant. She says if I continue sucking her beyond that point she feels discomfort. I don't know if that's the reason or if it's some other reason. Sometimes I'm allowed to suck a large amount of juice from her, but that doesn't happen often. In any case, this morning she allowed me to go on until she had an orgasm. I thought after that she would suck me and take the first ejaculation of the day, but instead she said she'd wait until the afternoon in order to get more out of me. I had a tremendous erection and I wanted to masturbate, but the merest hint of that always makes her furious. So the excitement produced by sucking her had to dissipate naturally. For some reason this morning that took a long time and Magda was aware of it. She teased me while she dressed, insisted I remain in the room while she put her makeup on and then her clothes. All of that has happened before, but this morning after she was fully dressed and speaking to someone on the telephone she called me to her and she told with gestures to get my head under her dress. When I did that, she immediately opened her legs to make room for my face, and in a moment I had my mouth pressed against the nylon gusset of her pantyhose while she continued talking on the telephone. This lasted no more than a few minutes, but when it was over I had an enormous erection again and evidently that was what she wanted. She ran her hand over it, fondled it through my trousers, and then she kissed my cheek and left the apartment.

When Magda returned home today, she seemed annoyed about something. This is always a bad sign, since I usually suffer for it in one way or another. Today she complained about the crowds in the department stores. She brought no packages home with her, so I don't know if she actually bought anything.

After she changed her clothes, she told me she'd like some tea. So I made a pot of tea in the kitchen, and then I brought it to her in the living room. She asked me about my day. "Did you calm down after I left?"

I told her that yes, I had calmed down. I said I read the newspapers and watched television awhile.

Then she wanted me to stand in front of her and drop my trousers and shorts. My hope was that she would immediately take my penis in her mouth and relieve the tension I'd been feeling all day. But instead she teased me by doing no more than looking at me, inspecting my penis and balls without touching me at all.

"You're too impatient for it," she said.

She ran her hands over the front of her dress, molding her breasts, then sliding a hand inside the low neckline to bring one of her breasts out in the open. As she teased the nipple with her fingers, she looked at me. "Do you want to come now?"

"Yes."

"You'd better have a lot of it this time."

I don't know why she said *this time*. She never complained the last time.

Instead of taking my penis in her mouth immediately, she first lifted her hand to my face and touched my lips. I knew what she wanted, and without any instruction I took her middle finger in my mouth and sucked it to get it wet. In a moment she withdrew the finger and dropped the hand down under my scrotum. She found my anus with her wet middle finger, and she slowly pushed the finger deep inside me.

She probed around a bit, found the spot she was looking for and seemed satisfied. "Yes, you're ready," she said.

Only then did she lean forward and take the knob of my penis in her mouth. As always, the scalding heat of her mouth made me come almost instantly. I spurted again and again in her mouth as she wiggled the finger inside me at the same time as she squeezed my balls.

The end of it was almost painful, but finally she finished and she pulled her mouth away. As she licked her lips, she looked up at me and for a moment her eyes were clear white and without pupils. It lasted only a moment, and then her eyes looked normal again. It doesn't bother me any more; I'm used to it now and it never frightens me the way it did in the beginning.

Up until last night I'd seen the doubling of her tongue only twice since that time in Egypt, and both times it happened when she had no idea I was watching her. But last night it happened again, and this time I think she knew that I saw it and she seemed bothered by it, as if she had revealed too much to me.

It began before dinner when I said I wanted to lie down and rest before we went out to dinner. She said fine, she would wake me in time for me to get dressed. I went to my room and slept for about an hour. When I opened my eyes, I saw the door connecting our two bedrooms was partly open. Magda usually likes the door closed, but sometimes she walks in and out of my room and the door remains open afterward when she forgets to close it. She's rather finicky about her privacy, and one of the reasons we chose this particular apartment was the arrangement of the bedrooms.

Anyway, when I rose off the bed and walked over to the partly open door to see if she was in her bedroom, I saw once again what I'd seen only twice before. She was standing at the full length mirror kissing her image. This time she was naked, evidently just out of her bath, her body still damp and parts of the mirror steaming with moisture. As she kissed her image, she extended her tongue, and for a second or two her tongue appeared to be doubled, neatly forked down the center, the two points fluttering against the glass to meet the other two points, the ensemble like four wriggling serpents dueling with each other. Then one of her hands moved between her belly and the mirror and she began rubbing herself, masturbating as she kissed the image of her lips. This excited me greatly. I'd seen her touch herself before, but I'd never watched her masturbate to an orgasm, and I was hoping she would do it now so I could see it. The rubbing of her cunt continued, her belly moving back and forth against the mirror as she kissed her image. Then after a while she slid her free hand around behind herself and between her buttocks, and in a moment it was clear she had a finger in her anus while the other hand continued rubbing her sex. This went on for about a minute, and then finally her body twitched out of control and she flattened herself against the mirror, made a horrible noise in her throat, and then opened her mouth to spew a black liquid against the glass. The next moment she turned, the black liquid smeared over her face, and she seemed to look directly at me. I immediately moved backward into the darkness of my room and I climbed into bed again. An instant later the door connecting our rooms slammed shut and I heard the clicking sound that meant Magda had locked it.

I lay there in the dark thinking about what I'd seen, wondering if she'd actually noticed me watching her. Would she finally come into the room and express her anger? But nothing happened. After twenty minutes or so, I switched on the light and I rose up to get dressed. We went out to dinner to a place we'd visited before, and nothing unusual happened. But after dinner, when we arrived home, Magda seemed more irritable than usual and it occurred to me it might be because of what had happened earlier.

I'd had only one emission during the day, and now she decided it was time for another. She told me to unzip my fly and bring my penis out, and after I did that she told me to masturbate. "Make yourself hard," she said. "I'd rather you worked at it yourself."

She watched me do it awhile, watched me stroke my penis with my hand as I stood on the carpet near her, and then she leaned back in the chair and pulled at her dress to uncover her thighs. She opened her legs to show me her crotch, but she was wearing pantyhose and I couldn't see too much.

As if reading my mind, she said: "It's enough for you. I'm not undressing yet, so this is all you're seeing of my cunt."

It made no difference, because I had no trouble keeping the erection and bringing myself to the point when I could tell her I was about to come so she could take the emission in her mouth.

But this time something unexpected happened. When I felt myself getting close, I slowed down the stroking with my fingers, but somehow it didn't work and I started coming. Two huge spurts came out and landed very close to Magda on the leather sofa where she was sitting. She stared at me in disbelief. I tried holding back the rest of it, but all I could manage to do was to have it gushing out over my hand. She rose up screaming at me. "You stupid fool, I was counting on it!" She came at me like a tigress, forced me down on the carpet and took my wilting penis in her mouth to suck out whatever she could. Then she licked my hand, cleaning it of the sperm that covered it. When she finished that, she remembered the sofa and she crawled to it over the carpet, reached it and started licking the sperm off the leather. Then she licked her fingers clean, and when she looked at me I saw the anger in her eyes.

"I think you did that deliberately."

"No, it's not true."

"You were spying on me before in my bedroom."

"Please, Magda…"

"Don't worry, you'll pay for everything."

I had to wait no more than an hour for the payment. She came to me while I was in my bedroom changing into my pajamas. She had a narrow Velcro strip in one hand, but I had no idea what it was for. She told me to take off my pajamas, and then as I stood naked in front of her she fastened the Velcro band tight around the base of my penis, tight enough so that it hurt even though I was still soft.

After that she opened her robe and she told me to get down on my knees and suck her cunt. Usually the reason for this is more to excite me than to dominate me, but this time I could see the anger in her eyes as she looked down at me.

I did what she wanted, kneeling on the carpet in front of her and getting my face between her thighs and my mouth on her sex. I licked her a long time, but there was no juice at all coming out of her, even when I licked her clitoris. When she thought I was excited enough, she made me stand up and she fondled my swollen penis and balls. Then she suddenly gripped my balls and squeezed them, and I felt a tremendous pain in my belly, either from the force that she used or because the Velcro strap was still tight around the base of my penis. In any case, I cried out in response to the pain and that seemed to satisfy her. She then sat down on the edge of the bed and she pulled me forward to get my glans in her mouth. She sucked hard at my penis, and when she suddenly released the Velcro strap I came with great force in her mouth. Now she squeezed my balls again, as firmly as before, but this time the pain was more bearable and I was able to finish ejaculating in her mouth. She continued sucking until there was no fluid left, and then she pushed me away from her.

"Do you love me?" she said.

"I adore you."

"If you love me, you'll always save it for me. You know how important that is for me, don't you?"

"Yes."

I think as far as anyone else is concerned, we appear to be an ordinary Manhattan couple. My friends and acquaintances know about Magda, know that I'm living with a woman, but they know very little about her and only a few of them have met her. I've more or less given up contact with everyone at Magda's insistence. It hasn't bothered me, because my closest friends are in London rather than here in New York, and because I really have no interest in seeing anyone. I've also stopped working because there's no need for it. Magda insists she has enough money for both of us to live comfortably, and for the time being I've agreed to the arrangement. On the rare occasions when it's convenient to spend money of my own, I have enough in my bank account to cover it. The fact is I'm happy that any work pressure that existed has been lifted, because I have absolutely no interest in it any more.

I'm not certain whether or not Magda has any friends in New York. She does talk to people on the telephone sometimes. If she has friends here, she never tells me about them.

I understand that I'm in a daze. I have no more concern about the world. All I care about is Magda and what we do together. I think she's correct about my reaching a physical equilibrium of some sort. I certainly don't feel any further weakening of my strength. I have the impression that whenever she allows me to suck her sexual juices I feel a bit stronger. When I asked her about it, she merely smiled and said nothing.

Monday afternoon.

Saturday morning she called me into her bedroom and she allowed me to lie on her bed and watch her while she dressed to go out. She knows how much this excites me, and of course the purpose is to get my juices flowing so that when she wants an emission from me there'll be enough coming out of me to satisfy her. I lay there on her bed, watching her as she walked around the room after finishing her morning shower, and as usual the sight of her naked body in motion produced a fierce erection. She glanced at the front of my shorts to see if she was having the effect she wanted, but after that she ignored it completely as she continued getting herself ready to leave the apartment. Her display this time was rather unusual in that after she finished doing her makeup, she dressed the upper half of her body while leaving herself naked below the waist for some time. I'd never seen her dress like that before, and the lovely picture she made walking around the room with her buttocks and belly naked while above her waist she was completely dressed was intensely erotic. After a time she glanced at my erection again, and by this time I was trembling as I lay there watching her. She smiled at me as she walked over to the bed, and she stood there looking down at me, teasing me because I had no idea what she would do next or what she expected from me. She leaned forward a bit to make her breasts dangle in her blouse, but then she seemed to suddenly change her mind about it and she turned her back to me and bent forward at the waist.

"Go on," she said. "But keep your hands off me." And then she reached back with her own hands and she pulled her buttocks apart as if to make sure I understood what she wanted.

My greatest fear was that I'd lose control and come while I did it. But I quickly slid forward on the bed to get my face against her buttocks, and as she continued to hold the cheeks apart with her hands I nuzzled into the crack and put my tongue to work. This particular caress is one that always excites her greatly, and this time was no different. But she kept me at it for only a minute or two, and then she abruptly pulled away and ordered me out of the room.

After dinner last night, Magda said she'd arranged a surprise for me. I had no idea what it was, and she seemed amused when I begged her for a hint. But she refused to tell me anything. All she said was, "I don't think you'll be disappointed."

So I waited, wondering what it might be, wondering what clever little enticement she'd cooked up for me this time. Then promptly at nine o'clock the doorman called up from the lobby to tell us we had a guest. Magda took the call, told him yes, it was all right, and now of course my curiosity was more intense than ever.

Several minutes later the doorbell rang, and Magda left me to answer it. When she returned she had a girl with her, a tall blond girl wearing bright red lipstick and a tight red dress.

"This is Dawn," Magda said. "And this is Jack. Would you like something to drink, Dawn?"

Dawn giggled. "Sure. Whatever you got's okay with me."

The girl wobbled a bit on her high heels, and I thought she might be already drunk. She was a little worn around the edges but still pretty, with a rather vacant stare in her eyes as she gazed at us, and then at the room, and then at us again. The blond curls fell over her shoulders and down her back, and the tight dress clung to what looked like perfect breasts and a perfect little ass.

"Hi," she said. She smiled at me, studying me a bit more carefully, and now I wondered how much Magda had told her about things.

Magda said: "Dawn is going to have a little party with us."

Yes, of course. It was difficult to imagine Dawn doing anything else. I tried to act calm and casual, but as I walked over to the bar to fix myself a drink my insides turned over with excitement. If this was what Magda wanted, all I cared about now was doing it.

We had drinks and made small talk in the living room awhile. Then Magda looked at me and said she thought I ought to change my clothes, get into something more comfortable. "Why don't you wear your new robe?" she said.

So I left them. It was obvious Magda wanted me away for a while. In my room I stripped my clothes off, and then I put on the new robe that Magda had recently bought me. I already had a strong erection, but by keeping my hands in the pockets of the robe I could hold the front of it out far enough to make the erection undetectable.

When I returned to the living room, I found a surprise waiting for me.

Dawn was sitting in an easy chair with her legs draped over the arms and her dress pulled back to her waist. Magda was on her knees in front of Dawn, her face between Dawn's thighs, her mouth busy at Dawn's cunt.

Not once in all the time we'd been together had Magda ever hinted to me that she might find it exciting to suck another woman's sex.

I sat down on the sofa to watch them. I was sitting off to the side and Dawn had her legs high enough so that I could actually see Magda's tongue sliding around Dawn's blond slit. Dawn wore black net stockings and a black garter belt, and I thought she looked quite fetching as she sat there with her knees raised as Magda sucked her. When Dawn looked at me, she seemed amused, with a hint of sarcasm in her smile. I wondered what she looked like naked. So far all I could see of her was the white skin of her thighs above the tops of her stockings and flashes of her cunt each time Magda moved her face to one side. Dawn's blond sex hair looked silky. Did Magda like her taste? I remembered one time Magda had kissed my mouth after I'd sucked her and she said she didn't mind the taste of her own cunt.

Watching Magda and Dawn had given me a tremendous erection. Dawn would look at me, then look down at Magda, then look at me again. I felt a great excitement as I thought of doing something with Dawn. Magda seemed oblivious to everything, very much involved in the sucking of Dawn's sex. Now Magda's mouth worked with more energy as she sucked hard, her nose and lips rooting in the blonde's gaping cleft as she sucked the girl's juices and swallowed them. Dawn groaned, and then suddenly she had an orgasm. She closed her eyes and shuddered, her hands gripping her knees as the spasms went through her. Magda continued sucking the blonde without letup, and with her eyes still closed Dawn turned her head to the side as she gave a final shudder of pleasure. The girl closed her thighs around Magda's head, her mouth hanging loose as she moaned through another climax.

When Magda finally pulled her mouth away from Dawn's cunt, her face was flushed and glistening with Dawn's juices. Magda looked at me, but whatever her thoughts were, nothing showed in her face as she rose up.

Dawn dropped her legs from the arms of the chair, pulled her skirt down and said: "Jesus, you sure know how to suck a pussy!"

Magda frowned. She found a tissue at the bar and she wiped her mouth with it. Then she looked at me and she asked me if watching her sucking Dawn had excited me. "Did it make you randy, Jack?"

I said yes. I showed her the bulge in the front of my robe. Dawn giggled and left her chair to come to me. "Well, look at that," she said with a teasing smile. She knelt down in front of me, her blond curls falling forward on her shoulders as she moved her hands up my thighs to my waist. I said nothing. I did nothing. I watched her hands as she deftly pulled my robe apart. Would Magda allow it? In a moment Dawn had my penis exposed, her small fist around the shaft, the knob bloated and dripping all over itself.

But Magda stopped her. "Never mind that," Magda said. "Get away from him. Why don't you get that dress off and show us what you look like?"

Dawn dropped my penis and she rose up and shrugged. "It's your party, guys." And then she began stripping her clothes off, moving her body, swaying her hips to some secret rhythm inside her head. First came the tight dress, unzipped at the sides, unbuttoned at the front and then peeled off over her head. She wore a sheer net bra with red lace trim, her full breasts and pink nipples clearly visible through it. Below that there was only the black garter belt and the black net stockings and the black high-heeled sandals. High up toward her blond bush, the insides of her thighs were glistening wet from the sucking Magda had given her. The blonde had a darling figure, a flat belly, a neat pubic triangle and a shapely little ass. She knew what she had, all right. She smiled at us, lifted her hands to the back of her head and teased us with a bump and grind. "I don't suppose there's a joint anywhere," she said.

She looked disappointed when I shook my head. In the meantime Magda had come over to me to gather the leaking fluid from the tip of my penis. Dawn giggled as she watched Magda lick my stuff off her fingers.

Magda said she wanted to see Dawn's breasts, and the blonde immediately obliged her. The girl's breasts drooped a bit when the brassiere came off, but they were still lovely to look at.

Magda then told me to sit down, and as I did so she started undressing. When she was naked, she took Dawn in her arms and they kissed. They had their breasts and bellies pressed against each other, and now Magda's hands dropped down from Dawn's waist to fondle Dawn's buttocks. The blonde giggled as she rolled her buttocks under Magda's palms.

Then one of Magda's hands slid between their bodies and I could tell Magda was exploring the blonde's cunt. Dawn closed her eyes and quivered as Magda fondled her sex. Magda was kissing Dawn's neck now, first her neck and then her chin and then her mouth. And then Magda bent her head to suck at one of Dawn's pink nipples. After a moment she pulled her face away, and now she removed her hand from Dawn's cunt and she brought her fingers to her lips. Dawn gave a throaty laugh as she watched Magda suck her fingers clean. "Hey, I guess you like me."

Dawn's hands became busy with Magda's body. She stroked Magda's buttocks, then moved a hand around in front to finger Magda's sex. Now each had a hand in the other's cunt, the two bodies wriggling against each other, and I could tell by the look in Dawn's eyes that Magda was getting to her.

Magda suddenly pulled away from Dawn, and she sat down and beckoned to me. "Come here," she said, licking her lips as she looked at my penis.

As soon as I came to her, she grabbed my balls and took my knob in her mouth. I lurched forward as I felt the heat engulf my penis, and before long I started spurting, emptying myself completely the way she liked it.

Dawn evidently found it exciting to watch us. She rubbed her sex with her fingers and made sounds of approval as Magda licked my penis clean. "I bet he had a nice load," Dawn said with a giggle.

Magda told me to lie down on the carpet. And after I did that, she looked at Dawn and she said: "Sit on his face. He likes that, and if he gets to suck enough juice he'll get hard again. That's what I want. I want him stiff again."

Dawn laughed. "Hey, that's kinky. I think I love it!"

As usually happened after an emission in Magda's mouth, I was exhausted, totally without energy. I lay on the carpet on my back as Dawn walked over to me, straddled my body and squatted on my face. Her buttocks came down on my head, and in a moment I had her wet sex grinding against my mouth. Now the world was shut out completely as I occupied myself with the smell and taste of the woman on my face. I sucked at Dawn's juices, and as I did so I shuddered with happiness as I felt the energy flow from Dawn's cunt into my body. I felt fingers stroking my penis, either Magda's fingers or Dawn's fingers, but all my attention was focused on the wet flesh pressing against my mouth, the drippings from Dawn's sex, the taste of a cunt other than Magda's. This was the first time in nearly four months that I'd been with any woman but Magda.

It wasn't long before my penis was erect again, and then Magda took it in her hot mouth and immediately sucked another emission out of me. She did this while Dawn continued to sit on my face, and it occurred to me we made a strange connection, the blonde's juices flowing into my mouth while my own juices gushed into Magda's mouth.

When Magda was finished with me, when my

penis was limp and useless to her, she made Dawn get off me and she attacked Dawn with the same vigor that she'd used with me. I had the impression that Dawn was now feeling for the first time the incredible heat of Magda's mouth. The blonde wriggled on the carpet and cried out, seemingly more affected by Magda's sucking than she'd been the last time. As I lay on my side and watched them, Magda pushed Dawn's knees all the way back and made growling noises as she sucked with abandon at the girl's cunt. "Oh Jesus!" Dawn cried out. "Oh Jesus, what you're doing to me!" Magda continued sucking without letup, and as she did so Dawn visibly weakened, her arms falling limp at her sides, her eyes closed, her face pale, her mouth open as she continued gasping for breath.

Magda raised her head and looked at me once, her mouth and chin dripping with Dawn's juices as she glanced at my limp penis. "I suppose you won't get hard again," she said, a croaking sound of frustration coming out of her throat, and then the sound becoming muffled as she bent her head to suck at the blond sex once more.

"You'll kill her," I said.

I meant it figuratively and not literally, but then a feeling of cold horror passed through me as I realized that it might indeed happen. Dawn was totally passive now, hardly moving at all except for an occasional twitch of her legs as Magda continued the sucking of her cunt. There was no sign of any more orgasms in Dawn, or maybe it was all one extended orgasm. Magda continued sucking the girl, drawing the juices out of her body, and I suddenly understood she would go all the way, drain all the life force out of the girl's body.

I thought of stopping her, but I was too weak. I

managed to raise myself on one elbow, but I was already too late. When Magda lifted her wet face again, her chin dripping with fluid, her eyes had no pupils, and it was obvious to me that Dawn was dead.

This is Sunday. I've waited three days before writing a report of what happened after the death of Dawn in our living room. My first thought after I realized that Dawn was indeed dead was that we had to get rid of the body. But Magda refused the idea completely. After wiping her face, she calmly told me the first thing we needed to do was get Dawn dressed and on the sofa. After that we would simply call the police emergency number and have them send the paramedics. "They'll discover she's had a heart attack," Magda said. "Come on, let's get her dressed."

I protested the plan. I told her I was afraid there would be complications. But Magda refused to even discuss it; she seemed annoyed at me, and for the first time I had the chilling thought this was not her first experience with this sort of thing. She had done this before.

We dressed the girl's lifeless body, first the underwear and then the tight little dress that showed all her curves. Her face looked softer now, as if she'd found peace somewhere.

"Don't get maudlin about this," Magda said.

When we finally had Dawn dressed, we struggled together to get her body onto the sofa. Once that was done, it was now time to call the paramedics. I dialed the number and gave the necessary information, and after that Magda and I sat quietly and waited.

I was less nervous now. People did have heart attacks, after all, even young people. But what would we tell them about our relationship to the girl? I asked Magda about that, but all she did was shrug and say it didn't matter. So then I was nervous again, afraid that something would go wrong with the authorities.

"Trust me," Magda said, and before I could answer, the doorman downstairs rang up and said the paramedics had arrived.

It all went as Magda had anticipated.

The emergency team pronounced Dawn dead of a heart attack and took her away.

As they carried the body out on a stretcher, a police detective arrived to ask some routine questions. He seemed interested only in Magda's legs, and as she sat opposite him in an easy chair she gave him a good show. It was Magda who answered most of the questions. She told the detective Dawn had been a casual acquaintance and he seemed satisfied. He finally closed his notebook, thanked us, looked at Magda's legs one last time and then left the apartment.

After the front door was locked, there was no longer any sign that anything unusual had happened. A blond girl named Dawn had been sucked to death in our living room, but now there was sign of it at all.

"You're too skittish," Magda teased. She said Dawn was only a whore and no one would miss her. "What did you think she was, a Park Avenue debutante?" Magda snickered at her own joke and left me sitting there as she walked off to her bedroom.

Later she came to my room and she fondled my balls until I had an erection. Then she took my penis in her mouth and she sucked it to produce an emission. As usual, she drained me carefully, and afterward she asked me if I'd noticed an increase in my vitality after I'd sucked Dawn's juices.

"Did you feel more energetic?"

I said yes, and when I asked her what it meant, she merely smiled at me and said nothing.

Of course I understand it. It means I'm becoming like her, I'm becoming a Lucullian vampire. Part of me is afraid, but that doesn't matter one way or the other. I'm completely in Magda's power and we both know that. She knows very well how much I love her.

It's Thursday evening now. This afternoon Magda came home from an excursion somewhere and she called me into the living room. She asked me about my day, what I'd been doing, and so on, and then she said she thought that from now on I ought to be more considerate of her. Why hadn't I been there to take her coat when she entered the apartment? When I said I hadn't heard her come in, she said that was nonsense, I ought to be able to hear the door open from anywhere in the apartment. "You're not deaf," she said. It was obvious she was annoyed, and I knew I would pay for it before long. What happened was that later on when she called me into her bedroom to take an emission of sperm from me, she denied me access to her cunt. She did this even though I was weak and obviously in need of it. "I'm teaching you a lesson," she said. Then she told me to sit down in a chair and refrain from moving.

After that she peeled her clothes off, teasing me with her nakedness, her hips wagging as she walked to her dresser and opened a package that she'd brought home from downtown. She lifted the object in the open package and showed it to me. "Have you ever seen one of these?"

What she held in her hand was a large dildo, a perfect replica of a thick penis.

She laughed when she saw the expression on my face. "You're not shocked, are you?"

Then she climbed onto the bed and she sat with her back against the headboard and her knees up and wide apart. Her notion was to both punish me and excite me by having me watch her use the dildo on herself, and of course it worked. I was punished because I had no access to the fluid I needed from her, and I was intensely excited as I watched the oversize instrument stretch the mouth of her cunt and push inside her body.

"Look at it," she said. "Watch it go in and out."

She introduced the dildo slowly, sliding it between the lips of her sex and then pushing it inside her vagina. She looked incredibly obscene, her dark eyes bright, her red lips pulled back in a derisive smile, her knees wide apart, the artificial penis now moving slowly in and out of her stretched orifice.

I felt even weaker now, and I hungered for the juices that glistened on the cylinder, despairing that I would survive this, hoping that she'd relent soon and let me suck her at least for a short time.

As if reading my mind, she said: "Beg me."

"Please," I said.

"Please what?"

"Please let me suck you."
With a laugh that was almost a cackle, she pulled the dildo out of her cunt and she began rubbing her enlarged clitoris with her fingers. She widened her knees even further, closed them, then moved them apart again. Then she pulled her fingers away from her sex, and with a hand on each widespread knee she finally called out to me:
"All right, come on. Get down to it and start sucking before you get too weak to do anything at all."
With a cry of gratitude, I threw myself on the bed and buried my face in her wet cunt.

Dinner in a restaurant last night. Magda seemed in a good mood and we talked at great length about various places we'd visited. For the first time I learned she'd actually lived in Budapest for several years. She said the city was nothing like what it used to be and that it was quite boring now.
When we arrived home, we continued the conversation in her bedroom. I lay on the bed and watched her as she undressed, and I enjoyed it immensely because this time she did it naturally and without artifice. She seemed too involved in telling me about her travels to think about teasing me. Or maybe she was teasing me all the time and I was just too insensitive to realize it. But all of that became irrelevant when she was finally naked, because it was then I noticed she had no reflection in the mirror.
I was shocked of course, but maybe not as much as the first time it happened because I've been

more or less expecting it would happen again sometime. The experience of it is quite remarkable: you see someone standing in front of a mirror and there's absolutely no image, not even a glimmer of anything. This time I was certain it wasn't merely an illusion produced by the angle of observation. She had no reflection in the mirror at all. Then she stepped away from the mirror a moment to hang her dress in the closet, and when she returned to the dressing table her image had returned. She stood there a moment running her hands over her body, and then she faced me and she said: "Are you up to it again?"

She'd already drained me twice during the day, once in the morning and then again in afternoon. But watching her move around her bedroom naked had given me an erection and she evidently knew it. She came toward me smiling, and before long I felt the familiar heat of her mouth closing around my penis, her fingers gripping my balls, her lips sucking without letup as she drew one more emission out of me.

Have been in bed the last three days. Maybe it's the flu. Or a general debilitation. Magda is annoyed, of course. She intimates that it would be too dangerous for me if she took sperm from me while I'm ill like this. So she stays away, asks about my condition, but makes no attempt to do anything with me. And since I know she can't possibly go more than ten or twelve hours without getting what she needs, my mind whirls with crazy jealousies of all kinds. Whenever she leaves the apartment, I imagine she's off to a rendezvous with another man. I imagine her getting what she needs from someone else, her mouth sucking at another penis, drawing the sperm from it, a look of satisfaction on her face as she pulls away and licks her lips clean. The image is intolerable. It becomes my obsession. I'm jealous of every man she meets and every man she knows, and this is true not only when I'm ill, as I am now, but at every other time as well.

She came to my room later and she said she wanted me to suck her because it might help me get well again. This time when she straddled my body, she did it so she faced my head and not my feet. Then she shifted forward until she had her cunt over my face and she pressed it down against my mouth. Her cunt became my world, the wet sex enfolding me, her juices soon streaming over my tongue.

Of course I adore her for it. She deliberately weakens herself in order to give me the energy I need.

Magda has told me she thinks we ought to leave New York and settle somewhere else. I don't mind the idea because I've been continually nervous about the Dawn affair, afraid something would happen to bring the police back to us. But then Magda said she'd like us to move to London and that made me unhappy. I'm afraid to live in London with her, afraid my friends there will discover us, discover Magda, learn enough to make me lose her. When I told her about my fears, she seemed amused. She patted my cheek and said: "Don't worry, Jack, I'll look after you." She teased me about it, and then she made me get on my knees and suck her through her panties. But as soon as she started to get wet, she pushed me away and told me I'd had enough of it. Then she hinted that in London she might arrange something for me, a way to keep my strength up without reducing her own. Yes, it's necessary. We can't go on this way. We do need to do something, to arrange something that will keep us both happy.

We leave tomorrow on the Concorde to London. I've regained most of my strength due to an extraordinary evening provided by my beloved Magda. What happened was that after dinner Magda came into my room with a cardboard box in her hands. She made me leave the bed and she stripped the covers and took the pillows away. Then she told me to get naked and lie down on the bed on my back. When I did that, she brought four dog-collars out of the cardboard box and she attached them around my wrists and ankles. Then she attached leather straps to the dog-collars, and she began securing me to the four corners of the bed until I was spread-eagled, stretched out on my back with my legs wide apart and my arms wide apart and behind my head. When she had my body fully extended, stretched to the utmost, she forced a pillow under my buttocks so that now my belly was the highest part of me.

She smiled at me and said: "You look lovely, Jack."

We'd never done anything like this before, and I trembled as I realized our relationship was entering a new phase.

She then fastened an elastic restraint around my

scrotum and penis, as close as possible to the pubic bone so that my genitals bulged out and upward. I already had an erection, and the elastic band around the base of my penis and the upper part of the ball-sac made the tumescence almost painful. Magda then went to the dresser and she opened the jar of Vaseline that was there. After dipping the middle finger of her right hand in the jar, she returned to the bed and she slowly introduced the greased finger inside my anus.

She asked me if the room was too cold for me, but I assured her it was fine. As her finger probed around inside my anus, she kept her eyes fixed on my penis. In a moment a spurt of clear fluid came out of the tip and she seemed satisfied. Using her free hand, she gathered the fluid off the glans with her fingers and then licked the fingers clean with her tongue.

After that she pulled her finger out of my anus, and then she climbed onto the bed and she straddled me facing my feet. My heart beating with excitement, I watched her mount me, watched her fingers guide my penis inside the gaping orifice of her vagina. As soon as she had her cunt settled firmly around my penis, she began rocking her body up and down with a slow but steady rhythm, each downward stroke punctuated at the end by a push that forced my penis to an ultimate depth inside her passage. The elastic band around the base of my penis and my scrotum prevented any ejaculation, although I thought it would happen when she reached back to hold her buttocks with her hands. Instead of that, my penis and balls merely felt as though they were swelling to the point of bursting.

Then the pain started and I groaned. Magda continued riding my penis another dozen strokes, and then she pulled her cunt off the tip of my organ and she used one hand to guide the knob to the dark ring of her anus. She made a guttural sound in some language unknown to me, and the next moment the anal sphincter opened wide enough to slowly engulf first the knob and then the entire length of my rigid erection.

Now the pain was even worse, the heat and tightness of her back passage making me feel as though my penis had been separated from my body. She rocked her hips again, her buttocks rising and falling as her backside swallowed and released and once again swallowed my organ. The sight of the orifice stretched wide and sucking at my penis brought my excitement to a fever pitch.

I started groaning again. She allowed it to go on another moment or two, and then finally she pulled herself off my organ and she whirled her body around to kneel between my spread-eagled legs and take my penis in her mouth. Her fingers worked at the elastic band, finally undoing it, and an instant later I exploded in her mouth with a great cry of happiness and relief.

A few lines written on the Concorde to London.

We sit beside each other, eating together, drinking together, giving the appearance of an ordinary couple. In three days I'll be forty years old. Only last week I thought my life was ending and I was frightened. Now I feel a new beginning, a new energy, a new bonding to Magda.

Or is it a new bondage, complete and irrevocable?

If that's what it is, maybe I ought to be more frightened than ever.

Part Three

IN LONDON TOWN

Chief Inspector George Drake, Scotland Yard, sat in his office gazing at a map of London. The map was on the far wall, and Drake thought it looked more than a bit frayed, bedraggled, the paper soiled in places, rotting after years of exposure to the filthy air.

Polluted, Drake thought. The bloody map of London was becoming as polluted as London itself. A man could hardly breathe these days, what with the chimney smoke and petrol fumes, the acrid smog that made his eyes water any time he was foolish enough to do a bit of walking. He wouldn't mind walking now, if had a reason to walk, some case that would take him out of the office and into St. James's Park, for instance. For some time now, he'd been bored with his work, fed up with it, dreaming constantly about his retirement. But that was a long time away, too long to be more than an idle preoccupation; he was still here, still in this shabby office, still a Chief Inspector in Her Majesty's Metropolitan Police.

The telephone suddenly rang, and when he lifted the receiver a loud voice squawked in his ear, barking at him, summoning him.

Drake said: "Yes sir, I'll be right there."

He heard the click on the other end and he put the receiver back in its cradle. The bloody Super, was it? Superintendent Rumbelow, his immediate superior, seemed terribly on edge this morning. Barking at him like that.

With a sigh, Drake left his desk and he walked out of his office.

Five minutes later he sat in the office of Superintendent Albert Rumbelow, listening to Rumbelow's grunting, watching him fill his enormous pipe.

"Ought to give it up," Rumbelow said.

"Give it up, sir?"

"Give up this bloody pipe. Rots the teeth, doesn't it?"

"Yes, I've heard that."

"Trouble is I'm addicted. Like one of those blooming druggies. Heard of the Berkeley Square mess, have you?"

"Berkeley Square?"

"The bodies, man. We've had three naked bodies discovered in rubbish bins."

"Oh yes."

"Two women and a man."

"Yes, I remember that."

"All of them naked."

"Unidentified."

"Yes."

"Apparently dead of heart failure."

"Yes."

Rumbelow grunted and seemed annoyed. "Well, what do you think of it?"

"Think of it, sir? I don't know. I've been working on the Lloyd's case."

"Yes, yes, the Lloyd's case. But what do you think of this one, three people dead like that, naked, all of them found in the vicinity of Berkeley Square. It's not an ordinary way to die, is it? I mean, naked in a rubbish bin?"

"No, it's not ordinary."

"Cardiac arrest in a rubbish bin."

"Yes, it's quite unusual."

Rumbelow nodded. "Foul play, don't you think?"

"Yes, I suppose so..."

"All right, get on it, Drake. I want every house in Berkeley Square investigated. Unusual goings-on, that sort of thing. Anything you might come up with. I want this business stopped before it becomes a scandal. We don't like scandals, do we?"

"No sir."

"Right."

"But what about the Lloyd's case?"

"The devil with the Lloyd's case, it's come to nothing, hasn't it? Give it to one of your Inspectors. I want you on the Berkeley Square case immediately."

"Yes sir."

"And Drake?"

"Yes sir?"

"Do come up with something, will you?"

Despite the heavy cloud of tobacco smoke, Drake managed to avoid coughing until he left Rumbelow's office. Damn the Super, Drake thought. His Eminence the Superintendent seemed to be in one of his moods. It was at moments like this that Drake wished Albert Rumbelow would fall off his horse the next time he went riding in St. James's Park. Then Drake thought of Rumbelow's wife, Olivia, and he felt appeased. For the past two months Drake and

Olivia Rumbelow had been engaged in a hot and secret affair, surreptitious meetings and frenzied couplings in unlikely hotel rooms. Drake now remembered their last time together, Olivia kneeling naked on a low bed with her rump wagging from side to side, the white moons of her buttocks shaking, her voice sultry as she coyly asked to be taken from the rear. He'd obliged her, of course. But the fact was, with Olivia he wasn't that fond of doing it from behind because it made him come too fast. She always tossed her hips in a way that made him lose control of things. Get her to slow down, Drake thought. But getting Olivia to slow down was like getting a horse to trot backwards; one might make the attempt, but the outcome was unlikely. Then Drake thought of Rumbelow again and he chuckled softly. He wondered what the Superintendent would think if he knew Drake had just the other day had Olivia groaning in a Kensington hotel room.

In the evening Drake lingered in a comfortable sitting room with his wife. Audrey was blond, slender, and forty, with a tendency to be sullen when he least expected it. She was now telling him how one of the clerks at Harrod's had been so sweet when she'd asked for his assistance. "He almost kissed my hand," she said.

"In Harrod's?"

"Yes, in Harrod's. But he didn't, did he?"

"I don't know."

"Oh George, you're not even listening."

"What did you buy?"

"Only an umbrella."

"Happy?"

"George, you're teasing me again. It's the job, isn't it? The stupid Yard always makes you so…"

"Bitchy."

"Yes, bitchy. Is it Rumbelow again? How's the old sod?"

"He says his pipe is rotting his teeth."

"Ugh."

Audrey now left her chair and she came to sit beside Drake on the sofa. "I bought something else besides an umbrella."

"In Harrod's?"

"No, in a little shop in Oxford Street. A blue peignoir. Would you like to see it?"

"Mmm, yes."

She gave him a teasing laugh and she hurried away to her bedroom. She was obviously in heat, eager to be tumbled after nearly a fortnight without it. He felt a moment of guilt as he realized he'd been too busy with Olivia Rumbelow to pay much attention to Audrey. But the guilt passed rather easily. He doubted any man could resist Olivia when she was determined to have him. The affair had been more or less Olivia's idea, begun at Olivia's initiative. Not that he was sorry for it. How could anyone be sorry, doing it to Olivia?

Audrey returned. She wore a filmy blue peignoir, the back trailing on the floor, the front open enough to show her legs covered by blue hose and her blue high-heeled slippers.

She smiled at him. "Tarty?"

"Very much so," Drake said. He thought she looked like an East End whore and it excited him. He rose up to take her in his arms and kiss her, all thought of Olivia Rumbelow out of his mind now as fondled Audrey's buttocks through her gauzy negligee.

"Here," she said. She opened the front of the peignoir and took her breasts in her hands.

He bent his head and he kissed her nipples, first one and then the other, and then he took one in his mouth and he sucked it firmly until he heard her moan with pleasure. She had lovely breasts, still shapely after all the years, the nipple in his mouth now stiff and succulent. When he slipped a hand inside the peignoir and between her thighs, he found she wore only a suspender belt and the stockings, no panties, the hairy mound naked against his fingers, the full-lipped slit already dripping its honey.

"I'm randy," she said in a throaty voice. "Let's go to my room, shall we?"

He walked behind her, following her out of the sitting room and up the stairs to her bedroom. Once inside the room, she quickly slipped out of the negligee, tossed it onto a chair and then stretched out on the bed to wait for him.

"Hurry, darling."

He wanted her badly now. He kept his eyes on her as he undressed, taking in the slender aristocratic body, the legs in blue nylon, the coral slit, the pink little mouth of her cunt fringed with dark blond hair that she now exposed more completely by moving her thighs wider apart. She moved a hand down to her belly, tickling the hairs at the top of her bush. Her eyes glittered when she saw how stiff he was. She held her arms out to him when he was naked, and he climbed onto the bed and quickly mounted her. She guided his penis with her hand, and then they both groaned as he pushed himself inside her cunt and began thrusting.

Nothing but grunting and sweating now. As he rested his weight on his knees and elbows, he felt her wrap her legs around his waist. She urged him on, grasping his buttocks with her hands, moaning into his ear, whimpering as he pounded her with more force, then finally crying out as he emptied his balls inside her hot passage.

"Oh dear, that was lovely," she said when he rolled off to the side.

"Are you all right?"

"I'm still tingling."

She cuddled close to him, and when he put his arm around her shoulders she reached down to gently stroke his wet prick. It was merely an idle touching, not really an attempt to get him interested again. He was too exhausted anyhow, and before long his minded drifted off and he closed his eyes. He thought of Olivia Rumbelow, comparing her with Audrey, one the mistress and the other the wife. Olivia was more exciting, wasn't she? If he had to choose between them, he'd take Olivia. But then how long would it be before he was just as bored with Olivia as he was with Audrey? His personal life, as always, was too bloody complicated.

Early the next afternoon, Drake called Olivia Rumbelow at home.

"You've been avoiding me," she said.

"That's not true and you know it."

"Busy?"

"The Yard never sleeps and all that."

"Why don't you visit me?"

"At home? Isn't that dangerous?"

"I'm fed up with seedy hotels. Please, darling. The servants are out and we'll have the place to ourselves."

He yielded finally. He knew it was dangerous, but

he felt a definite malicious pleasure at having Olivia in the Rumbelow house while Rumbelow was at his desk at the Yard. Oh yes, the idea was quite appealing. Twenty minutes after he spoke to Olivia on the telephone, she opened the front door of the Rumbelow house in Sydney Street and she admitted him inside.

She wore a white chenille robe, and he suspected that under it she was naked. She had a glass of wine in one hand. "Want some of this?"

"No, thank you."

"You're not annoyed that I asked you to come here, are you?"

"It is dangerous."

She took his hand and led him down the hallway. "Dear George. When I was a girl, I learned that nearly everything interesting in life is dangerous in one way or another. If you're worried about Albert surprising us, it won't happen. He never comes home during the day without telephoning first. I suppose he's afraid he might find someone fucking me."

Drake noticed how pretty her hair looked. She was blond like Audrey, but Olivia's hair was longer and more feminine.

He'd been in the Rumbelow house more than once on social occasions, and he was now surprised when she led him into the large sitting room rather than upstairs to one of the bedrooms.

She turned and smiled at him. "Are you sure you won't have a drink?"

"All right, but make it brandy, will you?"

He watched her as she walked to the bar to pour some brandy for him. When she returned, she handed him the glass, and then she immediately cupped her palm over the front of his trousers. "May I?"

He didn't bother to answer. He sipped the brandy

and watched her as she pulled the zipper down, slipped her hand inside his trousers and brought his penis out. She smiled down at it, gave it her full attention, stroking it with her fingers and making a sound of approval as it twitched upward. Then she abruptly dropped to her knees in front of him, took the knob in her mouth and started sucking it.

Drake enjoyed watching it. Here was the Superintendent's wife on her knees sucking his prick with complete abandon. It occurred to Drake that if one wanted a mistress, the most entertaining arrangement was to have the wife of the man who gave one orders.

Olivia pulled her lips off his penis, but she continued licking it. "He seems fit."

"He'll be even more fit if you take that robe off."

She laughed. "Do you want me naked?" He helped her rise, and then she pulled away from him and she unzipped the robe. "Off with those clothes," she said gaily. "I sat here last evening thinking about us doing it on that chair. Do you mind?"

When they were both naked, she came into his arms and kissed him, and then she whispered in his ear and said she wanted him to take her from the rear again. She wanted him to do it like the horses and dogs did it, poking her from behind with his big balls slapping against her.

"It's what I want," she said.

"All right."

"Lord, I adore your balls. They're twice the size of Albert's."

This was the first Drake had heard about the Superintendent's attributes, and what he heard pleased him greatly. Twice the size, were they? Well, she'd get a good fucking if she wanted it. She'd made him randy as the devil with her sucking and fondling and fingering. He cupped his hand under one of her full breasts and tugged at it. "Go on, bend over on the chair."

She had a luscious body, hips smooth, shapely, delectable, her belly gently sloping to a full bush of dark-blond curls. Her breasts were large but still firm, the brown nipples jutting, trembling now as she turned and moved toward the armchair. His penis twitched with excitement as he gazed at her swaying buttocks.

She knelt on the cushion of the armchair, leaning forward with her arms over the back. Then she moved her knees apart and arched her back to make her buttocks more prominent. Under the deep split of her buttocks, he could see the hairy fig of her sex, the wattles protruding enough to make her cunt look even more obscene.

When he moved up to her, he stroked her buttocks, running his hands over them, enjoying the smoothness of her flesh. Then he took hold of his penis and he rubbed the glans inside the slit of her sex. She made a sound of pleasure as he found the opening, and the next moment she groaned as he slowly impaled her.

"Oh, you brute!" she said.

"Don't move."

"Darling, I can't help it."

"Well, *try*, won't you?"

He pushed in slowly, pulled out again just as slowly. After a while the tension in his balls decreased and he realized he could last for some time. Gripping her buttocks with his hands, he found an easy rhythm that kept his penis moving continuously.

But before long she stopped him. "Wait," she said.

"What is it?"

"Would you like to bugger me?"

He said nothing for a long moment, his eyes fixed

on the closed whorl of her anus. It was something they had never done, but now as he gazed down at the brownish-pink orifice the idea appealed to him tremendously. "Are you sure?"

"Yes, I want it. You'll find some oil on the mantel."

He wondered if she'd planned it. What an amusement. He wondered if Rumbelow did it to her, if the Superintendent was in the habit of sodomizing his wife even as he condemned the act in others. Drake had heard Rumbelow more than once condemn it. As for him, he found the idea of condemning it ludicrous. If this was something Olivia wanted, he'd happily oblige her and enjoy it immensely.

He found the oil, a small plastic bottle with a nozzle, a pink label identifying it as a "love oil". Quaint, wasn't it? He brought it back to Olivia, pointed the nozzle at her anus and squeezed the bottle to get some oil out of it. Then he pushed just the tip of the nozzle inside the orifice and he squeezed again.

It's like oiling a machine, he thought. Now let's have the piston fit properly in the cylinder.

She gave out a long groan as he pushed the glans of his penis into the yielding sphincter. He had no trouble at all, not an instant of difficulty as his rigid organ slid into the heat of her backside.

"Dear George," she said, her voice a hoarse whimper, her hips swaying slightly as he pushed his belly against the groove between her buttocks.

"Am I hurting you?"

"No, not at all. Do it slowly, will you, but keep moving."

"It's a bit different, isn't it?"

She laughed. "But quite marvelous."

After that he stopped talking and he concentrated on what he was doing to her. The oil had made his penis glisten, and now it indeed looked like some pink metal piston pushing inside its companion cylinder. Olivia was making sounds he'd never heard before, low wailing sounds, bleating sounds, the noises of a woman running amok with pleasure.

Good Lord, what a lusty bitch she was!

He came an instant later, grunting as he slammed against her buttocks, his fingers mauling her flesh as the sperm jetted out of him with great force.

As he spouted inside Olivia, he felt like Lord Nelson in one of his sea battles, masterful, victorious, in full command of his physical being.

Afterward she made him lie on the sofa while she brought a wet towel to soothe and clean his genitals. She kissed the tip of his penis and said: "That was lovely, George."

"Yes."

"Do you do it with Audrey?"

He chuckled. "Does it matter?"

"No, I suppose not."

"It's not something we do. Or rather it's not something Audrey does."

"Silly woman." Olivia jiggled his balls with her fingers. "Where are you off to now?"

"Back to the grindstone, I'm afraid. I think I'll have a look at Berkeley Square. There's a new case I'm investigating, and Berkeley Square seems to be an important aspect."

"Berkeley Square? I've always thought Berkeley Square the dullest place in London."

Berkeley Square looked dull indeed. Drake parked his Rover in a No-Parking zone, placed an Official Business marker in the windscreen and left the car to stroll on the pavement.

He walked around the square, his eyes on the buildings, his mind wandering from thoughts of those bodies found in rubbish bins to thoughts of Olivia's buttocks to thoughts of the cloud of smoke over Rumbelow's head when he smoked his pipe.

Thoughts of Olivia soon pushed all the others aside. A quiver of pleasure passed through him as he remembered the visual details of what they had done together, the look of her anus stretched into a round mouth as it sucked on the shaft of his penis, the dangling globes of her breasts, the nipples elongated and stiff. Then he thought of Audrey. Only one time in their twenty year marriage had his wife ever permitted what Olivia craved with such exciting boldness. The occasion was a holiday in Scotland, he and Audrey motoring in the Grampians on the way to Balmoral Castle. They'd stopped at a place called Braemar, in a small inn with a cozy hearth and an innkeeper woman who seemed genuinely friendly. Audrey drank more than usual after dinner, and by the time they turned in for the night she was thoroughly bowsered. She later said she thought it was the altitude that had made her keep drinking. Altitude or no altitude, once they were under the covers in the dark of their room she wanted very much to be poked despite the inconvenience of her monthlies. They'd been married only two years and there were still things they hadn't tried. When he suggested they use "the other place", Audrey refused at first and then agreed after some coaxing. Drake remembered with amusement how he stumbled in the dark as he went to find his shaving soap. A few minutes later he had his penis inside Audrey's bottom, the two of them lying on their sides in the dark under the covers, Audrey wailing, telling him how much she hated it but at the same time making no move to pull away from him. When it was finished, she swore she'd never have it again and she made him promise he'd never ask for it. Now it was eighteen years later, and so far he'd kept his promise.

Like a bloody fool, he thought. George Drake, you're a bloody fool. How could anyone blame him for his affair with Olivia?

He did a complete turn of Berkeley Square, gazing at the houses one after the other, and then he climbed into his Rover, pulled the Official Business sign off the windscreen and drove away.

It took a few days, but finally Barzun, one of Drake's men, brought Drake a report on the houses in Berkeley Square.

Barzun said the only house that seemed a bit odd was the Hutchby house, the residence of the widowed Mrs. Agatha Hutchby. She had a reputation for being something of an eccentric, and it seemed the house was now occupied by some other people in addition to Mrs. Hutchby.

"What sort of people?" Drake said.

"A foreign butler, for one thing."

Drake sighed with impatience. "What else?"

"Individuals of suspicious appearance, according to the neighbors."

"Is that all?"

"The servants in the square appear to be gossiping about orgies and such in the Hutchby house."

"Orgies? What kind of orgies?"

Barzun scratched his chin. "I don't know. Wild parties, I suppose. It's not Bloomsbury, is it, sir? I suppose a party that's wild in Bloomsbury is an orgy in Berkeley Square."

"Quite. Now tell me what you've learned about the corpses."

Barzun pulled a notebook out of his pocket. He said he'd carefully read the medical reports concerning the three bodies found in the environs of Berkeley Square. He said he found it intriguing that in all three cases the examiner noted bruised genitals and a paucity of body fluids. In all three cases, the examiner reported his impression that the victims had suffered cardiac arrest during oral-genital sexual activity.

"Sucked to death." Barzun said.

"What?"

"That's the meaning of it, sir."

"I know that, you fool. But one doesn't lose body fluids doing that sort of thing."

Barzun lifted his eyes to the ceiling. "I've no idea, sir. I'm not an authority."

"It's preposterous."

"Would you like me to visit the Hutchby house?"

"No, I'll do that myself."

An hour later Drake was in Berkeley Square. This time he had no interest in doing a turn on the pavement. He went directly to the Hutchby house and knocked on the door. A full minute passed before the door opened, and there before him stood the butler.

Barzun had been right about the butler being a foreigner. He was a huge Turk, completely bald, with dark sleepy eyes and a dark curved moustache. He looked down at Drake as though Drake were an unwelcome annoyance.

"Yes?"

Drake cleared his throat and handed the butler his card. "Is Mrs. Hutchby at home?"

The butler looked at the card, his thick fingers making it seem insignificant.

"Chief Inspector?"

"Scotland Yard," Drake said. "Police."

"Drake."

"Yes, Drake. I'm Chief Inspector Drake of Scotland Yard. I'd like to have a chat with Mrs. Hutchby."

The butler was silent, and then after a time he said: "You wait." The door closed and Drake found himself standing alone on the steps.

Bloody cheek, Drake thought. He turned and looked at the square. Nothing unusual there, the ordinary scene, a large Daimler turning at the bend, the stately houses reminding him of Olivia's comment that Berkeley Square was the dullest place in London.

But in the Hutchby house they had a Turkish butler. Or at least Drake thought the man was Turkish. He might be Greek or Syrian or a Kurd or an Afghan. Why would anyone want a man like that as a butler? Did the man know how to serve tea when one wanted it?

The front door of the Hutchby house suddenly opened again, the huge butler gazing down at Drake, the dark eyes as sleepy as before.

"Come inside, please."

Drake climbed the remaining steps and at last entered the Hutchby house.

The door closed behind him and he found himself in a gloomy hallway. The butler took his hat, placed it upon a small table and led him forward. But they'd gone no more than a half dozen steps when a figure suddenly appeared from one of the rooms.

It was a young woman, a girl of twenty or so, and Drake felt a mild shock when he realized she was dressed in a nightgown. Oh yes, it was definitely a nightgown, white, lace-trimmed, the hem down near the floor. And her bare feet showing.

"Hello," she said in a sweet voice. "Are you the undertaker?"

"I beg your pardon."

"No, I guess not. I'm Sarah."

"Are you Mrs. Hutchby?"

With a vague smile, the girl now turned away. "On no. I'm not Mrs. Hutchby, I'm Sarah."

Drake watched her vanish through an open doorway, her white nightgown fluttering around her bare feet.

"This way, please," the butler said.

He led Drake into a cluttered drawing room, an old-fashioned room with old-fashioned furniture. The walls were covered with paintings and photographs, the mantel showing an array of small oval frames and various Oriental boxes.

Drake sat down on one of the two sofas that faced each other in front of the large fireplace. He thought of the girl he'd met in the hall and he decided the poor thing must be mad. First a Turkish butler and then a girl with mental problems in a white nightgown.

Then the door opened and a woman of fifty walked in.

Drake immediately rose to his feet. "Mrs. Hutchby?"

She was a woman of substantial figure, a pink face, brown curls, smiling at him. "Chief Inspector Drake, is it?"

"Yes."

"Do sit down, won't you? I've asked Mustafa to bring us tea."

Drake sat down, and Mrs. Hutchby sat down on the other sofa facing him. She wore silk, a brown silk dress with long sleeves, rather tight-fitting over her ample bosom, the hem long enough to cover her knees. She had surprisingly slender ankles for a woman of her proportions, and from what he could see of her calves they were fully curved.

"I met your daughter," Drake said.

Mrs. Hutchby stared at him. "My daughter? Oh, you must mean Sarah. Dear me, no. Sarah isn't my daughter, you see."

"Sorry. In any case I've met her."

"Is that what you wanted to talk to me about? Is it Sarah? Has there been some difficulty with dear Sarah?"

Drake assured her there had been no difficulty at all with Sarah. He told Mrs. Hutchby the reason for his visit was still vague. In any case, the visit was more or less unofficial, casual, for no purpose other than to ask her to help him. "I mean to help Scotland Yard," he said. "In that sense I'm here officially."

"Help you how?" Mrs. Hutchby said. "How can I help you?"

At that moment the door opened and the butler arrived with their tea. Drake waited while the tea was served, waited until the butler had left them and Mrs. Hutchby had settled down again. Then he told Mrs. Hutchby about the Berkeley Square case, the bodies in the rubbish bins, the unsolved mystery.

"How awful," Mrs. Hutchby said, her eyes fixed on him, more of her nylon-clad legs showing now, the full curve of one calf clearly displayed.

Drake was particularly impressed by her bosom. He imagined her breasts would be magnificent, pendulous when they were without support, the nipples like small pricks. He squirmed as he tried to keep his mind on more mundane matters, but for some reason he found it impossible. Was she flirting with him? Maybe she was. He had the feeling she was casting a spell over him. She was certainly showing more leg now than before, the edge of the silk dress pulled back, her legs crossed, one leg rocking slowly.

Then their eyes met and she smiled. "Are you married, Chief Inspector?"

Drake was taken aback. "What?"

"Are you married?"

"Yes."

"That's good. It's the married ones who know how to do it. The best fuckers, aren't they?"

"I beg your pardon…"

"Am I shocking you? But it's better to speak frankly, isn't it?"

A string of obscenities flowed out of her mouth, none of which made any sense to Drake, but hearing the words from her lips made him suddenly afraid that something awful was about to happen to him.

She smiled again, and for the first time he noticed her lips were actually painted a bright red. "Comfy?" she said.

"Yes."

"May I call you George?"

"Yes, if you like."

"Would you like me to sit over there beside you?"

Drake now realized he was lost. The woman was a witch and she could do as she liked with him. He felt powerless. He wanted to move but he found it impossible. He wanted to rise off the sofa, to bolt out of the room, but he could barely manage to move one of his legs.

"You haven't answered me," Mrs. Hutchby said.

"What?"

"Would you like me to sit over there beside you?"

"Why don't you lock the door first?"

She laughed, a cackling insane laugh that rattled him completely. Good Lord, what was happening to him?

He watched her as she rose from her seat to walk to the end of the drawing room. She locked the door, then turned and walked back to him. But instead of sitting beside him, she resumed her seat on the opposite sofa.

She cackled again, her massive breasts shaking under the silk of her dress. "Now look at it," she said. "You do want to look at it, don't you?"

And as Drake watched her, she pulled the edge of her dress back far enough to expose her thighs, the gartered tops of her stockings, and finally the pink gusset of her panties bulging with the bush of her sex.

Drake shuddered with both excitement and revulsion as he watched her fingers pull at the tight panties, continue pulling at the side of the gusset until the hairy slit of her cunt was exposed to his eyes.

"There," she said. "Isn't that better?"

He said nothing. He stared at the woman's thick-lipped sex and he told himself she was mad. Either Mrs. Hutchby was mad or he was mad. Or maybe they were both mad. No, he was sane and she was crazy. Dear God, where am I? he thought. Was it Berkeley Square or an asylum somewhere. He felt himself trembling, sweating, shuddering as he continued to gaze at the carmine split, the ripe sex, the pulpy gap that mesmerized him completely.

Mrs. Hutchby cackled again. "You're shy, aren't you? I adore shy men. Do you have an erection?"

"Yes."

"How lovely. Let me see it. Show it to me."

He told himself he ought to leave now, tell her his

business was finished and leave the house immediately. He ought to leave for the good of himself, for the good of the Yard, indeed for the good of England. He ought to run from this woman as fast as his legs could carry him, flee the house at once.

But then a voice on the other side of his head barked at him: Don't be an ass, George. Would there be any harm in it? He hadn't had a woman like this one since that Spanish bitch in Portobello Road offered herself to save her husband. Lord, what a quim, that one! And this one too. Tropical, it was. You could tell by looking at it the inside would be as hot as a baker's oven.

"Well?" Mrs. Hutchby said.

He unzipped his fly, slipped his hand inside the opening and brought out his penis, rigid, swollen, the pink knob already half exposed by the retracting foreskin.

Mrs. Hutchby made a sound of approval. "That's lovely, dear." She dropped a hand between her thighs and she began masturbating, massaging all of her sex with her plump fingers, her body jiggling, her breasts, her belly, her thighs moving as her hand moved. "What a handsome prick," she said. "Pull at the cowl, will you, I like to see all of the tip. There, that's better. Tasty looking, isn't he? Dear me, he makes my mouth water. No, don't stroke it, I don't want you spitting yet. Can you hold out?"

Drake managed a hoarse grunt. "Yes."

"Oh Lord, I'm hot. Creaming like this. Look at it coming out of me."

His voice breaking, Drake said: "Let's go to a bedroom."

Mrs. Hutchby laughed. "Is that what you want? All right, let's do that. Yes, it's a fine idea." She suddenly covered herself, pulled her dress down over her knees and smiled at him. "Come along, dear."

Drake fumbled with his penis, but he finally managed to push it back inside his trousers and zip the fly. When he rose up, Mrs. Hutchby held out one of her hands. "Come along."

He took the plump hand held out to him. He thought she'd lead him to the door at the far end of the drawing room, but instead she led him to another door, a smaller door near the windows that he hadn't noticed before.

He walked through the open door with her and he found himself inside a narrow passage, damp and dark, one presumably used by servants in another century, Mrs. Hutchby leading him along in the shadows, the scent of her perfume in his nose. Because of the narrowness of the passage, she had to walk in front of him, but she still held his hand, an arm stretched behind her, the heels of her shoes clicking on the wooden floor.

At last she came to the door she wanted. She opened it, held Drake firmly by the hand and quickly pulled him inside a bedroom.

Once the door to the passageway was closed, she turned and smiled at him. "Well then, now we're in a bedroom, aren't we?"

The room was square, furnished with a high bed and the usual accessory furniture, Victorian draperies and gilt mirrors on all the walls.

Drake had the sudden feeling he was being watched. He felt the skin at the back of his neck tingle. He looked carefully at all the mirrors, but he could see no sign of anyone behind them.

Mrs. Hutchby had released his hand and she was now busy undressing, removing her earrings, and finding himself unable to stand there like an oaf, Drake proceeded to undress also. He'd asked for it, hadn't he? Getting her on a bed had been his idea and not hers.

"Mrs. Hutchby?"

"Call me Agatha, won't you?"

"Is this your bedroom?"

"No, it's one of the guest rooms."

"I see."

What did he see? He saw nothing, but he had the feeling again he was being watched through one of the mirrors. Then he told himself he was too paranoid. There was nothing here except a randy woman who needed a man's attention. He had his trousers off now, and his penis poked out of the opening in his shorts like a stiff sausage. He watched Agatha as she slipped out of her dress to reveal her ample body covered by only a pink slip and the underthings beneath it. She had pretty shoulders and fleshy arms, and when she glanced at his penis her eyes brightened and she licked her lips.

"Is he going to make Agatha happy?"

"I don't see why not."

She giggled, squirming her shoulders, then lifting her slip and pulling it over her head. She tossed the slip away and she stood there in her pink underthings, a bulging brassiere and a panty-suspender belt combination to hold up her stockings. With a coy smile, she reached behind her to unhook the brassiere, then dropped it forward to pull it away from her huge breasts.

After she dropped the brassiere, she cupped the undersides of her breasts and lifted the globes upward. "Interested in these, are you?"

Drake felt himself blushing. He felt like a small

boy, awkward and stupid in the presence of such an abundance of female flesh.

Agatha seemed to recognize the state he was in, and in a moment she moved forward to push his head down to one of her enormous breasts. "Go on," she said. "Suck it if you like. Give it a good suck while I wank you a bit."

Overwhelmed with excitement, he gorged himself on the fat nipple, his body trembling as he felt her fingers close around his penis and shake it.

Then she dropped his penis and moved her fingers down to grip his testicles. "And what about these big balls?" she said. "Are they full up for Agatha?"

He wanted to suck the other breast, but she stopped him and pulled away from him. "No, that's enough of that. Let's get naked, shall we? You can get in me if you want that, but don't you dare come while you do it."

"I'll wear a safe," he said.

She cackled at him. "Never mind that; I'll show you what I want when it's time."

When they were both naked, she climbed onto the bed and then stretched out on her back with her knees raised. Drake climbed after her, moving between her open thighs, quivering as she took hold of his penis and guided it to the slit of her sex.

His organ pushed inside her without difficulty, and immediately he felt the liquid heat of her quim envelope him. He began thrusting, supporting his weight with his hands, his loins pumping vigorously. The jiggling of her huge breasts fascinated him, the globes like two large balloons bouncing wildly on her chest. He felt her fingers sliding under his balls and gripping them, twisting his scrotum as he continued sliding his penis in and out of her wet cunt.

"Are you close?" she said.

"Yes, I think so," he gasped.

With a powerful heave, she forced him out of her sex and pulled him forward with her hands. Understanding what she wanted, he shifted on his knees to get his penis in her mouth. Now he sat with his buttocks on her massive breasts, her fingers gripping his testicles again as she closed her red lips over the knob of his penis and began sucking it.

The heat of her mouth was incredible. His heart pounding with excitement, he gazed down at the scarlet orifice sucking at his organ. He felt her tongue and teeth on his flesh, her fingers twisting his scrotum, and in a moment he cried out as the sperm gushed out of him in a torrent.

She sucked relentlessly, pulling at his prick with her lips, swallowing his emission as fast as he gave it to her. When he thought she would stop, she went on and on, sucking hard, emptying his balls, sucking out the last drop of sperm from the tip of his penis.

When she finally pulled her mouth away, she smacked her lips, looked up at him with his sperm glistening on her teeth. "Glorious," she said. "You gave me more than I expected." She giggled as she tugged at his balls. "Any more? Would you like me to suck you up again?"

Drake blanched at the idea. "I'm afraid it's useless. In any case, I must be getting on."

Afterward, as they dressed, he thought of the medical examiner's report. Sucked to death, Barzun had said. Drake shuddered, fearing something still too vague to identify.

Mrs. Hutchby led him through the narrow passage and back to the drawing room. She wanted him to have more tea with her, but he thought it best to decline. He was about to leave when a woman entered the room, a tall dark-haired woman with eyes like black coals.

Mrs. Hutchby introduced the woman as Miss Clare. "The Chief Inspector is here to ask questions," Mrs. Hutchby said.

Miss Clare looked at him. "Oh?"

"Merely routine," Drake said. He noticed the look that passed between the two women. "I think I'll be leaving now," he said.

Miss Clare said to Mrs. Hutchby: "Agatha, have you been behaving yourself?"

Mrs. Hutchby seemed to tremble. "Magda, please..."

Miss Clare smiled at Drake. "Will that be all, Chief Inspector?"

In the evening when Drake thought of Berkeley Square and what had happened with Mrs. Hutchby, he castigated himself for having been derelict in his official duties. Good Lord, what a fool he'd made of himself! How awful to allow that repulsive woman to seduce him like that! Then he thought of Magda Clare and he felt a definite warming in his loins. That one was different. There was something incredibly seductive about Magda Clare. He regretted the sexual escapade had not involved Magda Clare rather than Mrs. Hutchby. Magda Clare, at least, would have made his transgressions worthwhile.

The more he thought of Magda Clare, imagining himself with her in some magnificently obscene pose, the more aroused he became. When Audrey brought him his brandy after dinner in the sitting room, he was affectionate to her, fondling her thighs as she stood next to his chair.

She smiled down at him. "Well, you're frisky, aren't you?"

"Let's go to the bedroom," Drake said. He was rather amazed to find his penis twitching so soon after the exhausting time with Mrs. Hutchby.

"Unfortunately, I'm out of turn."

Understanding she was having her period, Drake was annoyed, "I suppose we can manage something else."

Audrey didn't bother to ask what they might manage. In the past she'd never refused to give him a good pull-off when she had her monthlies. She now gave him a coy look and she walked away from him with a distinct twitch of her hips.

This time, however, he wanted something else. As soon as they were in her bedroom, he took her in his arms and he whispered in her ear. But when she realized what he wanted, she pulled away from him.

"Oh George."

"You've done it before."

"Yes, but I don't like it that much. You know I don't like it."

"You don't need to finish it that way."

"Promise?"

And so he persuaded her that if she would suck his penis until he was ready to spend, she could then finish him with her hand. It was evident she felt better about it now, and before long they were on the bed together, Drake's trousers and shorts pulled down around his ankles, Audrey leaning over his belly with his penis in her mouth.

He had one of her breasts out of her dress, his fingers toying with the nipple as he watched her mouth move up and down on the erect stalk of his penis. He enjoyed it immensely. She did this so rarely, he found it tremendously exciting to watch her go at it.

Then he felt himself about to come and he warned her with a grunt. "Now," he said.

Her lips made a wet sucking sound as she pulled them away from the tip of his penis. With her fingers curled around the shaft of his organ, she began a skillful pumping that soon had the sperm jetting out of his balls.

"There," she said, her eyes bright with excitement as she finished milking his prick. "Feel better now? You put out as much spunk as a young billy goat."

She was right about that. Drake was surprised at how much sperm she'd brought out of him after the draining he'd had by Mrs. Hutchby.

"I'm fine," he said.

Now that the danger of him forcing her to do anything she didn't like had passed, she seemed more relaxed. She said she'd read there were many women who disliked the taste of sperm and she hoped he wasn't annoyed with her.

Drake said: "I'm not annoyed with you."

"Some women like it and some women don't."

"Yes."

As she wiped her hands with a tissue, she told him she'd recently read an article about a tribe of vampires who sucked sexual juices. "What do you think of that? Isn't that gruesome?"

Drake stared at her. "What?"

He made her tell him more, but she remembered very little of the article.

"They're a special sort of vampire," she said. "That's all I know, really."

Two days later Inspector Barzun brought the identities of the Berkeley Square victims to Drake's office.

"We've got the lot," Barzun said.

"Confirmed?"
"Oh yes, sir."
The two young women found in trash bins had evidently been prostitutes, well-known in certain quarters. The man, on the other hand, was an American named Jack Lambert.
"Journalist of some sort," Barzun said. "He arrived in England two months ago."
Drake sat back in his chair. How strange this case was! In the first place, even if one strongly suspected foul play, all three victims appear to have died of heart attacks. In the second place, there was no motive yet apparent, if there was any rational motive at all.
"What else do you know about the American?" Drake said.
Barzun shrugged as he consulted his notes. "Not much, sir. Did a bit of travelling in various places. Resided at the Savoy a few days when he first arrived in London. He was evidently with a woman, connecting rooms and so on. A Miss Clare."
Drake stared at him. "What's that?"
"Sir?"
"The woman's name."
"Miss Magda Clare.
"Extraordinary."
"Extraordinary, sir?"
"I want you to find out whatever you can about the butler at the Hutchby house."
"The Turk, sir?"
"Yes, the Turk. Check with the immigration people. Also see if Interpol has a file on him."
"Yes sir."
Drake felt a twitching in his loins as he recalled his time with Mrs. Hutchby, the carnal delights, the sweaty connection they'd made, the way she'd insist-

ed on taking his emission in her mouth at the end. And of course afterwards he'd met Magda Clare, the tall dark-haired beauty, the woman who had apparently arrived in England with the American Jack Lambert, said American to be found two months later naked in a rubbish bin.

"There's a fellow named Cordwain," Drake said.

"Yes sir?"

"Professor Arthur Cordwain. He wrote an article recently about vampires and I want you to find him for me."

"Vampires, sir?"

"Find him," Drake said.

"Yes sir."

"In the meantime I'll be visiting the Hutchby house again this afternoon."

❖❖❖

When Drake arrived in Berkeley Square, he once again parked his Rover in a No Parking zone, this one on the side of the square opposite the Hutchby house. It was a clear day, the air brisk and clean for a change, and he enjoyed the walk around the square to his destination. When he reached the short flight of steps that led up to the front door of the Hutchby house, he thought he saw someone watching him from one of the front windows. But the curtain was quickly pulled closed and he had no chance to glimpse a face in the window.

He knocked on the Hutchby front door and waited.

In a few moments the door opened and the big Turk stood there glowering at him.

"Chief Inspector Drake to see Mrs. Hutchby," Drake said.

The Turk nodded and stepped aside to allow Drake to enter. The hallway was strangely dark and silent. The butler took Drake's hat, and then he led Drake down the long hall to the very same drawing room Drake remembered from his last visit.

"Wait, please," the Turk said.

Drake sat down on one of the sofas and waited. He surveyed the room, but he saw no sign that anything had changed since his last visit. When the door opened again, he expected Mrs. Hutchby to enter, but instead it was the butler bearing some tea for him.

"Mrs. Hutchby is delayed, please," the Turk said.

Drake nodded. He watched the butler leave and close the door, and then he leaned forward to pour himself some tea from the teapot. He sat back with his filled teacup, sipping from it, waiting for Mrs. Hutchby once again. At odd moments he looked at the smaller door near the windows through which she had taken him to a bedroom. He felt a quiver of arousal as he remembered their lusty time together.

The waiting continued. Drake finished one cup tea and he poured another. He was about to put the second cup to his lips when he suddenly felt weak, disoriented. He managed to place the teacup on the table, but after that he went to pieces completely.

Drugged, he thought. His astonishment only added to his helplessness. In a moment he slumped on the sofa in what appeared to him to be a voluntary muscle paralysis. His senses were intact, his remained conscious, his heart continued beating, but he was unable to move any muscles at all.

You've been foxed, old boy.

A moment later the door opened and Mrs. Hutchby entered the room with Magda Clare and the butler.

Drake could do nothing but look up at them helplessly as he lay sprawled on the sofa.

"Poor man," Mrs. Hutchby said with a giggle. "He looks awful."

Magda spoke to the butler in a foreign language, and the big Turk immediately moved to Drake, lifted the upper part of his body and removed his jacket. After that the butler rolled up the right sleeve of Drake's shirt to expose Drake's forearm.

Horrified, Drake watched Magda Clare remove a hypodermic syringe and needle from a black case. When she held it up, it was obvious the syringe was already filled with an amber liquid. The lovely brunette sat down on the edge of the sofa, lifted Drake's arm, and proceeded to jab the needle at one of his veins. When she had what she wanted, the vein securely penetrated by the needle, she emptied the contents of the syringe into the vein and then met his eyes for the first time.

Drake was already beginning to lose consciousness and he wasn't certain about what he was seeing. He thought he saw that Magda Clare's eyes had no pupils. But how could that possibly be? The ghastly image persisted until finally a blackness swept over him.

When he regained consciousness, he found himself slumped on the rear seat of a moving automobile. The paralysis continued as before; he was unable to move, unable to make a sound. He felt a stirring beside him, and in a moment Mrs. Hutchby came into view. She evidently sat on the rear seat with him, smiling at him now, her cheeks flushed.

Then he heard Magda Clare's voice from the front of the vehicle.

"Has he come around yet?" she said.

Mrs. Hutchby giggled. "Oh yes. He's looking chipper now."

Drake now found he could move his eyeballs if he exerted a great will and did it slowly. He managed to catch sight of Magda Clare and the Turk up front, the Turk driving. The car was apparently a Bentley. From the scenery that passed outside the windows, Drake suspected they were now on one of the trunk roads outside London.

Going where? he thought. He felt an urge to slip into the blackness of unconsciousness again, but he held on. Stay awake, he thought; stay awake if you want to survive this.

Magda Clare was telling them how much she adored the English countryside. She said England was such a tidy little country, cheerful and pleasing to the eye, its people so deliciously civilized. "How much further?" she said.

And Mrs. Hutchby replied: "Soon, darling."

"I'll want a bath."

"You'll find it quite pleasant, I think. There's a young gardener."

"Shut up, Agatha."

Mrs. Hutchby giggled again. She now leaned over Drake, close enough so that her round face occupied almost all his field of vision. "Fit, darling? Is there anything I can do for you?"

Magda Clare said: "Is he moving around?"

"Not at all," Mrs. Hutchby said.

She smiled at Drake again, brought a hand up to his cheek and patted it. Then she dropped her hand to his lap and he felt her fingers doing something to the front of his trousers. He managed to turn his eyes down, and he was appalled as he helplessly watched her unzip his trousers and slide her hand inside. He felt the fingers searching, fumbling, and then finally pulling at his penis to get it exposed.

She sat back now, sat erect and properly beside him except that she still held his penis in her hand. He felt her squeezing his flesh, stroking it, tugging at it as the Bentley continued rolling smoothly on the road.

Like a pet dog, he thought. Mrs. Hutchby fondled him as she would a pet animal. He remembered that afternoon with her on the bed, her lush curves, the two monumental breasts, the imperial buttocks. He felt a sudden surprise as he realized her stroking fingers were giving him an erection. Paralysis or no paralysis, his penis appeared to be one part of him that was still functional. Mrs. Hutchby was talking to Magda Clare again, but while they talked her hand continued to stroke his penis, tickle it and tug at it as he wondered if it meant he would survive this after all, if it meant his body would not fail him.

They finally arrived somewhere. Drake had no opportunity to notice any signs, but the car did slow down, leave the main road and continue on a smaller road through a rolling countryside. Then the Bentley made a sharp turn through a gate, and before long it pulled up in a circular driveway in front of a rather large and distinguished-looking manor house.

Where? Drake thought. Where the devil was he?

Mrs. Hutchby pushed his penis back inside his trousers and zipped the opening closed.

The big Turk came around and lifted Drake bodily out of the car.

Drake heard Mrs. Hutchby say something to Magda Clare about having him first.

"You promised," Mrs. Hutchby said.

Magda Clare seemed annoyed. "We'll see, Agatha."

His head bouncing up and down as Mustafa carried him from the car to the front door of the manor house, Drake could make out no more than the gravel path and the legs of the two women.

In a moment they were all inside the house, and from what Drake could see of the hall the house was indeed upper-class and well cared for.

As the women talked again, the butler carried Drake up the broad stairs and down a hall to a room. Inside the room, Mustafa effortlessly tossed Drake onto a wide four-poster bed and then turned and left him.

Drake's face was against the counterpane and he thought he smelled lilacs. His erection was gone and a deep despair overwhelmed him. Now he thought maybe he wouldn't survive this after all. Maybe he was already a dead man.

He lost track of time. He continued to smell lilacs as he lay with his face pressed against the counterpane of the four-poster bed. How many hours had passed since his visit to the Hutchby house in Berkeley Square?

Suddenly the door opened and he heard feminine voices. In a moment he was able to see two maids approaching him, giggling at each other, seemingly unconcerned about his state.

"Well, he's not a young one, is he?"

"I told you, lovey. I told you he wasn't a young one."

They rolled him over on his back and they began undressing him. They stripped him naked, giggling, one of the girls fondling his genitals, then her hand pushed away by the other girl who took his penis in her fingers and tugged at it with a laugh.

"Nothing much in this noodle. Come on then, let's put the cuffs on him, get him laid out proper before she gets angry at us."

For the first time Drake saw the restraints they'd brought with them, a set of leather cuffs and straps that he knew had only one purpose. He lay there helpless as they fastened the cuffs to his wrists and ankles. They then attached the cuffs to the four posts of the bed to get him spread-eagled on his back like a side of beef.

They stood there a moment looking at him, giggling, and then both girls turned, left the room and closed the door behind them.

His eyes fixed on the canopy over the bed, Drake lay there more frightened than ever.

Some time passed. He wasn't certain whether he'd been sleeping or not. But as he opened his eyes and came fully awake, he realized he had more mobility than before, at least within the constraints of his attachments to the posts of the bed. His muscles were still weak, but at least he could move some of them.

Then he heard the door open and close again, and a moment later when he turned his eyes to look he saw Magda Clare approach the bed.

She stood near the bed and gazed down at him, glancing with interest at his limp penis. Drake felt a great embarrassment at his nakedness in the presence of this strange and beautiful woman. Then Magda Clare said: "Well, Chief Inspector, I see you've partly recovered."

"Who are you?"

"My name is Magda Clare."

"Yes, I know that, but who are you?"

She seemed annoyed. "Don't be presumptuous."

"What sort of drug did you use to paralyze me?"

"It's an ancient Egyptian substance similar to curare. Quite effective, isn't it? You'll have more of it when it's necessary."

Drake groaned. "It might kill me."

She gave him a brittle smile. "No, I don't think so."

Suddenly he remembered what he'd seen at the Hutchby house, the look of her eyes when she'd finished injecting him, the eyes without pupils, ghastly, frightening.

He groaned again. He tried struggling with his bonds, but he was too weak.

Magda Clare now sat down on the edge of the bed and she reached out to stroke his genitals. She lifted his limp penis, looked at it, then dropped it again. She did the same to his scrotum. Then she took hold of his penis again and she began stroking it more deliberately, sliding the foreskin back and forth over the glans, tickling it, patiently coaxing the organ until it began to swell beneath her fingers.

Drake felt his heart beating faster as he watched his penis become erect, swollen, throbbing with his blood.

Magda Clare said: "There, that's better." She stopped stroking his penis and merely held it at its base. She squeezed it and watched the knob increase in size. Then she bent her head to take the glans between her red lips.

Drake cried out as he felt the heat of her mouth. The pleasure was so intense it overwhelmed his brain. He stared down at her, watching those red lips slide up and down the shaft of his penis. He felt his sap rising, the pressure in his balls...

She suddenly pulled her mouth away, her lips wet,

glistening. "No, not yet," she said, her fingers testing the firmness of his testicles. "You're not ready yet."

She waited a few moments. When the pressure in his balls abated, she dropped her head to suck his penis again. This time the movements of her mouth seemed more determined. Once more he felt his sap rising, the pressure mounting, and then finally he cried out and jerked his body as the sperm gushed out of his penis into Magda Clare's waiting mouth.

She drained him, using her fingers to milk the last of his emission out of him, sucking the tip of his penis and then licking it clean.

When she looked at his face again, he saw that now her eyes had no pupils.

She appeared to stare at him, but with what? Those horrible eyes, showing only glistening white corneas, ought to be completely blind...

In a moment she rose from the bed, and without a word she turned and left him.

Mrs. Hutchby said: "How are you, love? Full up and ready for Agatha?"

Drake opened his eyes when he heard her voice. He felt weak, helpless, without any strength at all.

"I may be dying," he said.

Mrs. Hutchby gave a snort of disapproval. "Nonsense, darling. Magda knows how to control these things. You might be feeling weak, but you're not going to die." She giggled. "Not yet, love. Certainly not until I've had my share of things. How is it now? Are you up to a little present for Agatha?"

She smiled at him coyly as she slipped out of her

robe. She was naked, her white body as lush as he remembered it, the huge breasts jiggling until she steadied them with her hands.

"She broke her promise," Mrs. Hutchby said. "Magda promised me I'd have the first turn with you, but she broke her promise. She can be an awful bitch sometimes. Sarah and I are planning to break away from her as soon as we can. We don't need her, do we?"

"Are you and Sarah like Magda?"

"What do you mean?"

"You're vampires, aren't you? Not the usual kind, but vampires nevertheless."

Mrs. Hutchby cackled at him, her red lips mobile. "Don't you think about that, because it might reduce your spunk. I want a good emission from you. I do need it desperately."

"Desperately?"

She looked amused. "Don't you know? Magda said I shouldn't tell you, but I don't see that it matters. The fact is, if we don't get enough of it we get weak and we die. Isn't that awful? But you're not going to let Agatha die, are you, darling? You're going to have a lovely packet of spunk for me. Mucho mucho."

She sat down on the bed now, leaned over him in a way that made her huge breasts swing against his thighs. She began tickling his penis, stroking it, coaxing it into an erection. He thought she'd fail but he was wrong. She knew precisely what she was doing, and before long she had his penis and balls tickled up enough so that his member began to swell and lengthen. She took it in her mouth before the erection was complete, and that of course brought him standing in no time.

She seemed to have no interest in the upper

part of him now. She held his testicles in one hand, the other hand squeezing the base of his penis as she sucked gluttonously at the glans. He thought her mouth was less hot than Magda's had been, but the pleasure he felt was almost as intense.

Before long she stopped squeezing the base of his penis, and soon after that her sucking mouth brought an emission out of him, a strong spurting of fluid that caused her to make sounds of approval as she continued sucking at the tip of his prick.

He thought she'd stop but she didn't. She kept on sucking him until his penis ached. She wanted more sperm out of him but he had nothing to give her. In an effort to get him erect again, she slipped a finger inside his anus and pistoned the digit in and out as she continued sucking his prick. But that didn't work either and she finally gave up.

"It's that bitch Magda's fault," she said. "I ought to suck you dry and kill you just to spite her."

And with that she put her robe on and walked out.

He slept.

When he opened his eyes, he was shocked to find the girl Sarah in the room. He remembered she hadn't come with them in the car. But now she was here, gazing at him with a soft smile, her eyes on his nakedness, on his belly, on his genitals.

"I always get my turn," she said, her hands now pulling at her nightgown to get it off her body. "Do you have anything left for me?"

Naked, she was sylphlike, her breasts like

apples, the nipples pink and pointed upward, a fuzz of auburn hair covering her mound. She gave a coquettish look as she climbed onto the bed to bend over his belly.

She began toying with his limp prick, her slender fingers lifting it, pulling at it, dropping it again.

Drake groaned and said: "I have a daughter your age."

Sarah laughed. "Really?"

"You're not as bad as the others, are you? Why don't you be a clever girl and get me out of these restraints?"

"Oh, I couldn't do that, Magda would be furious. Besides, I need to get something from you, don't I?" She curled her fingers under his testicles, lifting them, examining them. Then her fingers returned to his penis and she began stroking it slowly as she looked down at it.

Despite his desire to be uncooperative, Drake's prick had its own mind and it soon reacted to the girl's skillful fondling. His penis became erect, as swollen and extended as it had been with Mrs. Hutchby and Magda Clare. Sarah seemed pleased by it, and with a final jerking of the organ she dropped her head down to take the glans in her mouth and suck it.

Her mouth was definitely less hot than the others, more warm than hot, but still delightful enough to produce a quick response in his belly. After a while she slipped a slender finger inside his anus, and that fillip was enough to make him spurt in her mouth.

He watched her take the emission, watched her young lips sucking with relish at his gushing penis. After the spurting was finished, she cleverly squeezed the glans to get the last drop of sperm out of him. Then she licked the tip clean, smacked her lips and smiled at him.

"You're not salty at all," she said.

But he was already drifting off to sleep, his mind in a grey fog.

He dreamed he was in Hell, one of the rings in Dante's Inferno, his body on a rack and his penis in the mouth of a monstrous lizard.

Then he heard a babble of voices and he awakened.

This time they were all in the room, Magda Clare, Mrs. Hutchby, Sarah. And another girl, one he hadn't seen before. She was a blond girl, heavily made up, her breasts jutting in a short tight dress.

The blonde's eyes danced, her red lips working as she spoke. "He likes being tied up, does he? Gor, I love getting it when they're tied up. Makes me cream just looking at him."

She quickly peeled her dress off and climbed over him wearing only a red suspender belt and black stockings. Drake thought she might be a tart, maybe a local prostitute brought in to finish him off. He thought she'd hunch down to get his penis in her mouth, but instead she squatted over his face and then lowered her crack to his nose.

She giggled as she wriggled her hips from side to side. "Come on, dearie, use your tongue like a good boy."

In the dark, his eyes covered by her buttocks, Drake felt an eagerness that surprised him. Despite his weakness, he had an urge to suck her sex, to root in it. Mustering his strength, he began working his tongue and lips against the hairy slit. The girl made sounds of approval, and soon her juices were flowing.

He sucked at the drippings, and as he did so he gradually found his strength returning. The more juice he sucked out of her, the more fit he seemed to become.

Then, as he continued sucking the girl who sat on his face, he felt the heat of a mouth surrounding his penis. He thought it must be Magda Clare, since Mrs. Hutchby appeared to be talking to someone. He continued sucking the girl as Magda Clare sucked his penis, and now for the first time he felt the current of energy flowing from the girl's cunt into his mouth and out of his penis. As the girl's juices revitalized him, Magda Clare sucked the energy directly out of him.

And the others? Would they all have their turn?

What a pity he hadn't been able to talk to Professor Cordwain. Drake was certain now he'd be finished soon. They'd suck him dry and dead and toss him naked in a rubbish bin.

He heard someone giggling, and then he felt a new mouth on his penis.

Part Four

MAFERNIT'S TOMB

Audrey Drake first learned of the disappearance of her husband by telephone. On the evening following Drake's last visit to the Hutchby house in Berkeley Square, Inspector Barzun of Scotland Yard telephoned Mrs. Drake to ask if her husband had returned home. Audrey said he hadn't yet, and that she'd assumed he was working late at the Yard. Barzun seemed highly disturbed by this information, and he begged her to have her husband call the Yard immediately if by chance he did arrive home.

Audrey spent a restless night wondering about her husband, listening for his arrival, and finally falling asleep with the lights on and the radio blaring because she was suddenly afraid that something awful was happening.

In the morning Audrey called Scotland Yard. She managed to get through to Barzun, but he had no information for her. He said the Yard was working on it, and once again he assured her she'd be notified as soon as they had any information.

Three days later Barzun telephoned Audrey and said he'd like to visit her at the house. When she asked about her husband, Barzun said he'd like to tell her in person. Was George all right? Barzun said they didn't know, and he hung up.

Audrey waited for him. If anything had happened to George, she was determined to be brave, to put on a brave front, to show people how strong she was. Her mind was filled with horrible images of George shot to death by thugs in Soho, or blown to bits by the IRA, although she hadn't heard any news of an IRA bombing lately. Was this one of their quiet assassinations? But George never had anything to do with the IRA, did he? She fixed herself a gin tonic, and then she paced with it up and down the living room.

Barzun finally arrived. He walked in with his hat in his hand and a grave look on his face. "Good afternoon, Mrs. Drake."

"Tell me," she said.

"I'm afraid it's bad news."

Audrey closed her eyes. "Is he dead?"

"We have no evidence of that, but he's vanished."

"Oh dear."

"I'd like to ask a few questions, if I may."

"What?"

"Just a few questions, Mrs. Drake. It might help us."

"Yes, of course. Sit down, won't you? I'll have the maid bring some tea."

Audrey ordered the tea, and Barzun settled his bulk on a chair.

After the tea was served, the maid gone and the living room door closed, Barzun said:

"Can you tell me if he's done this before?"

Audrey stared at him. "Done what before? Vanished? Of course not."

"No, I don't mean that. Has he ever in the past gone off for a few days? It might have happened during a holiday, a time when the Yard wouldn't know about it. Has he ever done that?"

"No, never."

Barzun now shifted his body on the chair. "The next question is awkward, Mrs. Drake."

"Ask it."

"To your knowledge, has the Chief Inspector been a faithful husband?"

"Oh dear."

Barzun shifted uneasily. "I'm sorry."

"Is this really necessary, Inspector Barzun?"

"It might help us, but you needn't answer the question if you don't want to."

Audrey sighed. "I don't have any knowledge about George's infidelities, if that's what you mean. I can't say he's been faithful because I don't know. Now please tell me why the information would be of any importance."

Barzun shifted on his chair again. "Yesterday afternoon the Yard received a video tape delivered by messenger. The Chief Inspector appears on the tape..."

"Then he's alive!"

"We have no reason to believe otherwise."

"Dear God, what is it? Why is it so important to know about his infidelities?"

"The video tape shows the Chief Inspector with a woman, Mrs. Drake. In rather intimate circumstance, you see. Our assumption at the present time is that the disappearance of the Chief Inspector may be voluntary."

"Voluntary?"

"He may have decided to run off with a woman."

Audrey was silent a long moment. She decided not

to tremble. She wanted very much to tremble, but she decided to muster all her strength and avoid it.

"I want to see that video," she said.

Barzun seemed taken aback. "Oh no, Mrs. Drake. You really mustn't, it's too..."

"I want to see it."

Barzun insisted it would not be wise for her, not wise at all. But Audrey insisted, said she was the Chief Inspector's wife after all, said she'd complain to higher authorities, to the press if necessary. She was determined to look at the video no matter what.

Barzun finally relented and said he'd see what he could do about it. "I'll call you," he said. "I don't advise it, but I'll try to arrange something."

After Barzun left, Audrey sat alone in her living room feeling mixed emotions about what she'd learned. She was concerned about George. After nearly twenty years of marriage certain bonds had been forged and she had to be concerned about him. But she was also rather happy to be free of him. If she was indeed free of him. She supposed that no matter how this ended she could be free of him if she wanted. From Inspector Barzun's description of the video, Audrey gathered it might easily be used in divorce proceedings. If she wanted divorce proceedings. She was never sure about anything when it came to George, never sure of her feelings for this marriage. She did enjoy it occasionally. She played the role of the dutiful middle-class wife, kept the home going, looked after their daughter who thank God was now on her own in New Zealand. She entertained George when he seemed to want it, acted the tart when she thought it appealed to him. A woman had to do that, didn't she? A woman had to be coquettish and tarty and dress up in silly lingerie like a decorated bit of pastry. All of it to give him a stand so that he might poke her and get his pleasure from it. And her own pleasure? She became excited enough, but there was something always lacking in it. It was never sufficient for her. In the beginning she'd thought there was something wrong with her, but after many years she'd realized it wasn't her, it was George; he never cared enough about her pleasure; he never did and he never would. A woman friend had said it to her: "Some men are like that."

And now this new development. George and another woman. George maybe running off with another woman. Yes, he's done it, Audrey thought. Since she hadn't seen him in four days, didn't that mean he'd indeed run off with another woman? Was it possible she was indeed free of him now?

Did she want to be indeed free of him now?

She felt a keen exhilaration, a tingling all over her body and especially in her belly. Maybe it was shocking to be randy at a time like this, but she couldn't help it, and even if she could help it she wouldn't. Instead of dismissing the feeling, she expanded it, until finally she knew what she had to do and she left the living room and went into the kitchen to search in the refrigerator. In the vegetable bin she found a large cucumber, and she brought it to the sink to warm it under the hot tap. When she thought the cucumber was sufficiently warm, she carefully dried it, wrapped a paper towel around it and carried it up the stairs to her bedroom.

God bless the vegetable kingdom, she thought. She wondered how many hundreds of cucumbers she'd used. She wondered how many hundreds of thousands of cucumbers were being used by other women. She found herself giggling as she thought of that.

She locked her bedroom door. The maid was out, but it didn't matter, Audrey always locked the door when she engaged in one of her private entertainments. She quickly undressed, stripped all her clothes off, then climbed onto the bed with the cucumber in her hands. From the nightstand she lifted the plastic bottle of skin lotion, squeezed some out in her palm and carefully smeared half the cucumber with it.

She was trembling with need now, her heart pounding as she lay back on the counterpane with her knees raised. With an easy dexterity born of long practice, she used one hand to spread the lips of her quim and the other hand to slowly push one end of the cucumber inside the tunnel of her vagina.

A groan of deep pleasure came out of her throat as she felt the probing of her insides, the sensation of a heavy mass in there, the stretching of the mouth of the passage.

Now, as she held the cucumber in her left hand and began sliding it slowly in and out, jerking it, pushing it in, pulling it out again, she found her clitoris with the fingers of her right hand and she began rubbing it, tugging it, twisting its stiffness with more and more energy.

After the first orgasm, she continued right on.

After the second orgasm, she introduced the smallest finger of her left hand inside her anus and kept it in there as she continued pushing and pulling at the cucumber.

She lost count of the orgasms after that. She exhausted herself. When she finally pulled the slimy cucumber out of her vagina, she tossed it away on the counterpane and she gave herself one last climax with her fingers.

Then it was finished, her body drained.

Was she indeed free of George? She turned on her side and she began crying.

❖❖❖

The following day Inspector Barzun returned with a small video playback machine and a copy of the tape that had been mysteriously received by Scotland Yard. Once again he tried to dissuade Audrey from looking at the tape. "I really don't advise it," he said.

Audrey shook her head. "I must see it."

Resigned to it, Barzun suggested they view the tape in the Chief Inspector's den in order to have some privacy. Audrey agreed, and once they were in there she locked the door to keep the maid out.

Barzun immediately set up the equipment, loaded the tape, and they both sat down on George's leather sofa to watch the small TV set.

The screen flickered at first, and then abruptly there appeared a view of a bedroom, decently furnished, not too large, with a square old-fashioned bed under a large canopy. For several moments nothing happened, no movement at all, the camera evidently fixed in position. Then suddenly two figures appeared on the screen, one of them a plump woman of about fifty and the other George Drake.

Barzun said: "The woman is a widow named Agatha Hutchby, and as far we can tell this was done from behind a one-way mirror in a house in Berkeley Square."

Audrey's eyes were riveted to the screen. George and the Hutchby woman were now standing about five or six feet apart and smiling at each other as they undressed. Mrs. Hutchby was quicker than George, and in a moment her huge breasts were exposed, the white globes jiggling as she continued undressing, her red lips working as she said something inaudible.

Audrey was astounded as she watched them. How queer it was to see her own husband doing this sort of thing, to be an observer rather than a participant. She and George had often undressed like this preparatory to having a tumble on a bed. But here he was with a stranger, a woman with enormous breasts, now naked, her broad rump now facing George as if to entice him.

And in a moment George had enough clothes removed to show proof of his arousal. Audrey gazed at George's rigid prick, at the way it bobbed from side to side as he finished getting his clothes off, wondering if what she was seeing was real, wondering why she hadn't noticed all these years that George's balls swung about so much when he moved his body.

The two naked people on the screen approached each other. George immediately raised his hands to lift Mrs. Hutchby's wobbling breasts. She smiled at him as he squeezed the globes and tugged at her nipples with his fingers. As he did that, she took hold of his genitals with both hands, holding his balls with one hand as she stroked his penis with the other hand. Then she pulled away from his and she climbed onto the bed. She appeared to be talking to him as she rolled onto her back and raised her knees. George quickly climbed onto the bed and mounted her, one hand guiding his stiff penis inside her sex. Audrey felt her pulse quickening as she watched the connection being made, her husband's prick in the other woman's welcoming cunt. Was that the way she looked when he did it to her? She felt her knees trembling as she watched the two people on the bed begin a vigorous combat,

George's white buttocks rising and falling with a steady rhythm as he pistoned his organ in and out of Mrs. Hutchby's opening.

Audrey expected the congress on the screen to continue to an ordinary end, but she was mistaken. Mrs. Hutchby seemed to push at George, and in response he suddenly pulled his penis out of her sex. The organ glistening with wetness, he straddled the woman's thighs and shifted his knees forward until his buttocks rested on her huge breasts. Audrey shuddered, her eyes wide with astonishment as she watched George slide his prick into Mrs. Hutchby's open mouth.

Mrs. Hutchby sucked with obvious relish at the swollen organ. George began moving his hips, sliding his penis in and out of the open mouth, his own pleasure evident on his face. It wasn't long before he spent, his body shaking as he ejaculated between Mrs. Hutchby's red lips. She squeezed his testicles with her hand, coaxing the emission out of him as her mouth continued feeding on the rigid penis. With her lips stretched by the organ, Mrs. Hutchby turned her head and seemed to look directly at the camera. Audrey gasped as she saw the whites of the woman's eyes but no pupils.

"Oh my God," Audrey said.

A moment later the screen went blank, a flat grey, then after that only dense bands of random horizontal lines.

Barzun moved to the video playback machine and he switched it off. "I'm sorry, Mrs. Drake. But I did warn you..."

"Yes."

"I assure you we see all sorts of things in the Yard..."

"Yes."

"It's not unusual, you know. I mean the adultery aspect."

"Yes."

"Can I be of any help to you?"

"Why don't you fuck me?"

"What?"

"I said why don't you fuck me? You can't tell me that didn't affect you the way it did me. It did, didn't it?"

She took him out of George's den and into her bedroom. He seemed uncertain, unsure they were actuality doing it, maybe amazed at her boldness. But he did want it; she could see he wanted it each time she glanced at the front of his trousers. When they were inside the room, she locked the door and then she walked to the wardrobe and she began undressing.

"What do you know about that woman?" she said.

Barzun stuttered. "I—I don't know much. The house is empty now. It seems they've all gone somewhere."

"She has breasts like a cow, don't you think?"

"Big, yes."

Audrey avoided looking at him. But she knew his eyes were on her and she gave him a bit of a show as she undressed, the belly and bum teaser as she'd heard someone call it, showing herself front and back in her tights before she peeled away her blouse and brassiere to expose her breasts.

When she was completely naked, she turned for the first time to look at Barzun and she found him standing there with his fingers curled around a rather lusty looking prick with an arrow-shaped knob. She moved toward him and she took hold of his penis and balls with both hands the way she'd seen Mrs. Hutchby take hold of her husband in the video. Barzun, in the meantime, slid his arms around Audrey and dropped his hands down to fondle her buttocks.

"What's your wife like," she said.

"She has red hair."

She thought his balls weren't as big as her husband's, but she wasn't certain. So many years had passed since she'd been with a man other than George, she felt more than a little awkward about it. Eager to have him, she pulled Barzun to the bed and then left him and lay down on her back with her legs open. "Come on then. Get it inside me and do it."

He seemed excited by her, his eyes raking over her body and then gazing deliberately at her cunt. She didn't mind showing herself to him. She felt lewd. Keeping her knees up, she opened them wider to expose more of her sex to his eyes.

As he shifted forward, she watched the movements of his erect penis as it jerked up and down. Then he mounted her, raising her knees even further, guiding himself inside her sex and grunting as he thrust forward.

She felt an intense excitement as the spear of flesh stretched her opening and pushed in. He wasn't at all like George; he was more lusty, more animal-like. As he began moving inside her, she cried out in response to the exquisite sensations. She felt his balls slapping against her buttocks, and then before long the increased vigor of his thrusting as he started spurting inside her.

Lord, what a lovely prick, she thought. She'd adored every moment of the lovemaking.

"That's a piece, all right," he grunted as he rolled off her.

"You liked it, did you?"

"Come lie on top of me now."

Audrey was amused by the idea. She rolled over him, lay flat on his body with her head on his hairy chest. He was a big man, much bigger than her husband, with a broader and stronger body. She felt the mass of his genitals under her belly, the wet and still-tumescent flesh warm against her skin. His hands were on her buttocks, his fingers squeezing the globes rhythmically. The feel of his big hands mauling her bottom excited her, and before long she rolled off him again and she lifted his thick penis with her fingers and she looked at it.

"Will this be ready again?"

"It will if you want it. Keep tickling it that way and you'll see."

She toyed with it, stroking the limp prick, sliding the foreskin back and forth over the arrow-shaped glans. She looked more closely at his balls and she estimated they were indeed smaller than her husband's, more like pigeon eggs than George's fat plums. Before long she could feel Barzun's penis filling with blood again and her excitement was rekindled.

In the meantime he had his hands on her body, his fingers stroking her breasts and buttocks as she crouched beside him. Then he slipped his fingers all the way into the crack between her buttocks and he gently rubbed her anus.

"Would you like it here?" he said.

She froze, her body motionless, and she said nothing for a long moment. Then finally she said: "I don't know. I haven't done it that often."

"I won't hurt you."

"Are you sure?"

"Yes."

"All right, let's try it."

So many years had passed since the last occasion, she thought maybe she could tolerate it this time. Suddenly the idea of it excited her tremendously, the lewdness of it, the idea of him taking her there, making the adultery complete, allowing George's subordinate to bugger her.

She pulled away from him, and she knelt on the edge of the bed with her head down and her buttocks facing him. He seemed amused as he told her to change her position, to move closer to the edge of the bed.

"You're a lusty woman," he said. "I don't know why the Chief Inspector would want to bother with another."

She took that as a great compliment and she was pleased. "There's some skin lotion on the dressing table."

"Right."

She felt the pounding of her heart as she waited for him. What a lark this was! What a lovely lovely lark! All these years avoiding this with her husband, and here she was giving it so easily to Barzun!

She closed her eyes and remained motionless, her back arched, her knees wide apart. She heard Barzun return with the lotion, heard him shake the bottle, open it, squeeze some of the cream onto his fingers. And then she gave a quiet gasp as she felt his wet fingers touching her anus.

His hands were on her buttocks, one hand pressing the lower part of her spine, the other hand tickling between the globes. Then she felt the pressure against her sphincter, his glans rubbing against it, then pushing at it, pushing in, pushing in slowly, the rigid penis forcing its way inside her tunnel.

"Oh God!" she cried.

"Am I hurting you?"

"Yes, but keep going!"

He kept going until his belly was pressed against her buttocks, then he stopped and rested before he started moving again.

Now she thought of that time in Scotland, that night in Braemar when George had persuaded her to take him there. She hadn't felt anything then but an awful pain. But this was different. The pain was there, but as Barzun continued moving, sliding his penis in and out of her backside, the pain was slowly eclipsed by the most incredible pleasure. She groaned loudly, not caring who might hear it, her mouth open and her face covered with sweat as she felt the piston-like movements of Barzun's prick in her bottom.

He muttered something, a curse, a compliment, she had no idea what, the rhythm of his thrusting increasing, his belly slamming against her buttocks with more force, and then finally a deep bellow from his throat as he emptied himself in her backside.

Guilt followed very quickly. Before Inspector Barzun was even out of the house, Audrey felt a sharp guilt for what she had done. But she couldn't deny the pleasure she'd had. Dear God, she hadn't enjoyed a man so much in years!

❖ ❖ ❖

The next afternoon Olivia Rumbelow came calling to comfort Audrey. She'd heard from her husband about George's disappearance, and she wanted Audrey to know she was ready to do anything to help. "It's an awful thing," Olivia said. "But you do need to be brave about it."

Audrey thought Olivia looked especially attractive today, her pretty blond hair falling over her shoulders like fine silk. They had tea in the living room, talked about clothes, Olivia turning her slender ankles as she described some new Italian shoes she'd bought. Audrey realized she wasn't that fond of Olivia. She'd always thought of Olivia as a grasping woman, one of those women who always had to have things their own way. But Olivia did seem anxious to offer assistance, to help Audrey bear this trouble with her husband. Audrey tried her best to be hospitable to Olivia. She tried to place the musky scent of Olivia's perfume as she assessed Olivia as a woman, wondering how full-fleshed Olivia was, wondering what Olivia's clever dress was designed to hide.

As they sat beside each other on the sofa, Olivia began asking about George's last activities. "You might think of something important," Olivia said.

But Audrey doubted it. "There wasn't anything." She hadn't told Olivia yet about the Hutchby woman, but she decided to do so now. "No, I shouldn't say that, there was something. He'd been having an affair."

Olivia appeared to blanch. "An affair?"

"With a woman in Berkeley Square. I learned it from Inspector Barzun."

"Berkeley Square?"

"Yes, Berkeley Square. Is that surprising?"

Olivia seemed stunned. "I wonder why my husband hasn't mentioned it."

"Would he?"

"Yes, you're right. Albert is always so careful with confidential police information. But who is she?"

"I don't know much. She's a widow and her name is Hutchby."

"Are you sure?"

"Oh yes."

Audrey's intuition suddenly produced an explosive idea in her mind; she suddenly suspected that Olivia and George had been lovers. Yes, it was true, wasn't it? That was why Olivia was so stunned about George's affair with the woman in Berkeley Square. Olivia hadn't known. As Audrey gazed at Olivia's red mouth, she was more certain than ever that her intuition was accurate. She found her hands trembling as she imagined Olivia and George together. Olivia was now talking some nonsense about the people in Berkeley Square, but all Audrey could think of was Olivia and George, images of them together naked on a bed.

Before long Olivia finished her tea and she said she had to run along. She promised to return the next day if Audrey wanted it. "Would you like that?"

Audrey nodded. "Yes, if you like. It's very kind of you."

Olivia smiled her red-lipped smile, and once again Audrey thought Olivia's shade of lipstick was a bit too bright.

Shortly after Olivia left, Inspector Barzun arrived. He seemed awkward as he walked into the living room, as if he hadn't reconciled his official duties with what had happened between them. He had no real news about George, and as they sat sipping tea in the sunlit room, Audrey realized he hadn't returned to tell her anything at all about George. From the way he was looking at her, it was obvious the purpose of his visit was something else.

"You don't want to make trouble for yourself," she said.

"What?"

"You've come here to see me, haven't you? I mean there isn't anything new about my husband."

Barzun looked uncomfortable. "Well, no there isn't..."

When she brought him more tea, he leaned forward to rub one of her calves with his hand. She looked down at him and she said nothing as his fingers slowly stroked her leg through the stocking.

Then she said: "The maid's out."

He looked up at her. "I can't stay too long."

"But long enough, I should think."

He put his teacup down and he rose up and he gently kissed her lips. She liked it; she liked the sweetness of it. She suddenly yielded to the urge to touch him, and she slid a hand between their bodies to find his penis. What she found was an enormous erection, the heat of it through the cloth of his trousers exciting her tremendously.

"All right, let's hurry," she said, and she led him out of the living room and up the stairs to her bedroom.

They quickly undressed and joined each other on the bed. Audrey filled her hands with his genitals, excited by the firm length of his penis. She looked down at it as she stripped the foreskin back to uncover his glans.

Barzun made a sound of pleasure as he felt her fingers tickling his organ. "Give it a suck," he said.

She did nothing for a moment, but then she decided yes, why not? There was something about this one that made her want to do it. She hardly ever did it with George, but she wanted to do it with Barzun. His name was Edward, but she'd always called him Barzun and she couldn't think of him any other way now.

"Please don't come in my mouth."

He seemed surprised. "I promise."

She did want Barzun's prick in her mouth, and in a moment she bent her head to his belly and she took the tip between her lips.

She heard him groan as she ran her tongue over the arrow-shaped glans. The taste was pleasant, his flesh hot against her tongue. She took more and more of his penis inside her mouth, enjoying the bulk of it, the sounds he made, the feel of his balls in her hand as she began sucking him. She moved her mouth up and down on the stalk with a steady rhythm, but after a while she stopped it and she asked him to get it inside her.

"Hurry," she said, rolling on her back and then opening her legs wide. As he crawled to his knees, she slid both hands between her thighs and she pulled her sex open with her fingers.

Barzun seemed excited by her wanton display. His eyes hot, he stared at the open cunt. "Do you want me to lick it first?"

A shudder of excitement passed through Audrey. "Yes, do that!"

She pulled her knees up and opened them further. She felt her clitoris like a stiff little finger projecting at the apex of her slit. She watched him as he moved into position, as he crouched between her thighs and then lowered his face to her belly. She gasped as his mouth touched her. Keeping her knees pulled back with her hands, she moaned with pleasure as his broad tongue licked the groove between her labia.

"Oh, that's lovely," she said, and the next moment

she cried out as she felt him take her clitoris between his lips and suck it. George never did it enough, certainly never as well as this. She began thrashing about, keeping Barzun's head in place with her hands. Barzun finally stopped it and he pulled her forward to mount her. She had an orgasm at the instant his thick penis pushed inside her vagina, and then afterward she began building to another climax as he stroked in and out relentlessly. At the end she managed to get hold of his balls as he went off inside her, and as she felt the new wetness in her cunt she told herself she ought to be thankful to George for at least leaving Barzun for her.

Audrey passed a restless evening thinking about her husband and Barzun and Olivia Rumbelow. For the first time in her life she found her mind occupied with the intricacies of adultery. George had disappeared, but the wake of his disappearance had produced consequences Audrey had never expected. First there was her knowledge of George's adultery with that Hutchby woman, the infidelity witnessed with her own eyes on the TV screen. Then there was her own adultery with Barzun, twice now, and each time a great pleasure for her. And then there was also her intuitive certainty that George and Olivia were much more than social acquaintances, that Olivia was much more to George than the wife of his superior at the Yard.

Audrey felt a keen confusion as she considered these three adulteries. And underlying everything was the apparent awakening of her own sexuality, a new hunger making itself felt for the first time in years, maybe for the first time ever. She'd certainly never had the pleasure she was now having with Barzun.

Late in the evening, in her bedroom, she moved the cheval-glass to the foot of the bed, and then she climbed onto the bed and she lay there with her legs open looking at herself as she masturbated, staring at the red maw of her sex as she dipped her fingers in it. She rubbed her clitoris, gave herself orgasm after orgasm, and at the end she groaned with pleasure as she pushed one of her fingers inside her anus and simulated the movements of a penis in the tight opening.

When she finally fell asleep, the lights were still on, the radio still playing, her breasts and belly shining with a film of sweat.

The next day, as she'd promised, Olivia Rumbelow came calling again.

"How are you, darling? Are you all right? Not too unhappy to see me? Albert sends his regards, of course."

Olivia's lips were painted a dark pink today, and she wore a tailored jacket over a ruffled blouse. This time they had wine instead of tea in the living room. The two women sat on the sofa chatting, their friendship deepening as Audrey realized she welcomed Olivia's concern for her. Yes, she did need someone. And they had certain common interests, didn't they? Olivia's family, in fact, had known Audrey's family before she'd married George.

Olivia said: "You're very brave, darling."

"No, I'm not."

"I don't know what I would do in similar circumstances. I suppose I'd go to pieces."

But Audrey thought that was unlikely and she said so. She now viewed Olivia as a woman of great poise and charm. She realized she'd never really spent enough time with Olivia to understand her. No wonder George had wanted to make love to her. If he actually had, that is. She still didn't know, did she? All she knew about was that Hutchby woman, the Berkeley Square woman with those enormous breasts. Dear George, where are you? Audrey thought. As they sat beside each other on the sofa, she felt gratified that Olivia was so kind to her. Was it the wine? Suddenly Audrey felt terribly sad and she began crying, the tears flowing down her cheeks as she succumbed to the unhappiness she'd been feeling the past few days.

"I'm sorry," she said.

Olivia slipped an arm around Audrey's shoulders and reassured her. "It's understandable, darling. You've suffered an awful stress, haven't you? Here, lie down now. You can use my lap as a pillow."

Olivia made Audrey stretch out on the sofa with her head in Olivia's lap. Audrey sobbed quietly as she listened to Olivia's attempts to soothe her. When she stopped sobbing, when she was able to control herself again, she told Olivia how grateful she was. "You've been very kind to me."

"But I want to. Anyway, you're much too lovely to cry. I'm sure George wouldn't want it."

"Do you think he'll turn up?"

"Yes, I think so. I've always thought George was a very resourceful man. I don't know what's happened to him, but I'm hoping we'll have good news soon."

Olivia continued talking, her forearm across Audrey's breasts as she stroked Audrey's shoulder with her hand. Now Olivia pulled her arm away and she laughed softly. "There's more to you than I thought."

"What do you mean?"

"Your breasts. They feel more substantial than they look."

"They're too flat."

"Oh no, they're quite pretty."

Audrey wondered why they were suddenly talking about her breasts, but she didn't mind it. She felt warm and comfortable with her head on Olivia's lap, almost as if she and Olivia had been close friends for years and years.

Then Olivia did something surprising. She took hold of the low neckline of Audrey's dress with her fingers, and she lifted it in order to look at more of Audrey's breasts.

"Yes," Olivia said.

"Yes what?" Audrey said.

"Yes, I'm going to kiss you." And with that Olivia bent her head to kiss Audrey. The kiss lasted only a moment, but as she pulled her mouth away, Olivia ran her tongue over Audrey's lips.

"I like the taste of your lipstick," Olivia said.

Audrey quivered. "I think we've had too much wine."

"Have I shocked you because I kissed you?"

"I don't know."

"Then I suppose I ought to do it again so you can find out. Do you want me to?"

"Yes, I think so."

Olivia kissed her again, and this time the kiss lasted longer and Olivia's tongue slipped between Audrey's lips to wiggle about like a serpent. This time, when Olivia finally pulled her head back, Audrey found her senses aflame.

Olivia said: "Still shocked?"
"I've never done anything like this."
"Kissed a woman like that?"
"No, never."
"But you like it, don't you?"
"Yes."
"And I do too," Olivia said, her hand sliding inside the neckline of Audrey's dress, her fingers gently stroking the lace cups of Audrey's brassiere. "I've been having an affair with George," Olivia said.
"Yes, I know."
"You do?"
"I guessed it yesterday."
"You don't hate me for it?"
"No, of course not."
Olivia kissed her again, a much warmer kiss, her hand more aggressive as it fondled Audrey's brassiere-covered breasts. Audrey found herself comparing Olivia's touch with a man's touch. How strange it was to have her breasts touched by a woman!
"Here, let's have this down," Olivia said, her hands tugging at the shoulder straps of Audrey's silk dress, then pulling the top of the dress down far enough to expose Audrey's breasts. Audrey rolled to the side to enable Olivia to get at the catch of her brassiere, and in a few moments the brassiere was gone and Audrey was now naked above her waist.
"That's much better," Olivia said.
Audrey was fascinated by all of it. She'd thought lesbians were mannish women, females who affected a deliberate coarseness in order to imitate men. But there was nothing at all coarse about Olivia, absolutely nothing. Everything about Olivia was extremely feminine, especially the slender hands that were now stroking her breasts and toying with her nipples.

Do you want this? Audrey thought. She told herself yes, she did want it. She was finding the experience completely remarkable. Olivia's fondling of her breasts was causing her belly to melt.

She turned on her side and she buried her face against Olivia's belly. "I'm ashamed," Audrey said.

"Ashamed, darling? Ashamed of what?"

"Ashamed of my ignorance."

In Audrey's bedroom, they stood facing each other with their breasts bared. Olivia's breasts were larger, the nipples more pink in color. Audrey trembled as Olivia reached out to touch her breasts. Olivia's fingers fluttered over Audrey's nipples, teasing them, pulling at them gently.

"I like to enjoy life," Olivia said. "And sometimes it's more enjoyable with a woman as a partner."

She undressed Audrey, stroked her body, kissed her belly and bottom and then undressed herself. She gave Audrey a coquettish look as she lifted her breasts in her hands and arched her back to make her bottom protrude.

"I've been gaining weight."

"No, you're perfect."

"Not as thin as you are."

"It doesn't show."

"Really?"

They laughed as they fell on the bed together. George was forgotten now, only a dim presence and certainly not an obstacle between them. They closed their arms around each other, two warm bodies, a tangle of pink flesh on the counterpane. Olivia kissed Audrey's breasts, sucked at the stiff nipples before sliding her face downward to Audrey's belly.

On her back, her knees raised, Audrey groaned as Olivia dipped her mouth to kiss Audrey's hairy slit. She felt Olivia's fingers opening the labia, and then an instant later she groaned again as she felt the warm tongue vibrating against her swollen clitoris.

Audrey came. Olivia continued licking and sucking and Audrey came again. And then both women heard a sudden sound in the room and they looked together at the open door.

George was there. George was standing there looking at them.

"It's awfully stuffy in here," he said. "Wouldn't you like one of the windows opened?"

In the living room, George filled a glass with ice and poured some Scotch. Olivia had fled, shocked by the sudden appearance of George, by his discovery of her and Audrey in the bedroom, furious that he now knew her secret. "I'm not a lesbian!" Olivia screamed in the hall, and then she slammed the door as she left the house.

Contrite, Audrey now sat in the living room wearing one of her robes, her eyes on George, on his unhurried movements.

"It's awful of you," she said.

"What is?"

"You're disappearing like that."

"But I'm back now."

"What will the Yard say?"

"They already know it. They also know that I've resigned."

Audrey was stunned. She couldn't imagine George as

anything but what he'd been for the past twenty-five years: a Scotland Yard man. It seemed absurd that he was suddenly no longer part of it, absurd enough so that it frightened her.

"What will you do?" she said.

George shrugged. "Do? I don't know what I'll do eventually. But in a few days I'm traveling to Paris to meet a friend and I want you to come with me."

"A friend? Who is it?"

"It's a woman. Her name is Magda Clare and I want you to meet her."

"Oh George."

"Will you come with me?"

As reluctant as she was, George finally persuaded her. What else could she do? She was his wife, wasn't she? Now that he'd returned to her, she had no choice but to go with him.

"All right," she said.

When he looked at her, he seemed happy. He took her hand, and he led her out of the living room to her bedroom. "Tell me about Olivia," he said.

"Tell you what?"

"What was it like with her?"

Audrey blushed. "I don't want to talk about that. But you ought to know I know everything about you and Olivia. She told me everything."

"I'm not surprised."

"We don't need to talk about that either."

He sat down on the edge of the bed and he told her to take off her robe. "I want to look at you."

Audrey quivered. "Now?"

"Yes, why not?"

But it wasn't the ordinary thing he wanted. When she was naked, he lay down on his back on the bed and he wanted her to climb over him and get her sex on his mouth. Trembling with excitement, she straddled his body and shifted forward to settle her cunt on his face. He started sucking it immediately, and her pleasure was so great she cried out again and again.

Please God, don't let him stop it, she thought. She wanted it to go on and on.

They landed at Orly in the early afternoon and rode a taxi directly to the Hotel George V. Audrey was impressed that George had chosen one of the most expensive hotels in Paris. He'd always been careful with money and she wondered now what had changed. Was he suddenly rich? There were things about him that were different than before, a new attitude, amusement at circumstances that had previously provoked his irritation. She had no explanation for it and she decided it didn't matter. He was back with her, wasn't he? And so far it was pleasant. Sometimes extremely pleasant. She was afraid that if she asked too many questions all of it would burst like a pricked balloon.

At the hotel they had a sumptuous suite, more lavish than any she'd ever known, antique furniture, gilt-edged frames, brocaded drapes, two marvelous rooms of French splendor.

While she changed, George made a telephone call, and when he put the phone down, he said: "She's waiting for us."

Audrey quivered. "You've told me hardly anything about her."

"I haven't told you anything at all."

"That's what I mean."

"She has dark hair and she's beautiful."

"Is she British?"

"She says she's American."

"What does that mean? Is she or isn't she?"

"I don't know."
"Oh George. Are the two of you lovers?"
George looked at her as if he were considering the idea. "No, I don't think you could call it that. Not in the usual sense, anyway."
"It's too mysterious," Audrey said.
"You said you would trust me."
"Yes."
Twenty minutes later they met Magda Clare in the lobby of the hotel and Audrey immediately fell in love with her.

They had dinner at La Coupole. Audrey sat facing Magda, and George sat between the two women. The large room was crowded, people chattering at the tables, some of them men and women in evening dress.
"I love Paris," Magda said. She smiled at Audrey. "It's a marvelous city, don't you think?"
"Yes," Audrey said.
She wondered how old Magda was. She knew she was older than Magda, but for some strange reason she felt younger, much younger.
After they finished at La Coupole, they rode a taxi back to the hotel to have champagne in Magda's suite. Her rooms were even larger than those George and Audrey had, the furniture more exquisite.
After the second glass of champagne, Audrey realized she was getting potted. She blushed when she noticed Magda looking at her intently, and then a moment later Audrey's pulse beat faster as Magda approached her and touched her arm.
"Are you all right?" Magda said.
"Yes."
"Why don't you undress?"

Audrey felt a quivering in her belly. "Should I?"
"Yes, I think so. George will approve, won't you, George?"
From where he was sitting on the sofa, George called out: "Go on, Audrey."
Her mind confused, Audrey began removing her clothes as Magda stood there and watched her, as George watched her from the sofa. After she peeled the dress off, she wore only a black lace bra and flesh- colored tights. She rid herself of everything, feeling the heat in her face, avoiding Magda's eyes.
"Put the heels on again," Magda said.
Audrey did so, standing naked now wearing only her jewelry and the high-heeled black sandals she'd bought in that little shop in Oxford Street. She felt awkward because the others were still dressed, but it quickly passed. Suddenly she felt strangely proud of her nakedness, and with a casual turn she walked to the champagne bucket on the rolling cart and she poured herself another glass of the bubbly.
Magda seemed amused. "Come here, darling." And when Audrey approached with her champagne glass in one hand, Magda reached out to take hold of Audrey's breasts and fondle them. "You're more delicious than I anticipated," Magda said.
Audrey quivered. "I don't know very much."
Then a soft gasp came out of Audrey's throat as Magda dropped a hand down and cupped it over Audrey's mound. The brunette's fingers pinched the bulge of Audrey's sex. "Open your legs," Magda said.
Her eyes were locked with Audrey's, and Audrey quivered again as she moved her legs apart to enable Magda's slender fingers to probe between her labia. Magda smiled as she pushed her fingers inside Audrey's vagina and used her thumb to stroke Audrey's clitoris. The orgasm arrived quickly, Audrey shuddering from

head to toe as Magda's deft fingers churned in her wet cunt.

After that Magda pulled her hand away from Audrey's sex and she slipped out of her dress. Under it she wore only a thin suspender belt to hold up her stockings. She rubbed the neat black triangle of fur at the joining of her thighs, and then she moved to Audrey and she pushed at Audrey's shoulders to make it clear what she wanted.

Her body trembling, Audrey dropped to her knees on the carpet and pressed her face against Magda's dark thicket. The scent of it was strange, not at all what she'd expected, a strong musk, animal-like, almost overpowering. Yielding to the urge, she extended her tongue to lick between the thick labia. The incredible heat of Magda cunt immediately made itself apparent, and now Magda took hold of Audrey's head with both hands as she hunched her pelvis forward and rubbed her mound against Audrey's face.

"Suck it," Magda said softly. "Get it in your mouth and suck it."

Audrey did that. She opened her mouth and tilted her head to take in as much of Magda's flesh as she could. She felt Magda shudder, and then the next moment it was as if a liquid heat was pouring out of Magda's cunt and into Audrey's sucking mouth.

Audrey came. She felt the spasms in her cunt as she sucked at the brunette's drooling sex. She came again as she swallowed Magda's juices.

All three of them lay naked on a wide bed, a chain of bodies, the room silent, no noise in the room except the soft sounds of sucking, an occasional moan or a whimper, now and then a muted groan of pleasure.

Magda had George's swollen penis in her mouth, one finger moving slowly in and out of his anus as she moved her lips and tongue over the fat glans.

George's face pressed between Audrey's thighs, his nose rubbing her clitoris as he foraged with his tongue deep inside her vagina.

Audrey sucked Magda again, feeding at the trough of Magda's sex, pulling the juices out of the sex as fast as they gathered.

After awhile Magda pulled her mouth off George's penis and she announced that she'd be leaving in the morning for Egypt.

"This is my last time," she said.

She said it as if this were her last time on Earth.

Audrey and George remained in Paris another week. One evening after dinner, when they were alone in their suite, Audrey appeared in the living room wearing the black lingerie she'd bought that afternoon in the Place Vendôme.

George looked at her and smiled. "Spiffing."

She opened the diaphanous peignoir to show her legs in the sheer black stockings, the black lace suspender belt, the trimmed blond bush that covered her sex. "And the legs?"

"Marvelous."

She did a turn and lifted the peignoir in back to expose the white moons of her buttocks.

"And here?"

"Lovely enough to corrupt a saint."

In the bedroom, she removed the peignoir and she knelt on the bed with her buttocks in the air. George kept his eyes on her bottom as he hurried to get out of his clothes. When he was naked, he moved behind her and he quickly penetrated her sex with a single thrust of his rigid penis.

Audrey groaned, gently rolling her hips as he slid his organ in and out of her wet cave. "That's awfully good," she said.

George feasted his eyes on the black lingerie, the suspender belt and stockings that made her white buttocks so incredibly alluring. As he moved his prick in out of her sex, he touched her anus with the ball of his thumb. "What about here?" he said.

A shudder appeared to pass up and down Audrey's back. "You'll have to use something."

"Yes." He pulled out of her cunt and he brought the cold cream from the dressing table. "Cold cream," he said. "But I suppose we'll have it warm soon enough."

"Hurry," Audrey said.

They had done it only twice since his return, and her excitement was intense as she now she waited for it again. In a moment she felt him pushing in, his glans sliding inside her stretched opening, George making sounds of pleasure as he speared her backside.

"Are we returning to London soon?" she said.

George grunted. "No, not yet. I'd like to move on to Egypt in a few days, and then we'll see."

After that they stopped talking. Audrey reached underneath to hold his testicles as he started a forceful thrusting in her bottom. All she cared about at the moment was the sliding movement of George's prick.

On their second day in Luxor, they went to the Valley of Queens to look at the tombs. Audrey held George's arm as they walked over the paths from one edifice to another, past groups of tourists from various places, ladies with sun-hats, and white-haired gentleman with sunburned noses. George took Audrey to the tomb of Queen Mafernit. Audrey thought how strange it was that he knew where it was even though he'd never been to Luxor before. They stood at the sarcophagus that bore the death mask of Mafernit, and as Audrey looked at it more carefully she felt her knees trembling. The face of the mask was the face of Magda Clare.

"Oh George," she said in a weak voice.

"What is it?"

"It's her."

George seemed mesmerized by the death mask. "Yes."

"Will she ever return to us?"

"I don't know."

In their hotel suite, George sat on the sofa in the living room while Audrey knelt on a pillow on the floor and sucked his penis. They were both fully dressed, George with his trousers open and his rigid organ extending like a pink stalk into Audrey's mouth. Her head bobbed as she moved her lips up and down on the swollen member. After a while George made a sound of pleasure as he began spurting, and Audrey whimpered as she caught the gushing of sperm on her tongue and swallowed it. George looked down at her, watching her, watching the movements of her lips, and then when the sucking was finished Audrey looked up at him and a frightened groan came out of George's throat.

"Your eyes," he said.

"What is it?"

"They have no pupils."

Audrey patted his hand and smiled. "Darling George."

Dear God...